I0718046

ASHEN

CHRONICLES OF WARSHARD BOOK THREE

KATHERINE BOGLE

Patchwork Press

Copyright © 2017-2018 by Katherine Bogle

http://katherinebogle.com

Cover Design by Katzilla Designs

Second Edition — 2018

No part of this publication may be reproduced in any form, or by any means, electronic or mechanical, including photocopying, recording, or any information browsing, storage, or retrieval system, without permission in writing from Katherine Bogle.

❀ Created with Vellum

ASHEN

CHRONICLES OF WARSHARD
BOOK THREE

KATHERINE BOGLE

MAP OF
WARSHARD

For Nicole, who's never let anyone tell her who to love.

ONE

<hr>

Cold slithered across the bare nape of her neck. Adni shivered. A breeze inside the Cinder Mountains? Shadows fled from the flames of Renley's torch. Fire licked the oil-slick rag wrapped around the long branch.

But Renley's light wasn't the only illumination.

Cool blue, like the sky, grazed the jagged cavern walls. Wet glistened on its surface, and thunder roared inside the tunnel system. Somewhere ahead, rapids pounded the rocks.

Finally, she thought, *Father's treasure hunt is almost over.*

"Can you hear it?" Her father glanced over his shoulder. His gray beard strained over his face, stretched in a manic grin, its length only a reminder of how long it had been since they'd left home. Three? Four days?

"Rapids?" Renley's voice seized with excitement. He didn't see their father for what he was—a greedy madman.

Adni sighed, her breath fogging the cool autumn air. Only the bliss of a hot spring could ease the cold from her bones. After all, it had been months since they'd travelled to one.

Her fingers wrapped around the leather-strapped hilt at her waist - Adni's eighteenth birthday present. For years, she'd longed for a sword like the knights of Salander. She'd escape from this wretched place and convince someone—anyone—to train her. Once she had the skills, she could join the Salander army, or even the King's palace guard. She shook her head. After the Insane had been brought to justice ten years ago, there wasn't much need for armies anymore.

"Yes! We've nearly arrived, my boy!" Her father lengthened his stride; flying past the pulley system on the opposite wall, the one delivering fresh rainwater to the nearby village. His fingers tightened around the map he clutched. The dozen gold and silver rings on his fingers winked in the torchlight.

Renley grinned over his shoulder at her. Adni quirked an eyebrow and grimaced. Renley humored their father far too much.

His grin dropped. The flames of his torch turned his green eyes into emerald fire. He turned back to the coming tunnel, a frown curving his wide mouth. Renley was only fifteen, three years younger than Adni. He didn't understand the hundreds of trips that still waited him when treasure hunting stopped being fun.

"I knew today would end well when I heard songbirds this morning!" Her father rounded a bend in the rock.

They emerged in a large cavern, slick with mist from the pounding of a waterfall. At least it drowned out her father's insane mumblings.

Her father, Bran, paused by the edge of an underground lake. The brilliant blue-green water twisted into violent waves as it fled down a tunnel near the entrance of the cavern. A jagged hole in the ceiling, just above the tip of the waterfall, blazed with sunlight.

Adni's heart fluttered.

When was the last time she'd seen the sky? A week? A month? She couldn't remember. Though several skylights could be found through the mountains, they hadn't encountered any on their last few trips. She wasn't lucky enough to have one near their home either.

Her father pumped a fist in the air. She imagined his hoot of impending victory. She bit her lip to keep from rolling her eyes. "*It wasn't ladylike,*" her mother always said. Her fingertips brushed the red jewel of the amulet hung around her neck. The precious stone rested on her chest, nestled just below her collarbone. Her mother had given it to her so many years ago she could hardly remember its meaning any longer. Her siblings didn't have one, but her mother insisted she never take it off.

She shook her head. Maybe father was right about one thing. Her mother had always been eccentric, even in her youth.

While her brother and father raced for the stairs carved into the curved cavern wall leading to the cliff from which the waterfall bubbled, Adni pulled her sword from its sheath.

If her father insisted on forcing her along every one of his journeys, she'd at least take the time to practice her swordsmanship on the open ledge.

The heavy metal pulled her left and right as she twisted it, awkward in her unpracticed hands. It was far different than the wooden sword she'd fashioned years ago from driftwood. Its edges weren't as jagged, though they were certainly dull.

She narrowed her eyes at the uncooperative blade. She wouldn't let her lack of strength stop her.

Adni spun, swinging her blade out. The weight tore her off balance. Her stomach flew into her throat, and her eyes widened as her boot caught on a rock.

Her elbows slammed against the rough stone floor.

"Ow." She winced.

"Adni, what in blue skies are you doing down there?" Renley called over the thunder of the waterfall. He stood at the top of the steps, his eyebrows twisted with worry instead of amusement.

She glanced up, her cheeks burning. Damn. She had hoped they were too busy to see.

"Nothing!" Adni shook her head, her shoulder-length black hair flicking her cheeks. She stood quickly, dusting her thick trousers. Damp clung to her knees.

Renley waved her up the steps.

Adni nodded, but she was in no rush. While Renley disappeared back over the cliff side, Adni sucked in a deep breath. Cold hair filled her lungs. She needed to get used to the weight of her blade. Swinging her sword left and right, Adni steadied herself on the edge of the lake. How else was she going to join the Salander guards and be free of this mountain?

Her heart ached for the thick pine forests and open plains of the six kingdoms where her fondest childhood memories dwelt. It had been far too long since she'd lived in Warshard.

Adni wandered closer to the steps, bending her knees as she parried a non-existing enemy. The blade cut through the air, the metal glinting in the sunlight. She smiled. Her fingers tightened around the hilt. She could do this. She could learn. The native clansmen knew how to fight. Though they usually stuck to their bows and arrows, they were unbelievably fast with a dagger. Someone would teach her. And then she would go. She'd return to the home the Insane Queen ripped away from her ten years ago.

"Adni!" her father bellowed.

She winced. Cold seeped through the warmth blossoming in her chest. She bit back a snarl and sheathed her blade. Damn him, and his treasure hunts. Damn him and his constant need for her presence. Damn him, and everything he made her do.

Adni trudged up the slick stone steps, ready to share her irritation loudly with her father. He'd probably found his treasure and was ready to head home. Only he needed to gloat first of course. He *always* needed to gloat. Heat boiled through her limbs and tightened her fists.

She reached the top of the steps and froze.

The cliff side was flat and wide. The river leading to the waterfall disappeared into a narrow mouth at the far side of the cliff. Only blackness waited inside.

Where was the treasure?

Her stomach turned. If her father didn't find the treasure, she'd wish for his gloating, for his rage was second to none.

"Where is it?" her father screamed. His shouts echoed in the hollow cavern, carrying his words back to her over and over until they rung in her ears.

She gritted her teeth. *Damn.*

"I'm sure it's here somewhere," Renley said. His brows turned up as he glanced between them, frantically searching for what to do.

How could she tell him there was nothing to be done? If father's map lied, and there was no treasure to be found, the best they could do was flee before their father lashed out. Her cheek ached at the memory of his hand on her flesh from the last time he'd been disappointed.

Adni stepped up beside her brother. Her fingers brushed the fur wrapping the wrists of his jacket—similar to her own. His gaze met hers, and his lips pressed into a thin line.

Maybe he was old enough to remember their father's rage.

"The map is *very* clear!" Bran twisted to face them, his eyes wide and wild with lust for riches. His teeth gnashed together as he ripped the twine from the parchment. He splayed it between his hands. "It should be *here*!"

Light filtered behind the map, showing her every detail her father saw. The twisting tunnels, large caverns, waterways, and clues. She couldn't quite recall where he'd gotten the map, but the waterfall gushing beside a large X was unmistakable. They were at the right spot, with no treasure in sight.

"Maybe we took a wrong turn," Renley began hesitantly.

"There was no wrong turn!" he hissed. His face twisted in a snarl, fist clenched in front of him. His gaze flickered to Renley before falling back on his map.

Adni narrowed her eyes as she stepped in front of Renley. Her heart clenched with a need to protect her kin. Their father's gaze didn't rise from the page. He spun in every direction, looking at the map in every possible light.

"Head back to the camp," Adni whispered over her shoulder.

Renley's eyebrows rose as he met her concerned gaze. "What? I can't leave father now."

"Trust me."

Renley shifted from foot to foot, humming and hawing. "Fine." He spun for the steps and descended slowly, as if a thousand boulders lay on his shoulders.

She smiled. Ever the drama queen.

While her father's shuffling and muttering continued, Adni watched her brother go. Someone had to stay with their father and be sure he didn't hurt himself again. She moved to the edge of the waterfall, pushing her bare fingers into her pockets. Water sprayed a mist at the base of the falls, fogging the edge of the clear water.

Sunlight glazed the surface, a startlingly beautiful mix of greens. She revelled in the sun warming her cheeks, and turned her face to the skylight.

"Where is it?" her father's shout broke her reverie.

Her full lips twisted into a frown. She opened her clear blue eyes. Her mother always said her eyes might as well be the winter sky.

She looked back down into the lake below, ignoring her father's fury. Though it appeared still, the twisting current at the far end meant it was anything but. The underwater channel would be a dangerous one. She was sure many had lost their lives thinking it was simply a pretty pool to swim in.

"What is that?"

Adni glanced at her father. He leaned close to the edge, peering over her shoulder. His eyes widened as he leered into the clear depths.

She followed his gaze. Just in front of the waterfall's spray, something gold glistened at the bottom of the lake. She raised an eyebrow.

Could it be the treasure?

"You found it, my girl." His mouth stretched into a grin so wide his upper gums showed—pink and red, blotchy with color, just like his yellow, rotting teeth. "My good little Adanza."

Her nostrils flared. No one used her full name, not unless her father was drunk on the thrill of the hunt.

His fingers clamped down on her shoulders, digging into her skin even through the thick fur trim of her hood. He squeezed, pinching her skin.

She winced, and tried to step away. He held too tightly.

"You've always been my special little girl." His dark gaze shifted from the pool to her face. With his smile so wide, and his face this close, his wrinkles were far more apparent. "You'll survive it."

Her eyebrows furrowed. *Survive it?*

His fingers left her shoulders before his palms slammed into her back. Her breath fled her lungs and her eyes widened. The dark cliff side fell away. Her feet met air. The green-blue water flew up at her, gold glinting just below the surface.

Her heart rose into her throat where a scream ripped free. She hardly heard her father's cackle above the roaring in her ears.

Her whole body froze as pain and cold slapped her like the hand of winter itself.

TWO

Rapids rolled her back and forth in their violent grasp. No piece of her body was immune to the rocks colliding with every inch of her. Her hip slammed against something sharp. She tasted blood.

Her fingers fought for something to grasp, something to hold onto. Sharp rocks slipped between her fingers, slicing her skin. She'd hiss in pain if it weren't for her constant battle for breath.

Her lungs burned, wrenching tears from her eyes and every cry from her throat. She twisted for freedom, for the surface, but which way was it? With only darkness to greet her and rapids to throw her, she quickly lost track of up and down, left and right. Her mind swirled with panic.

What can I do? How do I find the surface?

Adni's heart pounded in her ears. She couldn't die, not like this. She wouldn't go down because of her father's foolish greed.

She clawed for the surface—whichever way that may be—but only water and rock met her fingers.

Damn him! Damn him, and his stupidity. Damn him and his greed.

Her chest ached and her head swam. Her muscles weakened with every stroke, every movement.

What would her mother say when father returned to their campsite without her? What would Renley say? She'd never been close with Bran, but her mother meant everything to her.

Fleeting images of her mother's long dark hair, curled around her shoulders, and the quirk of her lips as she smiled and laughed inside their home. Adni could almost smell the fish cooking over the fire as her siblings fought in the next room.

She could hear their voices, their clipped tones and quick tempers. Adni almost smiled.

This was it; her last battle, and she'd hardly even lived.

Adni closed her eyes and the images of her happy family drifted into the black.

* * *

PAIN BROUGHT her crashing back to reality. Adni gasped, her lungs and throat burning as she simultaneously vomited water and sucked in air like her life depended on it.

"Damn, I really thought you were gone there for a second." Warm hands rubbed her back as she puked up the last of the river. Her whole body shook. Cold like she'd never known seeped into every inch of her.

I'm alive?

Warm fingers prodded her bare arms and shoulders. Her coat was gone. When had she lost her coat?

"Only a few bruises…" the woman trailed off. "You're one lucky girl."

Adni shook her head. She reached for the amulet at her throat. Its touch always brought her comfort. Her fingertips brushed her bare collarbone. Nothing. Her amulet was gone.

"All the same, I think you should see a doctor immediately," the woman continued. Her voice was sweet with a slightly husky edge. It crawled under her skin and teased her brain. "You don't want to have survived the river, only to die of cold."

Her gaze racked the rocky shore. The river lay beyond her boots, much calmer than she remembered. Her soaking jacket lay in a wet pile beside her, but her amulet was nowhere to be found.

Mother would not be pleased if she found out.

"What's your name?"

Adni looked over her shoulder. A blonde woman, maybe a couple years older than Adni, kneeled at her back. Long waves descended to her breasts, like gold. Her dark blue gaze winked with mischief as she flashed a flirtatious smile.

"You are a pretty one, aren't you?" The blonde laughed. "You must be in shock. My name is Julian. I pulled you from the river." Her cheeks and the tip of her nose glowed pink from the chill.

"Adni," she said.

"*Adni*." Julian tested out her name like she wanted to know how it tasted on her tongue. "Unusual for these mountains, isn't it?"

Adni shook her head as she twisted to stand.

"Whoa there!" Julian stood with her, holding Adni's elbow as her head swam.

"Thank you." Adni's eyebrows furrowed as she swayed on her heels. How had she gotten in that river?

"You might not want to strain yourself." Julian's hands were warm on her skin. Adni had to resist leaning into them. "I really should fetch a healer."

Then she remembered.

Her father's hands slammed into her back, throwing her to the rapids below. She could have died. She *should* have died. And yet somehow she'd survived. Her fists tightened as fire burned through her chest.

He'd nearly killed her, and for what? For riches? For treasure? A treasure he'd never get, let alone see beyond the lake surface.

Adni gritted her teeth.

She'd put up with her father for eighteen years. She'd put up with his obsession, his greed, and his foolish lies. She'd put up with the journeys, the starvation, and a life of darkness inside the mountains. She'd lived in cold since the day her family fled Salander, flames licking their heels as everything she'd ever known burned with Ithrendel city.

And yet, he nearly *killed* his own daughter.

"Adni?" Julian shook her gently.

"I'm going to kill him," she hissed between clenched teeth.

Julian stiffened. "Kill who?"

Adni ripped away from Julian. Heat coursed through every inch of her, pulling her from the cold and into madness. Something shiny glinted on the floor.

Her sword.

She flashed a wicked smile as she plucked the blade from the ground and hooked it to her belt. Her mind raced with fury, crashing around her like the rapids had only minutes ago.

"My father." Adni wiped the wet from her face and fled into the darkness of the tunnel.

"Wait!" Julian called.

Adni soared over rock and water, passed bamboo pipes, and curious fishermen. The river weaved at her side, guiding her back to the campsite her family had set up downstream from the waterfall.

Blood lust burned through her in waves, stealing her breath and pushing her faster. She wasn't sore anymore. She hardly felt a thing aside from the heat washing through her bones.

She rounded a bend in the tunnel. A campfire roared beside a calm river. Two tents and several bedrolls stretched out beside it. Her mother, a raven-haired beauty, dried clothes over the fire, while her younger sister of twelve, skinned fish for dinner.

"*Where is he?*" Her scream wasn't her own. The rage inside it wasn't her own.

Her mother looked up as she adjusted a tunic on a long rod next to the flames. Her eyebrows furrowed as she looked Adni up and down. Her green eyes widened.

"Adni?" her mother's voice was small. "What happened?"

A growl ripped from her throat unbidden. "Where is my *father?*" she spat the word like she tasted something awful. "Where is he?"

Her mother glanced from her sister, to the river, and back to Adni. "Adni–"

"WHERE IS HE?"

Her green eyes widened, not only in surprise, but in fear.

But her mother's fear wasn't enough to cut through the blinding fury. It only strengthened her need to find her father and bring him to justice. He'd hurt this family for long enough. They didn't need him. It was time to end his tyranny.

A loud splash split the quiet left by her roar.

Adni spun towards the river.

On a small boat several yards out, her father grappled with two wooden oars, his eyes wide as he fought to paddle away.

"Father." Her nostrils flared as she leapt to the edge of the river. She hesitated, the toes of her boots inches from the calm water.

"Adni, wait!" Her mother jumped to her feet.

"There's no time!" Adni snapped. But she didn't continue forward. The dark river weaved around a distant bend in the enormous cavern.

The blackness of it curled beneath the surface, threatening to take her down again.

"Adni, please calm down." Her mother's warm fingers closed on her arm.

Adni snatched her arm away. "I can't!" Her voice broke.

Fire ate her resolve and fought to take over her mind. It stole her breath and forced her to take a step into the river. Cold seeped through her boot once more—but it wasn't enough to quell the fire.

"Adni, please!"

Adni took another step, as if her feet weren't her own.

"Adni!"

Cold lapped at her knees as her father's boat drew further and further away. He threw desperate glances over his shoulder as he splashed his oars faster. *Coward.* He was a damned coward. He wouldn't face her after nearly murdering her. He deserved to die. He deserved to drown in the cold darkness of the river like she nearly had.

She took another step.

"Adni, please listen to me!" her mother's voice was high, desperate.

Another.

"Adanza Seren, please!"

Her mother never used her full name. Maybe this was serious. Ice wrapped around her thighs. Her fingers closed on the hilt of her blade. Serious or not, she couldn't let this go on. Adni took another step.

"Adni, he isn't your real father!"

She froze like she'd been slapped. The fire wrapping her heart gave way with one exhale, leaving her frigid. Shivers descended on her spine and shook her shoulders.

What?

"Adni?" Her mother's voice was close and sweet. Her warm breath brushed Adni's shoulder. Gentle fingers descended on her arms. "Adni, it's all right." Her mother turned Adni back to the riverbank.

She led her from the river and sat her by the fire.

Adni's legs gave out and she collapsed next to the drying clothes.

"You're soaking wet," her mother tsked as she wrapped a dry coat around Adni's shoulders. "I'll get you some soup."

Her mother, Galia, known for her beauty and nearly ethereal presence, busied herself around the fire, preparing a pot on a wire hung above a cross of branches. She flew from one edge of the small camp to the other, gathering fish from her youngest daughter and potatoes from a rucksack.

Adni watched her work, her eyes wide and her mind racing. *Bran isn't my father?* Her eyebrows furrowed.

How could that be? Adni had the same dark hair as both of her parents, and blue eyes ran in her father's side of the family, not her mother's. How could she not be related to that man?

Confusion burned through her as her shivers slowly ceased. Her fingers tightened on the fabric of the coat. She pulled it close, fur tickling her ears.

Adni sat in silence, while her younger sister, Helen, looked between them with wide eyes. At least she wasn't the only one shocked into silence.

"What did you–" Adni began.

Her mother cut her a look. "We'll speak later, Adni." She glanced at Helen, and Adni understood. They'd speak in private once Helen was asleep.

Adni nodded. Her mother returned to work, stirring the boiling liquid inside the iron pot—one of the few luxuries besides wood they brought on the trip.

With the heat of her fury fading, as well as the cold of the river, she stared into the flickering flames. If she wasn't the daughter of a treasure hunter, then who was she? Who was her real father? And what was that fire that consumed her so completely?

Adni shook her head. Her mother stirred the soup, her brow set with calm determination. Adni envied her mother that. If she didn't get her fire from her mother, and didn't get it from the man she thought was her father, then where had the blinding anger come from?

Unease settled in her gut, even as she ate the soup her mother had prepared. The heat settled in her stomach, warming any cold left in her bones.

* * *

AFTER HELEN WAS SAFELY TUCKED into bed, her soft snores filling the quiet, Adni sat with her mother by the fire.

"Eighteen years ago, the six kingdoms were a lot different than they are now." Her mother twisted her thumbs around each other and bit her lip. She avoided Adni's expectant gaze. "War ravaged our lands for so long. My husband, he was gone for months at a time, taken to the warfront by King Brae."

The last King of Salander, before his son, Emeril, took the throne ten years ago.

"There was a time when your father was gone for more than six months. I was all alone, working at my father's tavern outside Ithrendel. I was so worried, and so lonely. I was sure your father had died."

"But he hadn't." Adni wrapped her arms around her legs, pulling them to her chest.

"But he hadn't," her mother confirmed. "One night, I was cleaning up the tavern by myself. My mother was ill and your grandfather went to care for her. As I put away the last of the goblets, a dangerously beautiful man entered the tavern." She paused, guilt clouding her green eyes. "He was so charming, and so kind. I hadn't had a man treat me like that in all of my life." She smiled ruefully. "I… took him to my bed that night. Before he left, he promised to return when the baby turned eighteen. Of course I was shocked. How could he know I would become pregnant from one night?" She shook her head. "And yet I did."

Adni's mouth hung open and her mind raced. "So this man… is my real father?" Dread settled in her stomach. The man who had raised her, and once upon a time given her flowers on her birthday, and crafted dolls by hand for her and her sister, that man wasn't really her father.

Her mother nodded. "Yes. When Bran returned a few months later, I couldn't hide the pregnancy from him, but he loved me, and accepted that I had made a mistake. He vowed to raise you as his own."

Nausea twisted her gut. "How *kind*." She didn't bother hiding her sarcasm.

Galia smiled. "My husband was different back then, before we fled."

Adni snorted. She hoped so. She couldn't imagine her kind-hearted mother marrying the man her father was today.

"There's not much else I can tell you about your real father, Adni. I'm sorry I didn't tell you sooner." Her mother met her gaze. Her eyes glazed with tears.

Adni's heart softened. She couldn't be mad at her mother, and she couldn't very well let her cry either. "It isn't your fault, Mother."

Her lips quirked. "You are so amazing, my daughter." Her mother reached across the space between them, and folded Adni in her embrace.

Adni laced her arms around her mother's neck, and hugged her back as the fire crackled beside them. Never had she imagined that the man who raised her, wasn't her biological father. And who was the strange man who'd sired her and claimed he'd return for her one day?

She shook her head and sat back.

Determination set her heart racing. Whoever her father was, she'd find him.

THREE

It took two days to return to their small village. The mountain tunnels were vast and difficult to navigate, but ever since the people of Salander had fled to the mountains, they'd mapped the passages. What the native clansmen knew, they shared, and in return the refugees of Warshard created a water system for the villages they set up, as well as the clans.

Adni had always been shocked by the stories her mother told her. When she was a little girl, Bran recounted tales of the natives living in the mountains, how they stole little girls in the night if they weren't good, and fed them to mountain cats. So when they arrived in the mountains all those years ago, the kindness of the clansmen had been shocking, to say the least.

Her mother smiled and nodded respectfully to the clansmen they passed. Their large hazel eyes and pale skin was beautiful in a strange way—like ghosts passing in the night.

The narrow corridors between homes opened up to their small front yard, with a wooden fence surrounding it. Though the *yard* was only stone; she remembered the endless grass of Salander, the way it stuck between her bare toes, and tickled the bottoms of her feet. She'd spent endless afternoons running through it with Renley and her grandparents' sheepdog.

"Finally!" Helen sighed loudly. Her thick brows descended over her eyes like angry caterpillars. Her little sister was not a fan of their father's trips either.

Galia glanced over her shoulder, a smile on her lips.

The front and sides of their house jutted from the mountain wall, much more put together then some of the rickety houses in their small village. Flames flickered from her brother's torch. He'd returned sometime in the night, and hadn't spoken a word.

Her mother unlocked the front gate and swung it inward, allowing her children to pass as she lit the torch tied to a fence post, a sign they had returned home, and their neighbors needn't watch for thieves any longer.

Stealing had become all too common in the mountain town.

Helen threw the front door open and stormed inside. For such a small girl, she really could make a lot of noise. Adni's lips quirked in a smile as she followed Renley into the darkness of their home.

Renley used his torch to light the fire in the center room. Flames burned to life, illuminating the firepit surrounded by stone. While Adni's taste in decoration was far more subdued, her mother's couldn't be tamed by a simple grayscale.

Brilliant red, blue, and purple curtains hung from the two doorways just outside the firepit room. On the right, the entrance to their parents' bedroom. On the left, the children's. Though their room was separated by more curtains, all three of them made do in the large room. They were much luckier than some, who shared one large room with their entire family.

Helen dropped her large rucksack, clanging with a pot and pan, to the floor. She stretched and flung herself down in front of the fire, lying on a fur rug. She draped her hand across her face like she was exhausted.

Renley grumbled something about their brat little sister as he stepped over Helen and into the back room, carved from the mountainside itself. The small cave was their kitchen, with stone shelves, and a long wooden counter on one side. In the center, their mother's fish scaling table was pristine as always, her knives lined up neatly beside a large bowl.

"Now, now, Helen." Galia shook her head as she entered behind them. She clucked her tongue and closed the front door. "Put away your things before you rest."

"*Mooom*," Helen whined.

Adni shook her head. She leaned her rucksack against the wall by the front door, and busied herself with lighting the candles spread throughout the living space. They'd bring extra warmth until the firepit grew a decent blaze.

"Don't *mom* me." Galia placed her hands on her hips.

Helen groaned and rolled onto her stomach. She pushed back up to her feet and sulked to the kitchen, her rucksack dragging noisily behind her.

"It's nearly dinner time. Wash up when you're done, children." Galia whisked through the firepit room to the kitchen, replacing their gear with practiced hands.

Adni smiled as her family flickered through the four main rooms of their home. They'd gone on so many trips through the mountains; they had the put-away routine memorized. No one bumped into one another or got in each other's way. They moved as one. But today there was one missing.

Her smile twisted into a frown.

Father was nowhere to be seen. But if he hadn't come home, then where was he?

She glanced around the firepit room, and froze. On the left-hand wall, a mantel dripping in colored fabrics and iron fire prods remained in place, but above it, an empty space glared back at her.

Adni's brows furrowed. Where was their mother's favorite painting? She wouldn't have taken it down. It was the only treasure she managed to keep from her parents' old home. Grandmother had painted the Salander landscape from atop a great hill—Ithrendel castle in one corner and the ocean in the distance, glittering with sunlight.

Mother would never have moved it. Not in one thousand years.

Her heart pounded in her ears as she twisted to search for other anomalies.

The fish drying rack on the opposite wall, though normally nearly full to the brim, had only three shrivelled fish left. She glanced at the weapon's hook by the door and the flint and steel box beside the fish rack.

The dagger vanished from the hook, and the flint and steel box was gone.

Her heart raced. No. This couldn't be. He wouldn't stoop *that* low, would he?

Adni leapt across the room and threw open the lid of the trunk below the mantel. A fishing rod was missing, as was their mother's crossbow.

Her heart sank.

"Adni?" her mother asked.

Adni ignored her and raced to their mother's bedroom. The red and blue curtains brushed her cheeks as she pushed past. The small room was nearly pitch black. She squinted through the dark as she found her way to the dresser on the far end.

She opened her mother's jewelry box. Empty.

Her fists tightened and her heart hammered in her ears. She didn't need to look for her parents' savings. She didn't need to scour the house for gold pieces or their water skins. Father was gone.

"Adni?" Galia brushed the bedroom curtains open. Candlelight flickered through her worried eyes. "What's wrong?"

"He stole from us. He took everything." Adni's shoulders shook. Heat built in her chest. She bit down hard on her lip. She couldn't lose herself to the rage again. *Mother needs me.*

"*What?*"

The surprise in her mother's voice chilled her to the bone. She didn't think her husband capable of it. But if Adni told Galia the reason she'd gone after Bran, that he'd nearly murdered his own daughter, she might reconsider.

"Your jewelry is gone. His dagger is gone. The fish are gone," Adni explained. She'd spare her mother the reality of what her husband had done to Adni, but she couldn't hide this betrayal.

Galia flew across the room. She set the candle by Adni's hands, which remained atop the smooth pinewood of the dresser. Her mother threw open drawers, many of which were empty, or tussled. She flew to the shelf built into the wall next. She tossed books aside and pulled a small copper box from the back.

Her gasp told Adni all she needed to know.

All of their money was gone.

Silence lapsed. Only the crackle of flames in the firepit room broke the uneasy quiet.

Adni looked over her shoulder. Her mother fell to her knees. Adni's heart leapt and her eyes widened. She raced across the room and kneeled by her mother's side.

"Mother?" her voice cracked.

Galia shook her head. Her fingers trembled around the empty copper box. "He's gone. My husband is gone."

Adni touched her shoulder gently. Galia looked up at her, her eyes brimming with tears. Adni's heart clenched. She'd only ever seen her mother cry the day Helen was born. Those had been happy tears, and these were nowhere close.

Wrapping her arms around Galia, Adni pulled her mother into an embrace. Galia clung to her daughter, her fingers tightening around Adni's jacket.

"I'm sorry, Mother. I'm so sorry," Adni said.

Her mother nodded against her.

Not only had her father stolen from them, but he'd run. He'd left them all behind. He'd left his wife and three children to fend for themselves.

And he'd left them with *nothing*.

How would they survive without money? How could they survive without food? Though Renley was good at fishing, and her mother good with a bow, they didn't have much to trade for bread, or vegetables. They'd have to live off of fish until they figured something out.

Adni shook her head. It wasn't fair. Her mother had worked just as hard as their father for everything they had. She'd stayed in these mountains, even when messengers came to tell them Salander was safe to return to. Galia had put up with her husband for over twenty years, and this was the price she paid?

Heat licked her heart. *No.* She wouldn't let her family go down like this.

"I'll get it back." Adni pulled away.

Her mother froze. "What?"

"I'll get it back from Father. *All* of it." Her lips pressed into a firm line. She could do this. She was determined.

Galia shook her head. "We can make it. We'll be all right."

Adni gripped her mother's shoulders. Galia had always been an optimist, but this time Adni had to be the realist. "We will starve without that money." Her lips quirked into a rueful smile. "And I won't let him get away with your treasure." Her mother's most prized possession in the world, the painting of Ithrendel, couldn't be gone forever.

"Adni…"

She stood. "I won't let him get away with this, mother."

Galia shook her head. "You're just like your grandmother used to be."

Adni smiled. Galia rarely spoke of her parents since they'd remained in Ithrendel to protect their livelihood. Adni still remembered the flames burning atop their old house as they ran from the burning city. "Good. At least I get it from your side of the family."

Galia stood, and wiped her eyes. "We will be all right."

"I know we will," Adni said. "But you'll be better than all right when I get back."

I'm really doing this.

Warmth blossomed in her chest. Not the fire of rage, but excitement for something new. Adni would leave her little mountain village, and she would find her father. Maybe even both of them.

* * *

ADNI PACKED A BAG, a fresh water skin, one of the remaining dried fish, a few boiled potatoes, some clothes, and of course her sword. While she readied her belongings, she made a plan. Her father could have only gone to one place: Salander. With all the goods he carried, the going would be slow. She might even be able to catch him before he fled the mountains.

She could do this. She had no other choice.

"Adni." Galia rested a hand on her arm. "Don't forget these." She placed a small box of flint and steel inside her bag, alongside a dagger, a small bottle of oil, and a rag.

"You think of everything." Adni smiled. She met her mother's eyes, which glowed with love. The back of her eyes burned. She'd miss her mother. She'd miss her terribly.

"Of course." Galia rested her hands on either side of her face, and kissed Adni's forehead. "May the blue skies bless your journey."

Adni nodded. Heat rushed through her. This was happening. It was really happening.

"One more thing." Galia pulled a rolled piece of parchment from the top of the mantel. She handed it to Adni. "You remember your lessons on map reading, correct?" Her mother raised an amused eyebrow.

Adni's eyes widened. She'd never been good at map reading. Her mother knew as much. "Yes," she lied.

Galia shook her head. She had to know Adni was lying, but she said nothing.

Adni took the map and tucked it carefully into the top of her rucksack. She flung the straps over her shoulders and secured them below her fur-trimmed hood.

"Goodbye, my love." Galia stepped back.

Adni blinked back tears as she embraced her siblings. Helen whispered a blessing, and Renley stared with a furrowed brow.

"Watch over mother." Adni raised her eyebrows at her brother.

He only nodded.

Adni turned to the door. If she didn't go now, she might never leave. Not with her mother's eyes shining with coming tears, and Helen's lip quivering like a baby.

She sighed and stepped out the door.

* * *

HER BOOTS KICKED up pebbles as she descended from the village to the riverside. The path would take her along the calm river for a while before she'd fall to the darkness of the tunnels. Though she carried a torch in hand, several lined the walls of the passage as it curved downward. A rope hung along the wall, in case the rock was slick with river water. In the spring, when the snow and ice melted, the lakes and rivers would swell and often spread over the narrow passages.

Adni descended carefully, glancing between the river and the path ahead. Though it shouldn't be a problem with the air crisp with chill, and spring far off, it was better to be safe than slip and crack her skull on the rock.

"Hey!" a female voice cut through the dull rumble of the river.

Adni stopped and looked over her shoulder. A blonde woman with shadowed blue eyes and thick lips bounced down the tunnel without a care in the world. Metal armor pieces clanged against one another until she came to a stop several feet from Adni.

Julian.

"Good, I caught you." Julian grinned, flashing perfect white teeth. "You look better."

Adni raised an eyebrow. "You were looking for me?"

"Of course. I had to make sure you were all right."

"I'm fine, thanks to you." Adni's stomach fluttered with gratitude before rolling with uncertainty. She didn't like feeling indebted to anyone, but without Julian she might have sunk to the bottom of the river, never to be found.

Julian shrugged. Her one metal shoulder piece glinted in the light. It was unusual to wear only half armor, or any armor in the mountains for that matter. *Who is this strange woman?* She wondered.

"Where are you going?" Julian asked.

"Salander."

"Lovely! I was headed that way, too."

"You were?" Adni looked Julian up and down. She didn't have any supplies aside from a sheath at her hip and a shield on her back.

Julian smiled. "Yes. I would love your company."

Adni shifted from one foot to the other. This was supposed to be *her* journey. Her quest. She hadn't thought about having anyone join her along the way.

"I do know the way out of the mountain," Julian continued. "Lots of shortcuts, too. We'll shave our travel time in half." Julian winked. This woman was all mischief. There was something dangerous about her carefree smile.

Adni's chest twinged. "How do you know the mountains so well?"

"I like to explore." Julian didn't elaborate.

Adni sighed. Her breath fogged the air. It would save her time if Julian really did know some shortcuts. Plus, she wouldn't need to pull out her map every twelve seconds. She shivered. She didn't want to end up lost either.

"Fine, we'll travel together until we reach Salander." Adni placed her hands on her hips. The hilt of her sword brushed her arm. Based on the size of the sheaths, Julian's sword was far larger than Adni's.

"Excellent." Julian linked arms with Adni and spun her toward the downward slope. "Onward, my new friend!"

Adni's eyes widened as she stared at the woman.

Julian simply grinned and led.

* * *

SUNLIGHT BURNED through the world like she'd never seen before. Adni's heart raced as she shielded her eyes. Knives of pain pierced her skull. The sun rose high in the sky, dusting the world with its rays. It had to be nearly noon.

"Haven't been outside those mountains in a while, have you?" Julian chuckled.

Adni shook her head. "Not in ten years."

Julian's eyes widened. "You're serious? You haven't seen the sun in *ten years?*"

Adni scoffed and rolled her eyes like her mother always chastised Helen for doing. "Of course I've seen the sun. There are plenty of valleys in the mountains where we cultivate what little land we can."

Julian took a deep breath like she was relieved. "Thank the blue skies. I thought you might be reduced to a blind mountain troll!"

"Mountain troll?"

"You haven't heard the stories of the trolls in the deep?" Julian wiggled her fingers and grinned deviously. "Legend has it, the trolls horde gold and pretty little girls who don't go to bed on time."

Adni snorted. "I do seem to recall something about creatures snatching little girls in my bedtime stories."

Julian winked as she spun toward the hillside.

From the cave mouth, they emerged atop a high hill, with grass, *real* grass, as far as the eye could see. Pine trees bordered the horizon, and curved around a small town at the base of the mountain. Smoke from wood stoves curled and dissipated into the sky, and the gleeful cry of children rose on the cool breeze.

Sun warmed her cheeks as she followed Julian. She slowly adjusted to the light, blinking less and less until she lowered her hand from her forehead.

"We should be able to resupply in town. Where are we headed?" Julian glanced over her shoulder as she maneuvered between the few sparse trees and large boulders atop the hill.

"We?" Adni adjusted the straps on her shoulder. As her cheeks warmed, so did the rest of her. Her fur-trimmed coat might be too warm for Salander's autumn.

"I'm invested in your journey now." Julian laughed, her voice high and pleasant. "It's like a story of old. The vengeful daughter seeks her thieving father to avenge her family and return wealth to the mountains. I need to know how this story ends!"

Adni scoffed, regretting all she'd told Julian on their way out of the mountains. "My life isn't a fairy tale, Julian."

"Not yet!" Julian flashed a grin.

Adni shook her head. Even after a day and a half with the mad woman, she still hadn't gotten used to her upbeat attitude. Her optimism rivalled her mother's, though her sanity had to be questioned. What sane person prattled on about trolls and legends constantly?

The red serpent on Julian's shield flashed in the sunlight. The paint was chipped, but the curved head and fangs were still visible. Adni'd never seen a sigil like it before, but then again, she hadn't had the resources to learn much about the six kingdoms beyond the main capitols and royal families.

Wherever she was from, it certainly wasn't the mountains. But maybe Eris or Wakefin? Her blonde hair, tan skin and blue eyes could be from either kingdom.

"Julian?" Adni asked.

"Yes, m'dear?" Julian called over her shoulder.

"Where are you from?"

Julian's shoulders stiffened for hardly a moment. She relaxed so quickly, Adni couldn't be sure if she'd truly tensed up. "Salander, of course."

Adni raised an eyebrow at Julian's back.

"My mother was from Eris, and my father from Salander. That's how I inherited these dashing good looks." Julian laughed and flicked her hair over her shoulder. Adni couldn't be sure if it was a real laugh, however.

They continued down the hill in silence, until the crack of wood and bustling of townsfolk rivalled the breeze rushing by her ears. The sun rose higher, and her back slicked with sweat.

Adni adjusted her hood and unhooked the clasps of her jacket. Cool air brushed her collarbone. She sighed with relief. She'd need to borrow a cooler jacket from someone, or layer up with a few of the shirts she'd packed.

"Welcome to Elmhurst!" Julian spread her hands to the village at the base of the hill.

The rows of homes, shops, and stables were nestled against the mountain, surrounded by a thick pine forest on one side, and hills on the other. They made their way onto a dirt road hardly visible through the overgrown grass, moss, and flowers. It twisted from the hillside, leading into town. The first village outside the mountains she'd seen in ten years. Adni's heart swelled with anticipation before clenching with unease. A hundred new adventures awaited for her in the six kingdoms, of that she was certain. But how much would she see given her quest? Once she found Bran and returned to the mountains, how long would it be before she was able to return?

Adni swallowed the lump in her throat. She'd soon find out.

FOUR

$\mathcal{A}$dni weaved through the unfamiliar town, full of tall wooden homes, stone forges and stables, to the market. The high roofs, and tan, smiling faces of Elmhurst's people surprised her into silence. She followed Julian down the main path, eyes wide and mouth agape.

She'd only been eight when her family fled Salander. Had the houses always been this large, and the sky this vast? Inside one two-story home they'd be able to house half the village. How many people lived in one home? Ten? Twenty?

The scent of fresh bread drifted down the street alongside the cut of pinewood and foul sting of horse manure. She wrinkled her nose. So many unusual smells, and not all pleasant.

"The market is up ahead!" Julian glanced over her shoulder. She was several feet ahead, and paused for Adni to catch up. "A lot different than the mountains, isn't it?"

Adni nodded. "There's so… much."

Julian chuckled. "Elmhurst is quite small, Adni."

Her brows furrowed and she cut Julian a sideways glance. "You can't be serious. Hundreds of people must live here."

"Maybe sixty or so."

Her mouth fell open.

"Be careful not to catch flies." Julian grinned.

Adni snapped her lips shut. "There are dozens of homes." She fought to comprehend this world where so few people had such abundance. She'd been lucky to only share a room with her two siblings in their four-room home. That had been luxurious compared to most in their village.

"Dozens of homes, and lots of open space. You aren't in the mountains anymore." Julian shrugged. Her metal shoulder piece clanged.

Adni shook her head.

She didn't remember there being so much space, and such large homes. Then again, even when she hadn't lived in the mountains, Adni had lived with her two siblings, parents, and grandparents in a two-story home with a tavern attached. That seemed like a luxury beyond compare.

The road widened before splitting in two. It circled around a large tent only to meet at the other side and continue into the distance. The market.

The center shop held fresh bread, piles of grain, bags of rice, and steaming sticky buns. Her mouth watered as the sweet scent slid up her nostrils. Surrounding the street were tents and stands of meat, fish, vegetables, and fruits. She couldn't remember the last time she tasted fruit.

"I'll gather some supplies while you search for your father." Julian's voice cut through Adni's reverie.

Her heart sank at the reminder. "All right."

Julian joined the locals milling across the road with their horses, mules, or children. Their chatter filled the air, and their smiles lit the market.

Adni took a deep breath. She had to remember her mission.

She spoke with dozens of kind, concerned citizens of Elmhurst, from shopkeepers to blacksmiths and children. No one remembered a tall man with a gray beard and dark eyes. They hadn't seen a stranger in days.

Adni continued down the street from the market, her heart heavy. Had she already lost her father's trail? Though she'd never been a good hunter like her mother, she'd hoped to inherit some of her tracking abilities.

The sweet scent of bread disappeared, replaced by dung and flies buzzing around her head. Adni swatted the small annoyances and narrowed her eyes at the stables at the end of the lane.

The barn doors were open with a dozen stalls inside. Most of the horses were in the outer pen, grazing on bales of hay. Their tails flicked at the same irritating flies.

Adni stopped. If her father had been there at all, he'd have gone to the stables. He couldn't very well walk across the entire six kingdoms with all the supplies he carried.

Her fingers closed to fists as she pushed ahead to the stable. Her hands were slick with sweat and her nails dug into her palms by the time she paused at the barn doors. Inside, a young man swept the hay strewn floor, flicking the long pale strands into a pile at the back, next to a large stack of bales.

Adni cleared her throat. "Excuse me."

The brown-haired man glanced up. "Oh, hello." His wide mouth quirked into a one-sided smile. "What can I do for you?" He straightened and leaned the broom up against a wooden post before clapping his hands together. Dust rained down from his dirty fingers.

"I'm looking for someone. A man. Have you had any visitors drop by recently?" she asked.

The man raised an eyebrow and his smile fell. Her father had been there. She knew it. "This morning. An older gentleman stopped by." He glanced at the barn doors. "Look, I don't want any trouble. Whatever that man did–"

Adni shook her head. "I just need to know where he went."

His hazel eyes flashed in the sunlight as he stepped closer. "He bought one of my father's horses and left for Ithrendel."

The capitol. What business did her father have there?

"Did he do something?" the man asked.

Adni worked her jaw back and forth. "Yes."

He quirked an eyebrow and waited for several long moments for her to elaborate. She didn't. "Okay. Was there anything else I could do for you?"

"How much for a horse?" She had to get to Ithrendel somehow.

His brows flew into his bangs. "I don't think my father would be interested–"

"*How much?*"

He sighed. "At least fifty gold coins."

Her heart seized. She didn't have any coins, let alone fifty. Her shoulders slumped.

The stable keeper scratched the back of his head awkwardly and shifted from foot to foot. "I'm sure you could get a ride in town with one of the farmers. They make runs every week." He glanced out the barn doors at the sky, judging the time of day. "Henry, the bread maker, will be heading to the capital soon. You might be able to catch him."

Adni smiled as her heart raced. "Thank you."

He shrugged and plucked his broom from the wall. "Good luck."

Adni nodded and left the barn.

* * *

HER BOOTS beat the dirt path as she raced back to the market. The bread maker was at the center of town, and if she caught him, she'd be headed to Ithrendel before nightfall. She could still catch up with her father. She was only a few hours behind. Though his steed would take him through the forests much faster than a trolley, they'd arrive within a day of him.

"Adni!" Julian waved from the shade of the bread maker's tent. Her smile lit her features, setting her tan skin aglow. At her feet lay a rucksack bulging with supplies. Something red and shiny peeked out the top. *Apples?* Her heart leapt with anticipation.

Her mouth watered as she slowed to a stop. "Julian," she panted. Her lungs heaved as she caught her breath. "I found his next move."

Julian clapped her hands together. "Brilliant. Where is he headed?"

"He bought a horse to travel to Ithrendel." Adni rolled her shoulders and straightened as her breaths evened out. She wiped the sweat from her forehead.

"What a coincidence! I was just speaking with Henry about his trip." Julian glanced at the bread maker, who was packing up shop for the day. "He's headed to Ithrendel in a few minutes."

"The stable boy said the same."

"Oh, there was a stable boy was there?" Julian grinned and waggled her eyebrows.

Adni scoffed. "I have no interest in stable boys, Julian."

Julian quirked a brow, a teasing smile playing on her lips. "Good to know."

"Oy, Julian." Henry stretched his back, veins bulging on his thick neck. "Did you say sometin' 'bout headin' to Ithrendel?"

"I did, Henry." Julian spun back to the shade of the tent. "You wouldn't happen to have room for two little ladies in your cart would you? It'd mean the world to me." Julian batted her eyelashes, her large eyes widening with innocence.

Adni choked back a laugh, covering her mouth with her hand. Julian clearly didn't mind using her charms to sway men in her favor.

Henry chuckled and his cheeks reddened. "Course 'not." He glanced at Adni, before his gaze fell back on Julian. "I'll be loadin' up in a few. You two ready to go?"

Julian glanced at Adni.

Adni nodded.

"Alrighty then." Henry motioned to the back of the shop. "Let's go."

* * *

FLAMES FLICKERED in the firepit at their feet as the sun dipped below the horizon. Adni stretched and twisted her shoulders to work out the kinks. They'd ridden straight through the woods all day, and if Henry was correct, it'd still be another day and a half to reach Ithrendel. Though she wasn't happy about the prospect, it was still better than being stuck in Elmhurst trying to swindle a horse from the stable boy.

Adni sighed and sat beside the dying embers. Henry snored from the back of the cart, and Julian sat across from her, her legs pulled up to her chest and her arms wrapped around them. The stance was protective. Something was off. Could it be the approaching city? Though Adni didn't remember much about Ithrendel, she could still conjure the faint excitement she felt when she was a little girl and her parents first told her and her siblings they'd be going into the city.

Though for eight years she'd lived not far from the city walls, her mother wasn't keen on crowds, and feared losing her children in the bustle.

"Are you all right?" Adni asked.

Julian's gaze flickered up from the flames. Orange burned through her normally dark irises. Her sullen expression quickly shifted to a flirtatious smile. Though the look had always seemed genuine before, this time it felt forced.

"I'm fine," Julian said. "Just thinking about the city."

"Thinking about Ithrendel makes you..." Was it sadness in her eyes? Or something else? "Nervous?" Adni guessed, unsure what emotion lurked in the depths of Julian's gaze.

Julian's smile wavered. "A little."

Adni crossed her legs and rubbed her ankles. "Why?"

Her gaze lowered back to the flames and her smile disappeared completely. "It's nothing, really."

Adni didn't believe it for one second. "I've told you about my father after having known you for only a few days." Adni smiled. "You can trust me."

Julian looked up, a question hiding in her eyes. She wasn't sure she could trust Adni anymore than Adni knew if she could trust Julian. But, if they were going to travel together, they might as well be more open with each other.

"Fine." Julian sighed. "Last time I was in Ithrendel, I was chased through the city by guards. I'm hoping no one remembers me."

Adni's eyes widened. Of all the things she could have said, she expected that the least. "Why did they chase you?" Unease rolled through her stomach. If Julian was some sort of criminal, she wasn't sure travelling with her was such a good idea.

"Because they thought me mad." Julian shrugged.

Adni paused, waiting for Julian to elaborate. "Why did they think that?"

"It's a long story." Julian left it at that.

Adni twisted her lip between her teeth. While she wished Julian would explain further, she didn't want to push someone to divulge their secrets if they weren't comfortable.

Unfolding the scratchy blanket Henry had given her, Adni curled up on her side by the fire, using her lumpy rucksack as a pillow. It had been a long day, and sleep pulled at her eyelids.

But before she could drift off, Julian broke the quiet. "Is finding your father the only reason you left the mountains? If they've been your home for so long, I imagine it was hard to leave."

Adni blinked awake, her eyebrows furrowing. She shifted uncomfortably, rubbing the lumps out of her rucksack. "It's not the only reason." Though it had been hard to leave the mountains, it had also been easy. She'd wanted to leave for so long that she'd leapt at the first chance.

"What is the second reason?" Julian asked. Her bright eyes watched Adni curiously.

The dying embers crackled inside the makeshift firepit dug into the earth. Adni paused for a moment to consider if she should tell Julian the truth. Even if Julian hadn't told her the truth, it didn't mean Adni needed to keep hers a secret.

"I want to find my real father," Adni admitted.

Julian stayed quiet for a long moment, her fingers balling into fists against her knees. "I can understand that." She didn't say anything more.

Adni watched the orange light fade from Julian's cheeks as the last of the glowing embers faded to black. She didn't quite understand

Julian's reaction, but then again, she didn't really understand a lot about the strange woman.

"Good night, then." Adni turned over, the coals continuing to warm her back on the cold autumn night.

"Good night."

* * *

THE TROLLEY CART bounced and bobbed over uneven ground as it disappeared over the horizon two days later. Henry waved a hand, silhouetted by the sun as it dipped toward the mountains on a side street winding around the city's outer walls.

It had taken far longer to travel to Ithrendel than she'd expected, leaving a sour taste in her mouth and nausea crawling through her stomach. The constant bounce of the trolley hadn't helped. More than once she'd lost herself to dizzy spells on the bottom of the cart. Luckily the hay strewn wood floor hadn't been the most uncomfortable thing in the world.

"Thank you, Henry!" Julian called as she waved goodbye.

Adni rubbed her sore shoulders and adjusted the straps of her rucksack. Her stomach ached with hunger. She hadn't been able to eat much while they travelled. Even the gorgeous red apples Julian had acquired weren't enough to entice her sour gut.

"Well, I should be going," Adni said. She had a mission to get on with, and picking up her father's trail in a city bigger than anything she remembered would not be easy.

Julian looked at her and her smile fell. "You can't be serious? After all you've told me of your father, I'm going to help you find him."

The protective edge to Julian's voice made Adni shift uncomfortably. She'd told Julian much about her father, including his change in the mountains, the constant treasure hunts, and his desperate attempt for more when he pushed her off the waterfall. She'd even revealed her second purpose for this journey; to find the man who sired her.

Adni shook her head. "It isn't necessary. I'm sure you have things to do."

Julian placed her hands on her wide hips. Her metal shoulder plate glinted in the dying sun. "I'm going to help you find him."

Adni sighed. Exasperated. There would be no convincing Julian. She was more stubborn than Renley on bathing day. "Fine."

At least Julian knew much of the six kingdoms, especially Salander and Ithrendel City. Hopefully her knowledge would come in handy. Someone had to navigate the winding cobblestone streets and tall stone buildings.

"Good." Julian's smile returned and the hardness of her eyes left. "Now, where should we start?"

Horns blared, and Adni jumped. Her eyes widened as she spun toward the city gates. They hovered less than twenty-feet inside the city, beside a guard tower next to the wall. The great wooden doors were open, leaning against the outer walls.

Horse hooves clacked across stone as a long procession entered. The street cleared of both soldiers and pedestrians, allowing the royal procession to pass. Two soldiers led the pack on white stallions, green flags atop long golden poles in hand. The flags billowed in the light breeze as a dozen soldiers marched in after, followed by a lavish pair with matching crowns.

"The King and his new Queen," Julian whispered. She pulled Adni back until their backs pressed against the tower. Wood splintered against her fingertips.

The two leading the pack passed and the royals drew closer. A man with thick brown hair, blue-green eyes and a kind smile, waved to his people. His golden crown winked in the light, and emeralds flashed. His long robe rested over his black stallion's back, reaching nearly to the end of its tail.

Adni racked her brain to remember the name of the new king. Her parents hadn't known much about him, as he was only a prince when they'd fled to the mountains.

"King Emeril," Julian said.

Adni glanced at the blonde. It was as if she'd read Adni's mind.

"His new Queen is Rona of Seaburn."

Rona was a beauty, with tawny yellow skin, dark hooded eyes and long raven hair. Her rosy cheeks dimpled with her smile as she waved shyly at the people they passed.

"I've never seen someone like her before," Adni whispered.

"She's a tribeswoman from across the sea. Rona was one of the soldiers to dedicate themselves to Queen Haven of Rythern. But after the war, many of the foreigners who came across the sea dispersed to start their own lives."

Adni raised her eyebrows. "How do you know all of this?"

Julian chuckled. "I travel, and I listen."

The royal procession passed, ending in another two dozen soldiers, all in the silver armor she'd always imagined wearing. Her heart leapt at the sight of their wide sheaths and thick shields. She still wanted desperately to be a part of them, and one day she would. Her fingers tightened on the hilt at her waist. Her heart ached to join the royal guard, to defend the nation she remembered so fondly.

She sighed. But for now she'd have to put her dreams on hold. She had a family to help first.

"Where should we start?" Julian glanced around the street as the small crowd dispersed.

Adni glanced at the lowering sun. It crested the castle peeks up ahead, just visible over the tall city homes. Ithrendel was built on a small incline, streets weaving upward to the main keep.

"I don't know." Adni reached for the amulet that always hung at her throat. Her fingers brushed her empty collarbone. She sighed. She missed her mother's necklace.

"It's getting late. We could begin in the morning," Julian suggested.

Adni twisted her lip between her teeth. She didn't want to give up. Not yet. Her stomach rumbled loudly.

Julian laughed. "Hungry?"

Heat flooded her cheeks. "Maybe."

Julian twisted her bag over her shoulder and plucked an apple from the top. She tossed it to Adni, who caught it with ease.

The skin was cold and slick in her fingers. Adni licked her lips. She hardly remembered the sweetness of apples. It had to have been at least five years since her mother had gotten hold of any. Adni sunk her teeth into the skin. Sweet and sour burst inside her mouth, flooding her taste buds.

A shiver worked its way up her spine and she bit back a moan of pleasure. "It's *so* good." She savored the taste, twisting the bite and gnashing it slowly between her teeth.

Julian's lips quirked with amusement. "That must be one good apple."

Adni smiled. "You have no idea."

FIVE

After the sunset, torchlight flooded the streets. Fewer and fewer citizens remained outdoors, while soldiers continued to patrol.

Adni and Julian searched for clues for several hours, coming up empty. It was difficult to describe her father to locals without him sounding like every other Salander man in his forties. But after speaking to innkeepers, shop owners, and several dozen soldiers, it seemed no one had seen a man with a painting and a crossbow.

"This is useless," Adni groaned. She leaned against the cold stone of an inn; the second they'd visited in city limits.

Julian's forehead wrinkled. "Don't give up yet."

Adni sighed. "I'm not giving up. Just tired."

"Why don't we stay here at the inn for the night? Tomorrow we can begin again. Maybe your father is staying outside the city walls. Or maybe with a friend somewhere."

Julian had a point. There was still plenty of ground to cover. Spending all night searching wouldn't do them much good.

"I don't have any gold for an inn," Adni said. They might be able to find a cozy barn though, or maybe a safe spot below a pine tree.

"I do."

Adni looked at her with wide eyes. "You do?"

Julian laughed. "How do you think I bought all these supplies?" She shook her bag for effect.

Adni flushed. "I thought you'd used your womanly charms, or something."

Julian gasped in mock offense. "Me? Well I never."

Adni grinned. "Fine, fine."

"Come on." Julian laughed and took Adni's arm. She pulled her to the inn door, and stepped into the warmth of a hearth and candlelight.

The smooth stone walls were covered in paintings and brass candle holders. Wooden booths lined the wall, and several small tables occupied the floor. Bar maidens rushed between tables with strange grace, twirling and spinning around one another and the patrons, who howled their laughter and stunk of beer.

Julian secured a room from the surly bar keeper and led the way upstairs, keys jingling in her hand. The small stairwell nearly brushed Julian's large shoulder plate. If she had one on either side, Adni wasn't sure the young woman would fit.

"I only got the room for the night, but if we need it for a second, it shouldn't be a problem," Julian said.

"How much coin do you have?" Adni raised a brow.

"Enough." Julian stopped outside a wooden door with a bronze three pegged to the door. She unlocked it with a rusted key and stepped inside.

Only one bed. Adni's stomach flipped. She glanced around the room. A dresser, a washbasin, furs and pillows, a small desk and a lantern. The shutters were drawn, which Julian opened first. Moonlight spilled inside, giving Julian enough light to find and turn on the lantern.

Adni had never once slept in the same bed as anyone but her parents, and that had only been when she was a child and thunder darkened the night. She wiped her sweaty palms on her trousers and stepped inside.

Julian didn't seem to notice her unease, busying herself with unpacking a few apples and a waterskin. Her blonde hair burned orange next to the lantern. Long shadows brushed her cheeks from her thick eyelashes.

Adni gulped.

"If you're still hungry, I bought salted meat and bread as well." Julian set her things atop the dresser and leaned her rucksack against its base.

"Maybe later." Adni lay her own bag on the other side of the dresser and removed her coat. She hung it on a hook by the wash-basin. The water was clear, but was it clean?

"The barkeep said the water was fresh. They empty and fill them every day," Julian said, as if anticipating her thoughts.

Adni sighed with relief. After days on the road, she was ready to wash up. But still, she paused and glanced over her shoulder. Julian continued to busy herself, smoothing the bed sheets, fluffing the pillows, and spreading a fur blanket over the bed. Adni's cheeks flushed, and her heart raced.

Why did she care if she slept next to another woman? Why did she care if she undressed in front of Julian? Adni shook her head. She was being irrational. It wasn't as if Julian was a man.

Adni dipped her fingers in the washbasin water. It was cool to the touch, a welcome relief to the heat building inside her chest and burning her cheeks. Trying to delay her disrobing, Adni removed her belt, and leaned her sword against the wall.

She removed her boots and paused at the buttons of her pants. Should she ask Julian to turn around while she washed? What would Julian think of her request? She'd think her strange, most likely. Women were naked around other women on bathing days all the time. But she'd never been nude in front of one who wasn't family before.

Adni bit her lip, self-conscious and uncertain.

"You're not the only one who needs a quick wash, you know,"

Julian said.

Adni jumped, and tried to cover the movement with a cough. "Apologies." She pushed off her pants, trying with all of her might not to glance over her shoulder. She pulled her shirt off next, leaving only her underclothes on. She busied herself with washing her skin, scrubbing as much dirt off as possible. Her skin felt as if it were vibrating, goosebumps running up and down her flesh.

Her heart pounded in her ears as she finished—not once looking at Julian. She pulled on a large shirt, which barely reached her thighs, and leapt into bed, clinging to the sweet safety of blankets.

Julian shuffled around the room as Adni quieted her pounding heart. Soft thumps hit the floor as Julian disrobed and water splashed quietly for several long minutes.

Adni's heart continued to race, and flush heated her cheeks. *Should I say something?* She gulped.

Her fingers tightened around the fur, which tickled her skin and warmed her in the chill night air. Every piece of her burned with confusion and curiosity. She'd never felt like this before. It had to mean something.

"It's nice to be clean isn't it?" Julian sighed blissfully.

Adni peeked from the safety of blankets and startled. Cold moonlight brushed the left side of Julian, from her wide hips and shoulders, to the curve of her back, while the warmth of the lantern set the right side of her aglow.

"Yes!" Adni ducked back under the blanket. She'd looked, and she hadn't meant to, especially in such a private moment. It wasn't right to spy on anyone while in such a vulnerable position. She swallowed the lump in her throat.

Her fingers trembled until the blanket slowly shifted. Adni froze.

"It's cold out here." Julian slipped under the fur.

Adni scooted as far away as possible, until her back pressed against the wall. Julian sighed, her hot breath brushing Adni's cheeks. A shiver wound up her spine.

"It is," Adni agreed.

Quiet descended between them. Should she start a conversation before they slept? Or should she let silence reign?

Her muscles tensed and her body remained rigid. Adni's mind raced with a thousand thoughts, none of which she could stop or cling to. Minutes dragged on, their breath the only sound.

She should say something. Something about tomorrow. Something about the plan they didn't yet have.

Adni cleared her throat. "Julian?"

Silence.

Adni waited for several long seconds. "Julian?"

Julian's breathing was even and steady. Her breath was hot on Adni's face. She was asleep.

Adni took a deep, shuddering breath. The dim light of the lantern lit the waves wringing Julian's face. It brushed her smooth skin and highlighted her sharp cheekbones, wide jaw and thick lips.

Shaking her head, Adni flipped onto her back and stared at the ceiling. She had no idea what was coming over her, or what the burning in her chest meant, but only one thing would cure it. Sleep.

She closed her eyes and waited. With a million thoughts drifting through her mind, she thought she might never sleep. But eventually she gave way to exhaustion and darkness.

* * *

THE SQUEAK of a floorboard sent her eyes flashing open. Adni breathed in sharply, her pulse pounding in her ears. Darkness greeted her. It was still night. Only the lantern had died and moonlight hardly filtered through the window.

She took a deep breath to steady herself. She'd heard something, but saw nothing. Maybe it had been in her dreams.

Creek.

Julian flew to her feet, throwing the blanket back as she darted toward the sound, a knife in her hand.

Adni's eyes flew wide and she sat up quickly as a man stepped from the darkness. He grabbed Julian's throat before she took a step off the bed.

Julian choked and Adni leapt for her sword—which suddenly felt much too far away.

White hair descended to the man's waist, and startlingly blue eyes stared into hers. She froze. She knew those eyes.

He smirked and tilted his head. Something sinister and curious flashed through the depths of his eyes. "It's good to finally meet you, Adanza." His voice cut like the blade Julian held. The knife clattered to the ground. "Especially after your mother hid you for so long."

What?

Adni's heart sped, though her entire body felt rooted to the ground.

"It's time for you to meet your real family." The man squeezed Julian's throat, forcing a strangled cry from her lips.

Adni leapt to her feet, Julian's pain ripping her from the cold that kept her still. "Let her go!"

Julian clawed at the man's pale fingers, his thick black nails puncturing Julian's perfect skin.

Fire rose inside her chest. How *dare* he harm Julian?

"I'll see you in a bit, my child," he said.

"My *what?*" Adni gasped.

The man raised a hand and blew sparkling purple dust from his palm. It flew into her face and lungs. She inhaled it, and with every breath, her limbs turned to lead. Adni fell onto the furs of the bed as a loud thump hit the ground. Julian? She lost consciousness before another thought could flicker through her mind.

* * *

Cold pressed against her cheek and shoulder. A haze lay on her mind like the first sprinkling of snow in winter. Adni shivered and pulled her blanket closer. Instead of fur, leather brushed her fingertips. Her eyebrows furrowed. *Why is my coat on top of me?*

Another tremble shook her shoulders. The fur hood tickled her ear. Hard rock stuck into her shoulder, side, and hip. The haze slowly fell away as her body's aches became more apparent.

Adni shifted onto her stomach and got her knees beneath her. Her hands pressed against the stone and pushed her up. The rock was smooth, almost polished. She shook her head to clear away the rest of the fog.

Where am I?

Adni startled as she sat back on her legs, kneeling on a stone dais. A large cavern opened up around her, with two passages forking off one side, and a throne on the opposite end. The dais she sat upon rested at the center of the cavern, which walls were smooth, but from the ceiling hung stalactites.

The obsidian throne oozed menace. There was something cold about it, as if it drained all light around it, and turned its twisting stone and metal into darkness.

Fire burned in six bronze bowls, with intricate carvings weaving through two straight lines, wrapping the dish like a bracelet. The flames were positioned two beside the raised platform of the throne, one on either side of the dais, and two beside the passages leading from the room. Between the passages a twisting metal statue arched in every direction, twisting and churning on itself like waves. She'd never seen anything like it.

Adni glanced around the huge space. Somewhere the drip of water echoed. She was back in the mountains. Her heart sank.

The damn Cinder Mountains.

"Adanza," the deep voice of a man boomed through the throne room, bouncing and echoing off the ceiling.

The white-haired man who'd choked Julian entered from one of the passages. His blue eyes darkened, and his wide mouth twitched into a menacing grin.

Her skin crawled as she slid off the dais and onto the floor. Her feet didn't freeze. She had her boots on. But she hadn't gone to bed with boots on. Her trousers and belt were on too. Adni's skin chilled. Someone had dressed her. Someone had touched her nearly naked flesh.

She bristled at the thought and held her jacket tight to her shoulders.

"Who are you?" Her voice was small, insignificant in the grand space.

"Your father." The man swept past the metal statue and down the small slope to the center of the floor. He stopped on the other side of the dais and held his hands behind his back. "My name is Solipher."

Adni glanced around the cavern. *Is this a joke? This* man is my *father?* The one who clearly kidnapped her and returned her to the one place she couldn't return to without her family's money.

"You lie," she squeaked, unable to find her voice.

Her heart sped. Even as she said it, she knew it was false. His winter eyes, pale skin and sharp jaw were all features she knew too well. They were her own.

"Come now, Adanza," he chuckled humorlessly. "You know that's not true."

Her nostrils flared. "My name is *Adni.*" Adanza never suited her.

Solipher smiled. "All right, *Adni.*" He raised both of his eyebrows at her.

"Where am I?" She bit off her words, trying to summon her courage, her strength—anything to compete with the cold fear stunning her useless limbs.

"Izenfir. Your home." Solipher slowly paced around the dais. Heat fell off him in waves, warming the cold in her bones.

"This isn't my home." Adni watched him circle her. He kept several feet between them until he returned to the opposite side once more. What was he doing?

"Maybe not in your mind, but it is the birthplace of your people."

Adni raised an eyebrow. What did that mean? "What are you talking about?"

Solipher smiled. "All will be explained in time."

She sighed. That was specific. Thoughts raced through her head, questions of where he'd been, why he'd left, and why he'd never come back until now. Her chest burned until she had to ask something—anything. "Why didn't you come back for me?"

His smile dropped. "I meant to take you on your eighteenth birthday, when I take all of my children home." His stony expression twisted into a frown. Danger flashed through his gaze. "But your mother kept you from me. She hid you from me," he scoffed. "From your own father."

Adni's fists tightened. "Why would she hide me from you?"

There had to be a reason. Aside from trying to spare her husband, Galia had never lied to her family.

"Fear, most likely." Solipher shrugged and returned to pacing. "Humankind has always feared that which it doesn't understand. We are no different."

Her brows furrowed. "We?"

"Yes. You may not be exactly like me, but you have my blood." He paused. "You have my power."

Her heart lurched and her voice squeaked. "Power?"

He smirked as he stopped by her shoulder. His icy gaze racked her from head to toe. Her nerves seemed to amuse him. "Yes."

Adni shook her head. She didn't understand. What power? What did he mean? What *was* he?

"I don't know what you're talking about." Adni stepped away. She'd always craved power, but could hardly swing a sword.

"Not yet, but you will." Solipher returned to the other side of the dais, his hands still poised gracefully at his lower back. His chest stuck out under fine black robes stitched with gold.

Adni glanced around the cavern once more. Her heart skipped. How could she have forgotten? "Where is Julian?"

A sound between a hiss and a growl rumbled from his chest. He narrowed his eyes. "You needn't concern yourself with humans any longer."

Adni stepped back. "I *am* human."

Solipher tipped his head back and laughed. His dangerous expression gave way to taunting, bright eyes. "You are *ashen*, my daughter. Part of me, and part of your mother. Do not lower yourself by calling yourself a *human*."

"But I am!" Her heart hammered inside her head. She had no idea what he was talking about. Everything was making less and less sense. Every nerve in her body told her to run. She had to flee. It wasn't safe there. But she couldn't leave yet, not without Julian. *If* Julian was there at all.

"You are *not*," he hissed.

Adni stepped around the dais, putting as much space between them as she could while making her way to the passages—her only way to escape. "Where is Julian?"

"In the dungeon with the other vermin."

Adni froze. The dungeon? What kind of place was this?

"But no matter, now that you're home, you can forget about the human world for now and concentrate on obtaining your truest power. It can all be yours. I sense greatness in you, daughter." Solipher's gaze followed her every step. Even as she drew away from him, he didn't move, only watched.

"I don't care. I don't want your power." Something in her chest twinged. A lie. Her heart betrayed her. Power was something she'd always desperately craved. Power to get away from the man she thought was her father, power to escape the mountains, power to join the Salander army.

Solipher snorted. "You can't lie to me, Adni."

Adni ground her teeth together. She hated that he saw through her. She didn't even know this man.

"Let me demonstrate the power you'll soon possess." Solipher's mouth twisted into a smirk.

The ice in his eyes turned to burning blue flames. He extended his hands on either side of him, his fingers splayed and palms facing the ceiling. He raised his chin and closed his eyes. Something dark curled in his palms. He exhaled loudly, almost blissfully, and with his breath, magic burned.

Black dripped from his fingers, falling like smoking waterfalls to the floor. It pooled around his feet, spreading like a pool of blood, before bubbling, rising and curling off the floor. It twisted like the metal sculpture at his back until long curved tendrils danced in the air, pointed like knives.

Solipher opened his eyes and lowered his chin. He met her gaze and smiled. "Behold... my power."

SIX

The darkness pulled all warmth from her bones. It left her cold, and shivering. Adni slipped her arms into her coat and held them tight to her chest. Her breaths ragged, she desperately sought to make sense of what she'd seen.

Magic.

That was the only explanation. Never had she believed in magic. She believed in duty, honor, and the first frost telling of the coming winter. She believed in what she was taught, what she saw for herself, and what she knew of the world. But that didn't include magic. That didn't include the darkness seeping from Solipher's fingers, or the awe that welled in her chest at the sight of it.

Her gut twisted with nausea. It didn't include the sudden desire that burned through her chest as the black encircled her, or the disappointment when it disappeared.

Her heart pounded faster. Some part of her wanted that power. *Hungered* for it. Something dark and hot blossomed in her chest. It scared her as much as it thrilled her.

Who am I? What am I becoming?

Adni leaned against the dais for support. Her fingers trembled and her breaths fogged the cold air. She couldn't get warm, no matter how close she got to the flame bowls.

"Daughter," Solipher's voice boomed. "Come." He turned towards the left passage and motioned her to him. Her body froze for a moment before her feet took across the room of their own accord.

She glared at the feet betraying her curiosity. If she was part of this man, then his power was hers. This magic was *hers*. And she wanted it more than she'd ever wanted anything.

"I'd like you to meet your half-brother, Kaldar."

Adni looked behind Solipher.

"*Kal.*" A tall man, maybe three years older than her, entered from the passage, his short hair shockingly white, and his grey eyes dead.

"Ah yes, you both prefer to shorten your names." Solipher's tone was flat. "At least you already have something in common."

Kaldar stopped beside his father, the spitting image of a younger Solipher, from his wide shoulders, so his long fingers and stern brow. "Sister," he greeted.

Adni worked her jaw back and forth. So she had another half-brother, too. She already had two siblings, adding another simply complicated things more. "Hello."

Something cold and dark settled in Kaldar's gaze. His expression was devoid of emotion, flat and lifeless. He stared through her as much as he stared at her. Is this what power did to them?

"Kaldar will guide you through Izenfir and introduce you to our way of life," Solipher explained.

Kaldar slid Solipher a sideways glance. "Has she embraced her power yet?"

Solipher shook his head. "Not yet."

Kaldar's cheek twitched as if this irritated him. His first potential emotion. "You should." He met her gaze. "Give up your humanity and embrace who you really are. Our family's power is nearly as great as the ancients." Solipher smirked.

Adni raised an eyebrow. She had no idea what he meant. "Ancients?"

"All will be explained to you in time, my child." Solipher's fingers brushed her shoulder. She stepped away.

"There is no feeling greater than this power." Kaldar extended his palm. Darkness swirled to life, writhing in his hand.

Adni gasped. Even such a small display sent her eyes wide and her heart pounding. Something tugged at her chest. Whatever this magic was—she needed it. She snapped her lips shut. But what was the cost of this power?

"Accept who you are, sister." Kaldar closed his fingers, and the darkness disappeared.

Adni cleared her throat. Her fingers twitched at her side. She needed to get a hold of herself. This was all too much information. "I'll think about it." She couldn't very well flat out refuse. "But I'd like to go home now."

"This is your home now," Solipher snapped. Heat rolled off of him. "You'll be expected to stay for a while like my other children." Solipher clutched his hands behind his back. "You'll be trained like all your siblings before you."

Her eyes widened. How many siblings did she have?

Though the urge to flee was strong, she didn't want to incur Solipher's wrath. It reminded her of the man she thought to be her father. Bran. She'd thought his temper worse than any other, until now. Where was the charming man her mother had described? Had it all been a ruse to seduce Galia?

"Go now." Solipher motioned to the passage doors.

Kaldar nodded and dipped in a small bow before he spun on his heels and proceeded toward the exit.

Adni glanced between the two of them before she quickly followed. She swiped her palms, slick with sweat, over her trousers. Her mind raced. Nothing made sense. Her life. Her family. Everything was falling apart. Everything she'd once known was gone. So many lies. So many secrets. And she might be the biggest lie of all.

"This way." Kaldar slowed his pace so she could catch up with him. His long legs had put some distance between them down the smooth stone tunnel.

"Where are we going?" Adni walked beside her half-brother, flashing curious glances under her lashes. They didn't have the same eyes, but they shared the same nose and jawline.

"To the cliffs. It's the best view in the Kingdom." His voice betrayed no interest, no curiosity, nothing beyond his duty to his father.

Adni bit back an irritated sigh.

Cold light filtered through the torchlight at the end of the tunnel. A clouded sky appeared over the edge of a high cliff. A storm was on the horizon, bringing darkness to the sky and wet to the air.

She pulled her coat tighter as they stepped from the protection of the tunnel walls, and out into the open air. Wind tugged at her coat and sent her hair flying. It slapped her cheeks and rushed inside her mouth.

Adni spit it out and pulled her hair back. The cliff overlooked a deep chasm, miles and miles wide. She could just barely see the other end, where snow-topped mountains rose all around. Pathways were carved out of the cliff sides, weaving downward, upward, into tunnels and cavern mouths. At the center rose a tower, carved from earth and balancing precariously on a tall, thin slice of rock.

The spire twisted out of the ground and into the sky. Windows were carved out of the sides, and a large metal door marked an entrance at the end of a narrow stone bridge from the cliff on which they stood.

"Welcome to Izenfir," Kaldar said.

Adni looked at him, but his expression was as flat as she'd ever seen it. "What is this place?"

"A sanctuary for our kind, and for theirs." He nodded at a few people milling around the cliff paths. Tall men dressed in regal robes, just like her father had. They wore gold, and jewels, brilliant colors and muted ones. Each was different from the other, but all had the same dangerous cunning in their bright eyes. The men and women who followed them were small in comparison, with graying skin and collars around their necks.

"What are they?" Goosebumps ran over her flesh.

"Dragons."

Her heart leapt, and a smile quirked her lips. "You're not serious?" Laughter curled around her words. She couldn't hide her amusement. *Dragons?* The mythical flying lizards that breathed fire. They were no more real than the trolls Julian spoke of.

Kaldar narrowed his eyes. Her lips snapped shut.

He *was* serious.

"But where are their scales? Their wings?" Adni's eyebrows furrowed as she battled with her own confusion. They all had to be delusional.

"They are in human form." Kaldar sighed as if it were obvious.

"So they can… transform into dragons?" Her voice hitched with disbelief.

"Yes."

"And we're… what? Half-bloods?"

"*Ashen,*" he corrected.

Adni shook her head. "You're all mad."

She stared over the cliff. The paths wrapping the chasm had dozens of tunnels. Some seemed natural, puncturing the earth in jagged lines, while others had large stone or metal doors, eight or nine feet high. Intricate carvings wrapped each of the doorways. Maybe they were separate dwellings. She looked down from the paths into the dark abyss at the bottom of the chasm. Miles down was the floor of the valley. People in rags and with pickaxes in hand, stabbed the stone floor and carted wheelbarrows of rock up the mountain paths.

"Who are they?" she asked.

"Slaves."

Adni spun toward him. "*What?*"

He stared back at her.

"There haven't been slaves in the six kingdoms in hundreds of years."

"We aren't in the six kingdoms."

Adni shook her head. Wrong. It was all *so* wrong. Whatever lunacy this was, she needed to get out and quickly. She froze. But the power they spoke of still called to her. It swirled like fire inside her chest.

She needed something, or someone familiar, something to cling to through all of this madness.

"Can I see Julian?" Her voice was small. She bit the inside of her cheek. If emotions were weakness to these people, she must be the weakest of them all.

He scoffed. "That woman you arrived with?"

Adni nodded.

"Fine." He paused. "As long as you come to worship the flames with me tonight."

She looked up. Worship the flames? What in blue skies did that mean? She sighed. Whatever it was, it'd be worth it to speak with Julian. Maybe she'd know what to do. "All right."

Kaldar turned back to the mountainside. Adni looked after him and startled. Her eyes flashed wide as she gazed up at the front of a castle. Though they'd emerged from a stone tunnel, she expected one of the same carved doors that marked the chasm. Instead, an enormous stone castle face was carved from the mountainside. Turrets rose on either side, spires rising from the top. Windows were etched from the stone, stained glass inserted into the otherwise dark rock.

"Come along." Kaldar motioned for her to follow. He led the way to the cliff side staircase. It curved downward, wrapping the chasm edge. Adni followed, her muscles like lead the further they descended. The wind died, trapped by the dark chasm walls with no escape.

No wonder they could keep slaves. Humans would never be able to climb the walls jutting from the earth. Her gut twisted. How would she escape up them either? Did she want to?

Before they reached the floor of the chasm, Kaldar turned inside a wide tunnel with a jagged entrance and no door. Torches lined the walls, and moans echoed within. Adni stopped.

Kaldar paused and glanced over his shoulder. "Are you coming?"

Cold slipped inside her jacket. Her jaw tensed as she nodded.

Adni followed Kaldar down the tunnel until the cold light of the sky disappeared and only torchlight remained. The tunnel branched off into many, a maze in disguise.

The tunnel widened into a cavern with cells carved out of the rock. Single cots lay inside, alongside a bucket and nothing else. Human shapes shifted inside the dark cells. Stone walls separated some of the cells, while bars separated the others.

Kaldar stopped half way into the cavern. He pointed to a cage. "That one." Shadows obscured anyone inside. "I'll be back soon." He turned and left without waiting for her response. His footsteps didn't echo in the cavern like hers did. He was quieter than a mountain cat stalking his prey.

"Adni?" Julian whispered.

Adni spun to the cell and leapt forward. Her fingers closed around the bars, her knuckles white. "Julian? Are you there?"

Julian's blonde hair and blue eyes appeared from the darkness. Her long fingers wrapped around the bars, smudged with dirt and specks of blood.

"What have they done to you?" Adni's heart pounded in her ears. Though she hadn't known Julian long, she'd put her in this mess. She'd allowed the woman to travel with her, and aid her in her journey. She was responsible for her imprisonment.

"Nothing but lock me inside this cage." Julian shrugged, but worry clouded her eyes. She smiled as if she were simply there of her own volition. "I'm fine, but how are you? Where have you been?"

Adni shook her head. "You wouldn't believe me if I told you."

Julian's jaw hardened. "Try me."

She shifted uncomfortably. "That man, the one who appeared in our room at the inn... he's my... father."

Julian's eyes widened. "*What?*"

Words poured from her mouth as she explained the magic she'd witnessed, and the things Kaldar had said.

"That's insane," Julian said once she'd finished.

"I know, but I don't know what to do." Adni leaned her forehead against the cold metal bars.

"You can't accept that power."

Adni looked up, her eyebrows pulled together. Julian had been far quicker to accept the things she'd said than Adni had been. She still didn't believe most of it.

"You don't understand what will happen to you if you do," Julian continued, her eyes pleading. "Please listen to me. No matter what they say. No matter what they do. You can't give in to it. You can't take their magic."

"Why?" Unease twisted her stomach.

"Just trust me."

"I don't even know you." Adni stepped back. Her heart raced. Did Julian know something about these people?

"Adni, *please*." Julian pressed her face against the bars. "We need to stop them, not join them."

Adni's fingers closed into fists. "How do you know that?"

Someone shifted in the cell beside Julian. They both glanced at the small, dirty girl inside. Whoever she was, she'd been there a long time.

"I can't explain now, but you need to listen to me," Julian continued.

Adni shook her head. "No, you need to explain yourself if I'm going to trust you."

Julian groaned her irritation and looked to the ceiling as if calling for the sky to assist her. "*Adni,* please."

"Sister." Kaldar's voice echoed in the cavern.

Adni spun to face her half-brother, while Julian's hiss filled the quiet. The woman shifted back into the darkness of her cell as Kaldar approached.

"It's time to go," he said. His grey gaze flicked to Julian's cell.

Adni sighed. "Fine." She hadn't gotten any help from Julian after all. All she was left with were more questions, and no answers.

SEVEN

"It's time to worship the flames." Kaldar led Adni from the dungeon to the staircase wrapping the chasm wall. He ascended quickly, his gaze stern and his jaw set.

Adni could do nothing but follow. She had no idea where she was or what she was doing. These people might be her family, but who were they? What were they? Though they claimed to be dragons, she had yet to see a scaled one among them.

The climb back to the castle front was long. Her thighs ached by the time they reached it. Exhaustion dulled her senses, and sweat slicked her back. The cold breeze was welcomed as the sun dipped toward the horizon.

Red light filled Izenfir, slowly lowering beyond the distant mountains.

"Stay with me," Kaldar said. She had no plans of doing otherwise, especially as they emerged on the wide ledge.

Dozens of men and women crowded the cliff in front of the bridge. They all faced the Spyre, quiet and still as they watched the windows on the top floor.

Adni glanced back and forth at all of them, confusion furrowing her brow. What were they doing? Kaldar led her through a few of them until they reached the center. She didn't see Solipher, and she didn't recognize anyone else.

The ones in robes reminded her of her father, regal, powerful, and with deadly cunning in their eyes. The others, dressed mostly in black leather hides and jackets, had the same dead expressions as her brother. *Ashen*.

Kaldar stopped and faced the Spyre just like the others. He held his hands behind him, holding his wrists.

Adni waited at his side, glancing between the others and the Spyre. No one met her gaze. All eyes were riveted on the Spyre as the sun descended ever lower.

Once the red glow crested the distant peaks, a glow lit the Spyre. A twisting ribbon of earth wrapping the spire burst into molten flames. It glowed, and something tingled along her skin. It pulled at her heart and mind, burning across her fingertips.

Her breath flew from her lungs as the others closed their eyes.

A second later, the flames disappeared and so did the sensation. Kaldar opened his eyes. He mouthed something, bowed to the Spyre, a mirror image of the others. He turned away and met her widened eyes.

"It's time to go," he said.

Adni's brows rose high on her forehead. "What was that?" she whispered, unable to hide the fevered edge to her voice. Her heart beat wildly in her chest, and her pulse pounded her ears.

"Father will explain to you later, but it's important you attend and worship every night." Kaldar had no passion in his voice, no stubborn faith, just certainty that she had to act and obey in the same manner he did.

"*Kaldar!*" The high voice of a woman cut through the pounding in her ears.

A woman with startlingly red hair and green eyes appeared at his side, wrapping an arm around his shoulders and leaning against his arm. Her curls fell over her hefty bosom, descending down her back over her black leather top. Coal lined her eyes and feathered away with her thick lashes. She smiled, her lips curving maliciously as she glanced from Kaldar to Adni. Her eyes glowed with excitement.

"Is this Solipher's new girl?" Her voice was sweet like a viper. Venom dripped from every word.

"Yes," Kaldar said. He didn't have any visible reaction to the gorgeous woman hanging off his arm. Was this another ashen?

"She's quite plain compared to you and your old sister." The woman laughed. Kaldar twitched at the mention of his *old* sister. "She didn't even inherit your beautiful hair." Her gloved fingers twisted through Kaldar's spiky white hair.

"Is this her?"

Adni turned. A tall man with long golden blonde hair, and a familiar smile wrapped an arm around Adni's shoulders. His soft robes pressed against her hands. He pulled her to his chest and kissed her forehead while inhaling a deep breath of her hair. He exhaled loudly, warming her scalp.

"Absolutely divine," he purred.

Adni's eyes flew wide. She took a step back, but his arm was like iron. It didn't budge.

"This is Adni," Kaldar said. "This is Lady Valeria and her father, Lord Dareys."

The same strange burn ran over her fingertips as Dareys squeezed her shoulder. "A unique name."

"At least something about her is unique." Valeria rolled her eyes.

"Be kind, Val." Dareys winked.

"*Never.*" Val held her hand to her chest as if the very thought offended her.

The pair laughed and tore away from Kaldar and Adni, linking arms as they turned toward the castle front.

"We'll play with the children another day," Dareys said. "I have a bone to pick with you."

"Whatever for, Daddy?" Val smiled, and slid a look over her shoulder as they disappeared into the dark tunnel.

Adni rubbed her arms as cold descended on her skin. Confusion filled her brain with exhaustion. Even her pounding heart had finally slowed.

"I'll show you to your chambers," Kaldar said. He turned to the cliff side. Adni sighed and followed.

* * *

After a long day and night, Adni slept well in her new chambers, even with questions racing through her mind about all the strange things she'd witnessed. The twisting ribbon of earth wrapping the Spyre had glowed like molten flames, only to disappear moments later. It was obviously a trick of the light, but the strange burn along her skin had been real. What did it all mean?

Adni sighed and opened her eyes. She'd been given her own set of rooms, carved from stone, and decorated with wood furnishings, dark tapestries, and thick fur carpets. She yawned and twisted around in the furs of her bed. They tickled her bare arms and ankles, calling her from sleep.

Candles burned throughout the bedroom, wax dripping over dark wooden tables and a stone mantel. They leant warmth to the otherwise cold air that brushed her neck. She shivered and sat up as a loud knock echoed in the hollow room.

She looked at the large double doors made of carved iron. One creaked open and a small girl with wide lifeless eyes and thin limbs peaked inside.

"Mistress, may I enter?" the girl squeaked.

Adni sat up, her brows furrowed. "Um, sure." She'd never been called *mistress* before. She wasn't the other woman to any man's marriage. Did the word have another meaning she wasn't familiar with?

The girl stepped inside. A small black dress fell to her knees, leaving several inches of bare leg between it and her boots. Her hair was pulled into a careful brown braid that hung down her back. She couldn't be more than sixteen.

"I have come to assist you and bring you breakfast." A tray

appeared at her hip as she closed the door and entered the sitting room just outside the bedroom. Thick dark curtains separated the rooms, draped from the ceiling to the floor. Adni hadn't thought to close them in case someone entered.

"Assist me?" Adni slid from under the covers and stood. Thick fur pushed between her toes.

"Yes, My Lady."

Now she was a *Lady*? Adni had no rank or station worthy of such a title, and neither did anyone she'd ever known. "I don't need any assistance, but thank you."

The girl finally looked up, fear clouding her large eyes. "There m-must be s-something, My Lady."

Adni raised an eyebrow. Cold stole her breath. Would this girl be harmed if Adni didn't accept her assistance? "I'm sure there's something."

Relief relaxed the horror in her eyes. "Thank you, My Lady."

"You can call me Adni."

"Lady Adni."

"Just Adni." She smiled.

The girl nodded slowly. Adni wasn't sure she'd accept just her nickname. "My name is Daniella."

"A beautiful name." Adni stepped from the bedroom and into the sitting room, with a large mantel on one side, a painting of the Izenfir chasm above it. A short table sat at the center of the room, with two plush maroon couches on either side. Daniella sat a silver tray upon it. Steam rose from eggs and sausages. Her mouth watered.

"Please, eat, My Lady," Daniella said.

Adni flashed her a look.

"A-Adni." Daniella's lips quirked slightly. "My apologies."

Adni sat on one of the sofas while Daniella bowed briefly before busying herself flitting around the sitting room, lighting as many candles as she could.

She took the plate and sat it on her lap, poising a silver fork in hand. Adni hesitated. While she adored sausages and hadn't had the luxury since she was a small child, Daniella looked as if she might crumble to dust at any moment.

She was a slave, and a poorly cared for one at that. Adni's heart twisted. This wasn't right. The six kingdoms had banned slavery for a reason. It was wrong. It was hurtful. It wasn't *humane*.

"Daniella." Adni cleared her throat. "Would you like some?"

Daniella paused by the mantel, a long match in hand. "Apologies?" Her thin brows furrowed.

"Come join me." Adni patted the sofa beside her. She had a feeling Daniella wouldn't join her without some kind of assertion.

Daniella glanced at the door, and back at Adni, as if her keeper might come bursting through those doors at any moment. But she licked her lips all the same and approached carefully, hovering beside the sofa.

Anger flared inside her chest. Kidnapping her and keeping Julian hostage was one thing, but enslaving *children* was another.

"Eat," Adni insisted. She held the plate out to Daniella.

After a long moment, Daniella finally sat. She took the fork Adni offered. It quivered in her hand as she devoured the cooked eggs in a few bites before taking one of the three sausages.

Adni let her eat, plucking only one of the thin sausages from the plate. She did need to eat something after all.

"Is this what you do here?" Adni asked. She ate slowly, unable to enjoy the savory meat or salty goodness. It tasted thick and heavy, like something she shouldn't be eating while others starved.

"I serve, I clean, and anything else my masters desire," Daniella mumbled between bites.

Adni's heart ached. "Do they treat you… all right?"

Daniella stilled. "Fair enough."

Once the plate was clean, they shared the cup of milk and returned the dishes to the tray.

Daniella's eyes brimmed with tears. "Thank you."

Adni smiled ruefully. "Any time."

A loud knock broke through the silence. Daniella leapt from the sofa and swiped the back of her hands over her mouth before she grabbed the tray and stepped aside, bowing her head.

Kaldar opened the door without being invited in. He stepped inside, a brow raised as he looked her over. "You aren't dressed."

Adni glanced down at the nightshift that had been laid out for her the night before. Her cheeks warmed. She'd been too concerned and hungry to think about what she wore in front of Daniella. Kaldar was another beast.

"No," Adni said. She stood, dark silk falling just above her knees.

"Get her dressed." Kaldar flicked his fingers at Daniella, not even sparing her a glance.

Adni's nostrils flared and she narrowed her eyes at her half-brother.

"Yes, My Lord." Daniella bowed and set the tray back on the table before rushing into the bedroom. She tore open a large wooden wardrobe with a mirror on the inside door. She glanced up, and met Adni's gaze for a moment. Her desperate glance beckoned Adni to follow and protect her.

Adni steeled herself and set her jaw. She followed Daniella into the bedroom, while Kaldar waited by the door, irritation clouding his eyes.

"You're training with Lord Kaldar today, My Lady." Daniella motioned to the wardrobe. "Trousers are here, and informal blouses here."

Training? Adni glanced back at the door. Solipher had mentioned the same thing. *All* of his children were trained in Izenfir. But what kind of training would they put her through?

Her stomach twisted with unease. "Thank you."

Daniella rushed back to the curtains separating the rooms and untied the bands clipping the curtains to the wall. Once the thick, dark velvet lay between her and Kaldar, Daniella visibly relaxed.

"Does he treat you poorly?" Adni whispered.

Daniella returned to stand beside Adni and the dresser. "N-no, My Lady." She pulled a pair of leather boots from the back of the wardrobe, along with a pair of high socks.

Adni raised her eyebrows.

"He is by far one of the better ones." Daniella met her gaze.

Adni nodded. "If anyone gives you trouble, I'll do whatever I can to stop them."

Daniella's lips twitched as if she might smile. "Thank you."

Adni picked a dark red blouse with three small buttons up the front of her cleavage, and a pair of black leather pants. The only colors available were dark, her tastes exactly. She slipped off her nightgown and slipped on her clothes. Daniella helped tie her hair back, slicking it away from her face and into a ponytail.

By the time they returned to the sitting room, her coat in hand, Kaldar's cheek visibly twitched with impatience. It was good to know *some* emotions remained after whatever switch he'd flipped.

"Let's go." He spun on his heels and fled into the dark corridor.

Adni gave Daniella one last long look before following.

* * *

TRAINING TOOK place on a flat ledge overlooking the valley. It was the widest she'd seen, nearly the same size as the throne room she'd first been introduced to. A dozen men and women with the same lifeless eyes as Kaldar's fought each other on the far side. Some fought with swords, others with fists, and some with magic.

Adni stopped at the top of the slope leading down to the training field. Fire flashed from the fists of one man, while a woman launched stones with the flick of her wrist.

Lord Dareys stood behind the man with flames in his fists, his jaw set and his fingers rubbing the scruff along his chin. Valeria stood opposite them, a smirk on her lips and fire in her palms. At a twitch of Dareys' fingers, Valeria leapt into the air, a crazed look in her eyes as she spun and swiped fiery claws at the tall blond man that had to be another of Dareys' children.

So Adni's family's darkness wasn't the only magic. Whatever they were, be they ashen or dragons, each lineage must contain a different set of gifts. After all, most of the ashen didn't look like one another. None were related to her and Kaldar.

"This way." Kaldar led the way down the slope to the flat expanse.

Wind tore at her ponytail, flicking her hair against her bare neck. Adni pulled the fur of her hood closer to her nape.

"I want to see what you can do," Kaldar said. He flexed his fingers as he turned to face her.

Adni stopped several feet from him. "What I can do?" Her stomach twisted. She could hardly swing a sword, she had no experience in fistfights, and she had none of this magic that surrounded her. Her gaze flickered to the flames flying through the air not twenty-feet away. Valeria's howl of triumph was chilling as she pinned her blond brother to the earth.

Her mouth went dry and her heart leapt. She couldn't stop herself from wanting this power any more than she could stop her own kidnapping.

"Yes." Kaldar shifted into what resembled a fighting stance, his hands up and his feet apart.

Adni stepped back. "I don't have any fighting experience." She could wield a bow, and hit a rabbit running fifty yards away, but she had no bow, and Kaldar wasn't a rabbit.

"Then it's time you get some." Darkness curled around Kaldar's hands. He swung a fist, and black exploded from his fingers.

Adni's eyes flew wide as she leapt to avoid the blast. Her heart raced as it sailed by her arm, within inches of skimming her jacket. What would it feel like for that darkness to touch her? Would it burn? Sting? Or was it more physical than she realized?

Kaldar threw another punch. A wave of black exploded from the ground, flying through the air, ready to squash her.

Adni spun out of the way. Again, it moved within inches of her.

Her heart rose into her throat, fear and excitement a bizarre mix. Her limbs tingled with something unfamiliar, that same desire for magic burning underneath her skin.

Kaldar's eyebrows furrowed, descending low over his eyes, darkening their gray depths. She could feel the heat of his anger from seven feet away. He threw two more punches, one ball of dark flashing low, the other high.

Adni leapt without thinking, before pressing herself to the ground. Both shots missed. Kaldar didn't give her a moment to catch her breath. A snarl on his lips, he threw four this time.

Black flashed by her on every side as she twisted to avoid them.

Her heart pounded in her ears as she sucked in deep breaths. She'd avoided all four, though she hardly understood how. It was as if she could sense the magic flying by her.

"You're insufferable!" he growled, flashing his teeth and narrowing his eyes. "I can feel your power, and yet you refuse to wield it! You shouldn't be so weak and just accept it like the rest of us!"

Adni stepped back. "Life isn't just about power." The lie in her own words cut through her excitement like a knife. Of course life was about power. The power to survive. The power to live. The power to protect those you love, and the strength to keep on protecting them when things got hard.

Kaldar scoffed and rolled his eyes. "You'll rethink that when you experience a hurt like none other." Anger twisted his normally poised face, and clouded his eyes.

The fighting beside them stopped. Someone shouted, though she hardly heard them over Kaldar's low voice.

"What do you mean?" Her brows furrowed. Did their turn to the dark have something to do with pain? How did the ashen get their powers? There was so much she had yet to understand.

"When all you can feel is pain, and all you want to do it turn it off, you'll make your choice." He smirked as if he'd won some kind of battle. But still, Adni didn't understand.

"What pain could be that great?" Though she felt the pull to power like she'd never felt anything before, if she had to somehow turn off her humanity, turn off her love, her kindness, and her feelings, she wasn't sure she wanted it.

"Loss." Kaldar's smirk dropped. "When you lose *everything*."

A twinge of panic flashed through her chest. "What are you saying?"

"Solipher killed your mother for hiding you from him."

Her heart dropped. Her fingers went cold.

What?

Adni stood frozen to the spot, a block of ice as all warmth drained from inside her. Her eyes widened as she stared at Kaldar. He wasn't smiling. He wasn't joking. He was serious.

The man who sired her, killed her mother.

"You're lying," the words tumbled from her lips as she backed towards the slope out of the training field.

Kaldar's lips flattened. He wasn't.

Adni spun on her heels and flew from the training field. Her boots kicked up rocks and her heart raced with her feet. She couldn't think, could hardly breathe. She raced across the ledge surrounding the chasm until she reached the castle front.

Fear, shock, and rage had her legs pumping until she reached Solipher's throne room. He stood by the dais, long white hair descending down his back, over black regal robes. Two others, one in gold robes, and another in navy, hovered beside him. They glanced up at her entrance.

He turned as she stopped at the door. His lips parted to speak, but she beat him to it.

"You killed my mother?" her scream was hollow. She couldn't believe it. She wouldn't. Not until she saw proof. But every inch of her burned to know.

Solipher's eyes went dark. He looked at the two with him. "Would you excuse us?" One sighed dramatically and the other nodded curtly. Both fled the opposite passage before she could scream again. "Yes, Adni."

All the air flew from the room, taking her breath and her sense. "You *killed* her?" Her words hardly rose above a whisper.

Solipher swept away from the dais, crossing the room in a fraction of a second. One hand brushed the tears from her cheek, while the other cupped her shoulder. "Yes, my daughter. She kept you from me, and she had to be punished."

"Punished?" Her head swam, and her knees shook. She couldn't believe this. She wouldn't. "I don't believe you."

Solipher frowned and his brows pulled together as if he actually felt sorry for her. "It is the truth."

Adni shook her head and tried to pull away. He didn't let go. "Why would you do this?" Her voice rose with the panic his words brought. What if he *was* telling the truth?

"It had to be done."

"No it didn't!" she cried. "You didn't have to hurt her! You could have left her alone!"

"I had no other choice."

Fire flared to life inside of her. "No other choice?" Her scream echoed off the walls. "You *chose* to murder her!"

Adni yanked back, freeing her cheek, but not her arm. His fingers clamped around her forearm like iron. "You need to accept this, Adni."

"No! I won't." Adni again tried to pull away. "I don't believe this. Not for a second. My own father wouldn't kill my mother. You couldn't."

Desperation welled inside of her, burning through her like ice. Her mind flew in all directions; unable to accept the possibility he wasn't lying. Her heart pounded in her ears and her head swam. *He's lying. He has to be.*

"If you won't accept it, I'll show you." Solipher pulled her closer and grabbed her head between his hands. His nails dug into her scalp, sending bites of pain through her hair.

"Let go of me!" Adni grabbed his wrists.

"See for yourself."

Darkness descended over the world like a blanket. Only blackness existed in this world, until an image slowly formed. Torchlight flared to life. It lit the outside of her home in the mountains. Something moved closer, a shadow slipping through the quiet of her village, passed the front gate and through the front door.

Laughter rang from inside. Her family's laughter. Her mother hunched over a boiling pot of stew, stirring the thick contents while Helen tried unsuccessfully to cross-stitch on a piece of white cotton.

She'd never been good with a needle and thread, much to Galia's dismay.

Renley sat on the other side of the firepit, his knee up and his arm laid lazily across his knee, how he always sat while waiting for dinner after a long day of fishing. He hated cooking, and for good reason. He'd nearly poisoned the family at least once.

A creak cut through their laughter. Her mother looked over her shoulder. Galia's eyes flashed wide and her mouth dropped open as she spun to stand.

Shadows spilled across the floor. Helen jumped up, a cry at her lips, and Renley leapt for the weapon's chest below the mantel.

A black spike thrust through her mother's chest. Blood burst from her lips.

Adni cried out as the vision pulled her deeper. The scent of copper was thick in the air. Embers flickered from the fire as Helen ran for her bedroom, and Renley leapt to defend his mother.

Galia hit the floor with a thump. Renley leapt, but a hand flashed out, sending Renley flying into the wall. His head smashed against the mantel and he fell to the floor lifeless.

"Stop it!" Adni begged. She couldn't take anymore. Not her mother. Not her brother.

The shadow continued through the firepit room, to the bedroom. The curtains parted. It was nearly pitch black inside. Whimpers permeated the quiet.

"N-not Helen," her mother's voice stuttered.

The shadow glanced back.

Galia inched across the floor, pulling herself with one hand. Blood pooled below her body as she dragged herself.

"S-stop it, *please!*" Adni said.

The shadow turned away and entered the room, it stepped inside, where curtains parted the large room into three spaces. The whimpers came from Adni's section, where Helen always hid when their father was on a tirade and she was too scared to do anything else.

The curtains parted, revealing a small bed, with a bow hanging off a hook beside it, and a leather quiver leaning against the nightstand.

"Please, no!" Adni moaned. She couldn't take one more second of this. She understood; Solipher *had* killed her family. But she couldn't watch it. She couldn't watch the execution of the only people she'd ever loved.

Tears streaked her cheeks as the vision shifted. The shadow kneeled next to the bed and peeked under. Helen's scream was deafening, and mingled with Adni's own. *"Stop!"* she cried.

Adni fell to the ground and the blissful embrace of darkness behind her eyelids. Solipher's vision disappeared as sobs racked her body and she trembled on the floor.

Her family was dead. Everyone she loved was dead. She'd never hug them again, never make a new home for them, never see their smiling faces. She'd never see her mother's proud smile as she shot down their dinner, or feel her warm hands as they held hers.

Despair encompassed every inch of her being. It shook her core and blinded her to all else. She would feel like this forever. This pain. This sorrow. She'd feel every second of her family's pain, and *see* every minute leading to their deaths. The vision would replay again and again before her eyes until she couldn't take it anymore.

She needed it to stop. She needed it all to just *stop*.

"You see, my daughter. I spoke the truth," Solipher whispered, his voice almost soothing. "But you don't need to feel this pain. You can let it all go. Reach inside yourself. Find your humanity. Find your pain, and your despair. Find it and turn it off. Like the switch of a lantern, let it die like the flames."

Adni's sobs racked her body as she pressed her face to the cold rock. Tears burned her cheeks as pain rippled through her body, heart, and soul.

How could she stand to feel like this forever? She could hardly take another moment of it. Her mother's face as she crawled across the ground, desperate to save her daughter, flashed before her eyes. Adni choked on a sob. Her fingers wrapped around her ears.

"Just turn it off, Adni." Solipher's words wound around her mind like a safe place she could hide.

Just turn it off. That's all she had to do. She had the key. She could turn off the pain. Turn off the despair. Turn off the hollow left in her chest.

"That's right," Solipher purred. "You can do it."

Adni trembled as she reached inside herself. She grasped her pain, her family, and every desire for a future. She took it all and she shoved it inside a box. She found it and she let it go.

With one last quivering breath, she let everything she'd ever care about fall to the void. She let them go. She let it all go.

EIGHT

A dni kneeled on the stone floor, her mind blank and her breathing evening out. She sat back on her heels, her brow relaxing and her shoulders dropped.

"I'm proud of you, my daughter." Solipher squeezed her shoulder. "You've done well." He stepped away. "I'll give you a moment to settle." His footsteps retreated out of the throne room and down the passage until they disappeared.

Hollow. She felt hollow. Empty nothingness sat in her chest where her pain had been. Cold pressed through her leather pants and into her skin. But it didn't make her shiver. It didn't bother her like it should have. Like the death of her entire family should.

She stared at the ground as she tested out the nothing. Her fingers clenched and unclenched as she pictured her mother. Nothing. Her sister. Nothing. Her brother's lifeless body.

Nothing.

"Adni!" Julian skidded to a stop in front of her. She kneeled, and held her hands to Adni's cheeks. Warm like the sun on her skin.

Adni looked up into blue eyes lit with concern.

"Adni, are you all right?"

"I can't feel anything," Adni said.

Julian's eyes widened and her mouth fell open. "Adni, please tell me you didn't. Please tell me you didn't give in."

Adni met her gaze. She didn't need to say a word.

Horror blossomed in Julian's eyes. "We need to leave, *now*."

"Leave?" Adni's eyebrows furrowed. "Why would we leave?" Hadn't they just arrived only a day ago? Why would they leave their new home already? Adni had new rooms, far larger than she had before. She had a new sibling, a live one, a new father, and a new family.

Why would she ever want to leave?

"Adni, listen to me. You'll start to get some feelings back in a few minutes, but they won't be you. This isn't you." Julian gripped her shoulders tightly. "You'll be left with rage, and hate and an unquenchable desire for power. You'll crave magic like you've never craved anything in your life before. It will consume you. It will *be* you. You need to turn it back on before it's too late."

"Why would I do that?" She'd escaped her pain. She's escaped her sorrow. Why would she want that back? Anger, hate and power sounded better than pain.

"*Please*, Adni!" Julian shook her. "If you won't turn it back, then we need to go before we're found. I can help you, but we need to *go!*"

Footsteps sounded in the passage.

"Damn it!" Julian rocketed to her feet, pulling Adni with her. She spun towards the passage entrance.

"Adni?" Kaldar asked. He rounded the bend, and his eyes widened. His nostrils flared and his lips pulled back in a snarl. "You!" He leapt across the room faster than she could follow.

Darkness flared around his fingers, curled like talons as he reached for Julian.

Something inside her chest lurched to life. Adni twisted in front of Julian, throwing a snarl of her own at her half-brother. The sound ripped between her teeth, a noise she'd only ever heard from mountain cats when they got too close to the mountain-dwellers' hens.

"Stay away from her!" Adni hissed.

Kaldar reared back at the last moment. A storm burned within his eyes. "Here I've come to congratulate you on finally making the right decision, and you're consorting with *that*!" He motioned at Julian.

A growl rumbled in her chest.

Kaldar lowered his hand, his magic disappearing. He rolled his eyes and laughed. The sound held no humor, only irritation and mockery. "You're going to keep a human now, are you?"

Adni's nostrils flared. "She's *mine*." Her chest burned as she narrowed her eyes. Julian wasn't to be harmed. Whatever she was to Adni, she was still hers.

"Humans are fun pets, my *sister*, but that's all they are." Kaldar stepped back. "One day father will choose a proper mate for you. Someone ashen, not *human* like this foul *thing*."

Thing? Adni grinded her teeth. A feral beast leapt under her skin, pushing her to attack. But she held back. She didn't know how to use her magic, if she even had any. Kaldar on the other hand, wielded his with ease. She'd fight him one day, but today wouldn't be it.

"Put the beast away, Adni." Kaldar rolled his eyes. "I won't harm another's pet." He crossed his arms.

Adni worked her jaw. She wasn't sure she believed him, but the hostile fury was gone along with his magic. "Fine." The embers burning in her stomach slowly faded as she straightened and dropped the defensive arm she held in front of Julian.

"Return your pet to her cage," Kaldar continued. "She won't be harmed."

Adni nodded as she slid around Kaldar. Julian followed her, as did her half-brother, all the way to the dungeon.

* * *

Kaldar waited at the entrance to the dungeon while Julian stepped inside her cage. Adni closed the cell door and turned away.

Julian reached through the bars and grabbed her wrist.

Adni faced the cell.

"Adni, covering up your pain with darkness will only make it worse." Julian squeezed her wrist gently, as if trying to comfort her. "Let pain and love back in."

Adni pulled her wrist away. "Why would I do that?" She raised an eyebrow. "Why would I want to go through the pain of my family's death over and over?" The words didn't stir anything inside of her. She knew they should, but they didn't.

Julian's eyes flew wide. "What? Your family is dead? How?"

"Solipher killed them."

Something dark flashed through Julian's eyes. She bared her teeth. "He killed them and yet you choose to side *with him?*"

Adni stepped away from Julian's cell. "I don't see it that way." She wasn't siding with her family's killer. She was siding with the ashen, and with who she truly was. She was siding with power. She was embracing the magic that gave her life.

"Adni..." Julian shook her head. The rage in her eyes quelled to sadness. "You're only making this worse on yourself."

"Sister," Kaldar said. His tone was edged with irritation.

"Goodbye, Julian." Adni turned to the dungeon entrance.

"Adni, please be careful." Julian sighed.

Adni glanced over her shoulder as she followed her brother back into Izenfir.

NINE

$\mathcal{A}$dni sat at breakfast the next day, chewing sausages and eggs mechanically before getting dressed. Her teeth gnawed through the tasteless food, a simple necessity to keep on living.

"Are you finished, My Lady?" Daniella hovered on the other side of the table.

She glanced up, unable to recall why she'd corrected Daniella the day before. "Yes."

Daniella nodded, her brows pulled together as she took away the rest of the food. Adni didn't care that Daniella ate what remained. It made no difference what happened to her leftovers.

Adni stood, smoothing the front of her nightgown before she went to her bedroom to fetch a fresh set of clothing. Solipher would arrive any moment to bring her to training. He mentioned there was something he wanted to tell her in the morning, but didn't elaborate further.

Adni had mostly been left to her solitude after she'd returned Julian to the dungeon. Cold nothingness floated inside her as she drifted through her new morning routine. Daniella hardly said a word as she pulled Adni's hair back, slicking it tight to her skull before wrapping a thick band to keep it in place.

"Have a good day, My Lady." Daniella bowed as she stepped away from Adni and headed for the door.

Adni watched her go. Yesterday she'd felt so strongly about Daniella being a slave. But now her chest didn't ache at the sight of the little servant girl. Why should it?

Daniella slipped from the room moments before a knock interrupted the quiet.

"Come in." Adni stood and made her way to the door.

Solipher opened it. He smiled at her approach. "Good morning, Adni."

"Good morning," she said.

"Are you ready for your training?"

"Yes." Adni plucked her coat from the sofa and slipped it on as Solipher led the way out. She clipped it in place, the fur hood brushing her neck, the trim making her wrists itch.

"Your initiation ritual will be in a few days' time," Solipher began. "You'll be bound to our family by the Holy Fire."

Adni glanced at her father as she walked, but said nothing.

"Once you're bound to the fire, we will be your true family." He smirked. "But you already know that now."

"Yes."

"You'll also be able to sense magical beings more strongly throughout the world, like the rest of us, and hunt them should you choose." He shrugged, as if this were a normal thing to say. "Some of my children have pursued them, and others have not. Your brother, for example, doesn't bother with them. Though he is still in training, I imagine he might choose to stay in Izenfir unless I ask him to leave."

Adni nodded. She understood wanting to stay, or not caring to leave. There was no point in going now.

"I will tell you more when the time comes." Solipher stopped as they reached the slope to the training field.

The other ashen were already gathered, some practicing, like

Valeria and her kin, while others, like her brother, watched on the sidelines.

Solipher glided out onto the ledge, his hands held behind his back as he turned to face Adni. Kaldar slipped from the mountain wall to join them. He stood beside Adni, his white hair flashing in the morning light.

"My children, you make me so proud." Solipher's lips twisted into a devious smile. "It's time to bring Adni into the fold, Kal."

Kaldar nodded.

"It's time you learn how to use your shadow magic, Adni," Solipher said.

Adni raised an eyebrow. "So that's the power you both use?"

Solipher raised his chin. "Kal, please demonstrate."

Kaldar splayed his fingers, his palm to the sky. Blackness swelled in his palm, twisting and churning.

Adni's eyes widened slightly. Her chest twinged with lust. Lust for the power Kaldar possessed.

"This is shadow magic. Only our family line possesses it." Solipher smirked proudly. "The other lines–" He nodded in the direction of the other ashen. "–Have their own magic. Fire. Earth. Air."

As if to solidify his statement, Valeria leapt through the air, flames bursting from her palms. She threw them at her brother, and he rolled out of the way.

"Some of our lines are long, like earth and shadow, while others are shorter, like fire."

"Longer?" Adni's eyebrows furrowed.

"Some lines are more mixed and have had more generations, especially in the early years of our kind, but others have shorter, more direct lines," Solipher explained. His cheek twitched in irritation as if he were angry that their line was longer. Maybe a longer line meant less power. That was the only explanation she could think of.

"Today I want you to use your magic, Adni." Solipher's gaze sharpened. "You can manifest your power with your mind. I want you to picture the darkness on your fingers, your hand, in the air." Solipher nodded for her to give it a try.

Adni opened her palm, mimicking what her brother had done moments ago. Her fingers danced against the air as she pictured the same swirling darkness Kaldar held in his palm. Heat shot through her fingers and burned the center of her hand. Her limbs tingled and the hair on the back of her neck stood at attention.

Black flickered over the pale creases of her hand. Her heart jumped.

The heat disappeared, as did the black.

Solipher sighed. "A fair start."

Kaldar smirked and shook his head. He closed his palm and his magic disappeared.

"Try again." Solipher paced in front of them, his ice-like stare roaming from his children to the other ashen and back.

Adni nodded. She cupped her hand in the air and called the heat back to her fingers. It coursed down her arm and into her hand, prickling her skin like needles. Black flared to life like an ember before dissipating. She frowned, irritation flashing through her chest. She wanted the power inside of herself so badly. Why couldn't she conjure it?

"Take off your coat," Solipher said.

Adni looked up. He had stopped his pacing and stared at her levelly. Adni stripped off her coat and lay it on the ground. Wind whipped her ponytail against her neck. Cold slithered inside her shirt. She clenched her fists.

"Try again."

She splayed her palm and called back the heat. Cold, wet air slicked her skin, pushing up the sleeves of her shirt. Adni shook her head and furrowed her eyebrows in an attempt to concentrate. She stared at her palm, calling back the heat. Warmth tingled in her chest and down through her arm, but it didn't reach her hand.

"Try harder," Kaldar snapped.

Adni glared at her brother. Heat leapt inside of her, and darkness pooled in her palm.

"Excellent." Solipher chuckled.

Kaldar shrugged and crossed his arms. "Now try it in combat."

"Great suggestion." Solipher stepped to the side of the training field.

Adni glanced between them. Solipher wanted her to fight Kaldar already? She'd already proven yesterday that she had no power, only luck at evading his. Would it be different this time?

Kaldar took several steps away before turning to face her. He held his hands up and parted his feet like he had the day before. Adni mimicked him, clenching and unclenching her fingers, as she tried to call the heat of magic back to her hands.

"Begin," Solipher said.

Kaldar lunged forward, swiping his hands at the air. Darkness flared from his movements. Adni spun out of the way. Any heat in her palms fled as cold assaulted her limbs. Why was she forced to fight in the cold while Kaldar wore a warm coat?

She ground her teeth and clenched her fists.

Her brother lunged again, sending darkness in a wave straight for her head. Adni ducked, flashing her hands out in a protective stance. The darkness sailed right over her.

Kaldar snarled, his features twisting with rage. Adni straightened. She had to concentrate to bring back the magic, but Kaldar would take any pause to his advantage.

Adni circled Kaldar, and he did the same. She focused on pulling heat into her hands, blocking out the cold of the mountains as black embers burned her palms. She needed more. More magic. More power. She tried to breathe life into the black flames, sucking in breaths slowly as the darkness amassed inside her hands.

Kaldar threw a fist at her, instead of magic.

Adni ducked, but his ankle snaked around hers, kicking her feet out from under her. Her back slammed against the ground, and air exploded from her lungs. The burning in her hands disappeared in an instant.

"Nice try, sister." He cackled.

Her nostrils flared as she sat up, taking a moment to catch her breath. "That wasn't fair."

"All is fair in war, Adni," Solipher chastised.

Adni stood, angry heat flooding her chest. How dare Kaldar try to embarrass her in front of their father?

Kaldar smirked as their dance continued. He threw punches, and kicks, nearly landing every blow. But his magic sailed by her time and time again as she dodged and ducked. His eyes narrowed and he growled in frustration every time she escaped his magic unscathed.

Though her own frustration built at not being able to amass her own power, she took satisfaction in the anger twisting his face.

Swiping a hand through the air, Kaldar sent another blast of black at her.

Adni stepped out of the way, with an ease that was almost comical.

"You infuriating wench!" Kaldar snapped. Adni smirked. "You may think you're strong, but you'll never be powerful like my old sister! *She* was great. *She* took down kingdoms. She killed thousands and left fear to ravage every land in her wake." He laughed. "You can only dream of being half as powerful as she."

Adni's eyebrows furrowed. What had happened to this old sister?

"Kadia was great indeed, Kal, but she still fell to a mere mortal." Solipher narrowed his eyes at his son. "You'll do well to learn from her."

Adni's heart lurched painfully. She barely clamped her teeth down in time to stop her gasp. The insane Queen Kadia was her sister? The madwoman who destroyed the six kingdoms ten years ago, and fell to the blade of the Immortal Queen? They were related?

Her mind reeled and she stepped back. A crack snapped through the emptiness inside her chest, leeching fear into her bones.

Kadia had destroyed her life, her family, killed her grandparents and thousands of others. She'd set her home, Ithrendel, aflame and probably laughed as the city burned.

But with this new information, a lot made sense. No one ever knew where Kadia got her power. No one knew where she'd come from, or how she'd summoned her shadow soldiers.

Kadia had been ashen, just like her.

Her heart raced as she turned to the edge of the chasm. Wind slammed against her chest, the bracing cold suddenly welcome over the heat burning through her. She didn't like these feelings. The uncertainty disturbing the calm. Adni took a deep breath. She called back the emptiness, the hollow inside of her. Though she quelled the panic rising, the crack remained.

"I'm done with practice for the day," she said. Her fists tightened.

A long stretch of quiet descended on the training field. She could feel Solipher and Kaldar's stares, but she didn't look back.

"All right." Solipher placed a hand on her shoulder. When had he gotten so close? "We'll begin again in the morning."

Adni nodded. She didn't look at her brother, or her father as she grabbed her coat and fled the training field.

She didn't know where to go. Her chambers? The throne room? Confusion stirred inside her. She shook her head. Adni let her feet lead her, and the next thing she knew, she was in the dungeon.

"You're back," Julian croaked from the darkness of her cell.

Adni paused by the passage entrance. She shouldn't have come, and yet there she was. Kaldar had called Julian her pet, but that wasn't true. Julian was something else. But what?

"Come here," Julian said. She leaned against the bars, her long fingers wrapping around them.

Adni sighed. Her warm breath fogged the chill air. She kneeled in front of Julian's cell, her face nearly level with Julian's. "Are you all right?" What else did one ask someone who was imprisoned?

Julian nodded. Her cheeks were streaked with dirt, and her eyes were bloodshot, but she appeared fine otherwise. "How are you?"

"Fine."

"You're still...?" Julian trailed off.

"Yes."

Julian slammed her fist against the bars. The rattle of iron echoed through the dungeon. "Adni, you need to turn it back on before you forget what being human feels like. Just remember what makes you, you."

Adni's eyebrows pulled together.

"Remember your family, even if it hurts. Remember the sweet taste of apples, and how sick it makes you feel to ride in the back of a trolley." Julian's eyes widened with desperation. "Remember what makes you *human*."

Adni leaned away. A spark flashed through her, but she quickly squashed it. She'd already had something crack her once today; she couldn't let it happen again. But what would Julian think of the revelation she'd had? Adni's fingers wrapped around the cage bars. She had to tell someone. "I'm related to the Evil Queen."

Julian looked up, her eyes wide. "Then you know what she is now."

"Yes."

Julian shook her head and leaned her forehead against the bars. "I have a plan, Adni. I can get us out of here and take down Izenfir for good. There will never be another Evil Queen. We can stop them." Fire blazed through her dark blue eyes, even in the low light of torches.

Someone shifted in the cage next to Julian's. Adni glanced at the small brunette with big blue eyes and determination set in her jaw. The girl pulled herself across the dirt floor until she leaned against the corner closest to Adni and Julian. She nodded.

Julian glanced between them, some sort of exchange flashing between the two women. She looked back at Adni. "This is Astrid." Her fingers wrapped around Adni's. They were warmer than the heat of magic. "She's the sister of the Queen of Rythern." She smiled. "And she's going to help us destroy the Spyre."

TEN

"You're the missing princess?" Adni asked.

Even in the mountains, it was a well-known fact that Princess Astrid of Rythern had disappeared during the war. She'd been sent away for her own safety, but once the war was over, she was nowhere to be found.

Astrid nodded. "I've been here for years." Her voice hitched. "I don't know how many anymore. We were lost in the mountains for so long after the war. We couldn't find a way out, but eventually *they* found us." She mustered a glare towards the entrance of the dungeon.

"We?" Adni raised a brow.

"James, my guard."

From the quiver in Astrid's voice, it was clear James was far more than her guard.

"I haven't seen him in weeks. They enslaved him with the others. He visits when he can, but it's been so long since I've seen him." Tears welled in her bright eyes. "I'm afraid he's dead." Astrid's hoarse voice broke as tears spilled down her cheeks.

Adni's heart lurched, forcing another crack into the empty void.

She squeezed the bars like she needed them to hold her up. Julian tightened her grip on Adni's trembling hand.

"We can get out of here, all of us," Julian said. "We can flee the mountains to Rythern and come back with an army."

Adni shook her head and ripped her hand away. She stood abruptly, her mind racing and her limbs shaking. "You're just trying to confuse me."

Julian sighed and stood. "You know that isn't true."

Adni paced back and forth in front of the cages, her heart pounding in her ears. If she didn't clamp down on the emotions seeping through, her mask would shatter, and with it, her power.

"Don't let the darkness consume you, Adni," Julian continued.

Adni spun toward her, a growl on her lips. "What do you know about fighting this darkness?"

Her words echoed off the cavern walls. Adni took a deep breath to calm herself and turned to the exit. She fled the dungeon as fast as she could.

* * *

Kaldar met with Adni not far outside the dungeon, apparently sent to escort her. His lips twisted in a snide smirk as they left the tunnel. Wind rushed against her chest as they ascended the steps to the cliff.

"Went to visit your *pet*, did you?" he mocked.

Adni's cheek twitched and she glared at him under her lashes. "She isn't my pet." But Adni had called her *"mine"*. She wasn't sure what she was saying at the time, but some part of her still didn't want anything to happen to Julian.

"You cage and visit her like a mutt. Of course she's your pet." Kaldar rolled his eyes.

Adni hissed her irritation. "Never mind."

They ascended in silence. Her gaze roamed down into the chasm. Darkness licked the edge of the valley, so far away from the sun. Slaves roamed the chasm floor and the ledges surrounding it. Her mind went back to Astrid, and what she'd said about James.

86

"Why do they keep slaves?" she asked.

"They?" Kaldar snorted. "You're one of us now."

Adni narrowed her eyes at him. He knew what she meant, and yet still she didn't consider herself one of them.

Kaldar slid her a dubious look. "Why do you care about slaves?"

Her nostrils flared. She didn't care about anything. Not anymore. At least she didn't think she did. "I don't."

"Then why ask?"

"Curiosity." Adni bit the inside of her cheek. She didn't want to let Kaldar know it was anything more than that.

Kaldar flicked his fingers through the air in a dismissive motion. He led the way back to her chambers in silence.

* * *

As night fell on Izenfir, Adni fought her restlessness by pacing her bedroom. She'd already eaten dinner, attempted to conjure her magic again and again, but the more she tried, the less she could create. Thoughts of her day flitted through her mind without permission.

The Evil Queen who destroyed the six kingdoms all those years ago was her sister. Astrid was the missing princess of Rythern. Julian wanted to bring down Izenfir. And what were they using slaves for?

Adni shook her head and gripped her hair. She called back the emptiness, the lack of feeling she so desperately craved. It didn't return. Had the cracks in her mask really gone so deep?

She sat down hard on the edge of her bed. Fur tickled her fingers.

She'd never be able to sleep like this. Not in a million years. Adni rolled her shoulders and stood. If she wasn't going to sleep, the least she could do was cure some of her curiosities.

Adni plucked her coat from the sofa and fastened it tightly around her chest and waist. She pressed her ear against the door to be sure no one was around. Nothing. Good. She opened the door and slipped into the dark hall.

Torches were hung every few feet, lighting her way down the tunnel. The passages had grown familiar, even after only a few days.

She had a feeling it was something to do with magic. How it tingled at the back of her mind when she wondered which way to go, or paused too long at an intersection.

She reached the cliff with no problems, slipping out the large double iron doors that marked the entrance of her family's home. The chasm was even more daunting at night. Torches lit the stairs and ledges wrapping the walls as they zigzagged into blackness. She could no longer see the base, only a large bottomless void.

Adni shook her head and began her descent. The stairs were wide enough for two people to walk comfortably side by side without fear of falling over. But the further she descended, the less frequent the torches became. Shadows pooled between the bits of light, concealing the steps she needed to take in order to continue below.

No stars lit the sky. No moonlight led her way. In Izenfir all was dark aside from the few scattered flames.

Whispers drifted on the wind, desperate, angry, and sad. They twisted around her like the harsh breeze, pulling her deeper until she reached a tunnel. Mumbles flowed from within. Flames burned atop a large blazing fire nestled in the rock. Half a dozen forms sat around it, speaking in hushed voices.

More tunnels curved from the main cavern, twisting into the earth, where she assumed the rest of the slaves slept.

"They're working us harder than they ever have," a man with a raspy voice and thick beard whispered.

"We must be close to whatever they're looking for." A woman with gray hair and eyes nodded grimly.

"I'm afraid if we go any deeper, the earth will scorch off our feet." A younger man shook his head.

They were all so thin, so frail, their skin graying and burns lining the bottoms of their feet, which they cooled on the cold rock of the cavern. They hugged their knees, or lay on their sides, barely conscious enough to hold their conversation.

What were the dragons digging for? Clearly there were different groups of slaves, from ones like Daniella who served the ashen, to these people, who dug in whatever mine the dragons had created.

She'd only scarcely seen the jagged hole at the bottom of the chasm, with slaves wheeling large barrows of rock away from the site. Others toted pickaxes as they chipped away at the entrance, or disappeared into the dark hole.

"Maybe we'll get lucky and the heat will kill us." The older man chuckled humorlessly. He shook his head as he stared into the flames.

Adni hovered in the entrance, unsure what to do. Should she ask them about her father, or the ashen? Should she find out more about the slaves? Or should she ask about James for Astrid?

"Who's there?" The younger man shot to his feet. He swayed precariously, and winced as if it hurt to stand.

Adni froze. She hadn't made her decision yet.

"Who are you?" the man snapped. His blue-green eyes were shadowed with anger and fear.

Unsure if she was allowed to be this far into the chasm, Adni stepped forward hesitantly. She'd have to tell them something, but she couldn't give them her name. "I'm looking for someone."

The six seated around the fire exchanged glances. Did they know what she was? The fear in their eyes told her they did.

"What do you want with them?" the woman stood, stronger than the young man despite her age. Her fists clenched at her sides and she glared daggers.

What did she want with James? "To make sure he's all right." That might sway them.

"You want to make sure one of us *slaves* is all right?" The young man laughed. "What do you care?"

Adni's jaw hardened. Flames of irritation flared inside her chest, surprising her by calling heat to her palms. Why would her magic burn now?

"Lady Adni?" Daniella appeared in one of the tunnel entrances. She was just as frail as Adni remembered, but her eyes were far more alive. "What are you doing here?"

"You know this one, Dany?" the young man spat.

Daniella narrowed her eyes at him. "Yes, she's the one who fed me."

The young man's eyes went wide. "What?"

Daniella rolled her eyes and marched across the cavern. "What are you doing here, My Lady?"

Adni glanced between her and the others. "I'm looking for a man named James."

Daniella nodded, her big eyes set with determination. "I'll take you to him."

"Dany," the young man snapped.

"Shut up." Daniella glared at him before turning to the passage she'd emerged from, and disappeared back inside. Adni followed, glancing over her shoulder as the young man stared after them.

The tunnel was narrow, and low. If she were a few inches taller, she'd have to duck to weave through it. They emerged, a few steps later, in a smaller cavern with a fire lit and two women sleeping soundly in the corner, wrapped in wool blankets on the cold floor.

On a mat beside the fire, a young man with dark brown hair, a short beard and hollow cheeks lay. His feet were wrapped in linen stained red, and his face was pale and blotchy. A cloth lay across his forehead. He didn't move.

"That's him." Daniella stopped beside him. She kneeled on the stone floor and took the rag from his forehead, dipping it in a bucket of water and wringing it out before returning it to his forehead.

Bruises marred his bare chest, purple around his ribs and brown near his throat. He'd been badly beaten by someone.

"What happened?" Adni kneeled by James's other side. Her heart fought against her, pounding loudly and threatening to return her pain.

"Two of the ashen guards beat him when he collapsed. He's had a fever ever since," Daniella explained.

James's eyelids fluttered before he opened his eyes. He looked around the cavern, at Daniella, and at her, seemingly in a daze.

"James." Daniella smiled. "You're awake."

"So I am." James coughed loudly, his whole body shaking with the effort.

"Someone is here to see you." Daniella nodded at Adni.

James raised his brows half-heartedly. "I didn't know we were accepting visitors now."

"Hush," Daniella shushed, like a younger sister who didn't want to see her brother suffer.

"Astrid sent me," Adni said.

His eyes widened and he grabbed her hand. Sweat slicked his skin, and he was hot to the touch. "Is she all right? Is she being taken care of? Have they been feeding her?" His fevered eyes filled with panic and concern.

"She's all right," Adni patted the back of his hand awkwardly. Another crack snapped through her like emotional whiplash, sending her limbs trembling as she held his hand.

"Thank the blue skies." He lay back, still as if that's all he needed. Not food, not water, not rest, just to know his love was safe.

Another snap flashed through her chest. Her heart twinged. Her mask was crumbling. The heat inside her was leeching away. She needed to escape these people forcing her to feel. Adni let his hand go and stood.

"I need to leave," she said. Her heart raced, her pulse thumping in her ears.

"Please, tell Astrid I love her." James closed his eyes, and his breathing evened out.

Adni spun on her heels and fled faster than the wind itself.

ELEVEN

er initiation day had come. Today she would accept the Holy Fire, and with it, the magics and powers it gave. Her body burned for it, craving the power living inside of her. Though she'd been given a taste of her family's power, now she'd be given the rest. Solipher said it would enhance her gifts and bind her to the family, giving her greater magic than she could ever imagine.

Adni sucked in a breath and exhaled slowly. She wanted that power. She wanted the magic. But with every waking moment, her chest ached with something else. Julian. Astrid. James. They were all cracks in the darkness holding her together. If she gave it up, she'd lose her power. She'd lose her family.

Kaldar led her up the cliff and across the bridge to the Spyre.

The tower rose from the earth, twisting into the sky, nearly as high as the surrounding mountains. A thick, dark ribbon wrapped around the entire thing, the cord that glowed with the sunset and burned like fire.

If she accepted the Holy Fire in the initiation ceremony, she'd feel the fires of the ancients before her, or so Kaldar said.

"The ceremony will take place in a couple of hours," he said. "I'll leave you in the preparation chamber where you'll be cleansed."

Cleansed? She raised an eyebrow.

"You'll be bathed, polished, and dressed. Nothing more."

Adni nodded.

The iron doors to the Spyre opened to accept them, two large muscled men standing on either side.

The main chamber had smooth stone walls, and floors of obsidian. Strange twisting iron sculptures littered the floor, and a winding stone staircase sat in the center of the large room.

Kaldar led the way up, passing more iron doors with strange carvings, until her legs burned and her limbs grew weary from the climb.

"Here we are." At the top of the staircase were twin iron doors carved with strange patterns and two large circular bone handles. Kaldar pushed open the doors, and motioned her in first.

Adni stepped inside, expecting another dark stone room. Firelight blazed through the open space, illuminating white walls with gold trim. The trim outlined diamonds across every inch of the wall. Several windows were etched from the stone. North. East. West. But, South was another set of iron doors. The faces of dragons were carved into these doors, giving them horrifying grins and huge teeth.

At the center of the room, on a crystal dais, a large glass orb hovered, twice the side of a horse's head. Flames burned within, orange, red, yellow, white, mixing and flickering inside the orb, as bright as the sun.

The Holy Fire.

Something unseen pulled her toward it, beckoning her to the flames. Her eyes widened as she stepped across the obsidian floor.

"Wait." Kaldar grabbed her wrist, a protective glint in his eyes. "Not yet."

Adni looked back at him.

"Soon." For the first time his irritated gaze softened into understanding. He knew the pull she was experiencing, the need to be close to those flames, the need to touch them.

Adni swallowed the lump in her throat and nodded.

Kaldar led her to the doors off the main room. The light disappeared behind them as they entered a dark corridor. A few torches lined the stone hall, but nothing more.

Through another set of doors at the far end, a nearly identical room to the Holy Fire's chamber waited. White and gold walls, plush white couches with thick furs and pillows. A glass vanity with a large mirror. An ivory bathing tub, and closets nearby. There she would be prepared to accept the Holy Fire.

"You'll be attended to shortly." Kaldar stepped back toward the door. "I'll see you at the ceremony, sister." None of his normal bite edged the word when he called her 'sister'.

For the first time Kaldar seemed as if he were human once, and maybe even warming up towards her.

"Until then," Adni said.

Kaldar excused himself, leaving Adni to admire the beauty of the chamber. As she glanced around the room, she held a hand to her chest. Cracks littered the fortress around her heart. She wished he hadn't left her alone. Solitude would be the end of her self-made mental walls.

NOT FIVE MINUTES after her arrival, half a dozen servants entered to bathe and dress her. Clothed in the same attire as Daniella, they weren't as worse for wear as the slaves who dug out the bottom of the chasm. Still, their skin was pale and their eyes sunken.

Even if emaciated, they didn't waste time in pulling and prodding her into a bath, washing every inch of her before dousing her hair in sweet smelling oils. She'd never been bathed before, never had another person touch her so intimately, but she didn't care.

She couldn't. Adni had settled back into the emptiness.

Try as she might to put them back together, cracks still permeated her mask, but not completely. Her heart still hammered, and her stomach still twisted, but she got through the bath with no embarrassment over her nakedness. Once they were finished, she was dried and primped.

Her nails were cleaned thoroughly and her hair was wrapped into curls. Though her hair normally brushed her collarbone, with curls, the ends of her black hair tickled her bare shoulders.

The servants sat her in front of the mirror, continuing their whirlwind of preparations. Her hair framed her face beautifully, showing off the hard edge of her jaw and sharpness of her cheekbones. The shorter hair made her look older than eighteen.

Before she was fully dressed, they plucked her brows and powdered her cheeks. Adni had never worn makeup in her life, and tried her best not to sneeze as powder climb up her nose and strange instruments were shoved around her eyes.

When they were finished, they rushed her to a wardrobe where the ladies hummed and hawed over which outfit would impress Solipher best.

Adni shifted uncomfortably. She'd never worn anything as lavish as silk, or as pretty as purple. She'd dressed most of her life in cotton and leather, or whatever else her mother could find.

As they pulled dresses from the black wood armoire, her eyes widened.

"No," she said.

They stopped to look at her, as if they hadn't noticed she was a person capable of thought this entire time.

"No dresses." Adni would remain firm on that.

After a few minutes of clucking, they shoved her into tight black leather pants, a red silk blouse and a corset with black strings. Air fled from her lungs as they tightened it around her waist. She hissed and glared at the maidens, who shied away or yelped under her intense gaze.

Once the strings were done up, she stepped into black boots. They covered her wrists in black pearls, and golden rings before settling a red amulet on her chest.

Adni froze. It wasn't exactly the same, not rectangular like hers had been, but more of an oval. Her mother had given her the necklace when she was young, before they'd even fled Salander. It was supposed to be her lucky charm, her protection.

Sharp pain stabbed her chest. She slammed her teeth down on her tongue to hold back a sob.

"Leave!" she commanded.

The ladies leapt with fear and fled as fast as they'd come.

Adni stared at herself in the full-length mirror. The belts wrapping her hips were just like the ones she had worn at home, but fancier, steel instead of iron clasped, black leather instead of brown. With her hair curled, her face was framed just like her mother's. She could be the spitting image of Galia as a teenager.

Her heart lurched, threatening to send her falling into pieces.

"No," she hissed. "You will not crumble." She glared into her own eyes, fierce like ice in her reflection.

She wouldn't give up this power for her *feelings*. She wouldn't give it up for pain.

The curtains at the window fluttered as someone brushed through.

"Adni?" Julian stood outlined by the cold blue sky, white-topped mountains in the distance beyond her shoulders.

Adni's heart thumped faster. Why had she come? She was the last person Adni needed to see right now. Every meeting with Julian broke something inside of her.

"What are you doing here?" Adni snapped. The cold that had settled inside her warmed at the sight of Julian's dark blue eyes and careful smile. Since when had Julian become careful? She was the reckless one.

Julian held her hands up as she approached, as if Adni were some kind of wild beast. "I'm here to rescue you."

Adni scoffed. "I don't need rescuing."

Julian sighed and lowered her hands. "You may not know it, but you do. You can't stay here with these people. They aren't good. They're evil, just like Kadia was, and they'll make you like her."

Her chest twinged. Like Kadia? That was the last thing she'd ever wanted to be before she'd let the darkness consumed her. Even through the lost for power, and anger writhing in her belly, she didn't want to be like Kadia.

"The power isn't worth it. Nothing is worth giving up who you are." Julian motioned at the door. "That's what this ceremony will do to you. It'll take away the human part of you for good. It'll leave you with hunger and hate. You'll never love anyone or anything again."

Adni shook her head. "Julian, I can't do this with you right now. Someone will be coming for me any moment."

Julian stepped closer. Her breath fogged the air between them. She took Adni's hands and squeezed her fingers. "Adni, listen to me. You don't want to go through with this."

Panic welled in her chest, tightening around her heart. "Y-yes, I do."

Julian's pretty lips twisted in a rueful smile. Another pang flashed through Adni's chest. She missed Julian's flirtatious smile and carefree attitude. She was so serious since they'd arrived in Izenfir.

"No, you don't," Julian said.

Adni ripped her hands away. Confusion flooded every inch of her, threatening to pull her into a never ending well of despair. She fought for breath as she turned toward the window. "Stop," she said.

"I won't." Julian's fingers rested on her back.

"Stop it." Adni shook her head.

"Never."

Adni turned to face her, a cry on her lips. A cry for her to go away, to stop, and leave her to her fate.

Instead, Julian pressed forward, hand on Adni's cheek as she kissed her.

Heat blossomed inside Adni's chest, burning through the rest of the cold. Her lips parted in a gasp. Julian wrapped an arm around her waist and pulled her closer. Her fingers gripped Adni's hair, and her sweet lips pressed against hers.

All sense of thought and feeling escaped her. Her legs went numb and her fingers trembled as they wrapped around Julian's cheeks. Adni kissed Julian back with every bit of strength she had left.

Her heart raced as their kiss deepened and Julian nipped her lower lip gently. Adni shivered and pressed closer, but Julian pulled away.

The warmth of Julian's lips left, but her hands still hovered by

Adni's cheeks and hair. "Adni?" Julian's voice was low and husky, sweet and tempting.

Adni opened her eyes. Julian's dark blue gaze had brightened with hope, with affection, with a desperate need to have the real Adni back.

She nodded. "Hi." Tears burned the back of her eyes as everything she'd pushed down for the last few days came rushing back. Adni's throat hitched and her legs gave out. Julian held her up, wrapping Adni in her arms. Adni buried her face in Julian's hair.

"I'm so sorry," Julian whispered, her breath hot on Adni's ear.

All Adni could do was nod and cry. Her mother was gone. Her brother was gone. Her little sister was gone. Everyone she'd ever loved was gone. All she had left in the world was Julian.

As her despair waned, heat burned through her bones. She didn't have her family anymore because Solipher had taken them from her. Solipher had killed them, and Solipher would *pay*.

Adni got her feet under her and slowly released Julian. Julian planted a kiss on her forehead before she stepped away.

"What are we going to do?" Adni swiped the back of her hands across her eyes, removing whatever makeup remained.

"I have a plan." Julian turned to the window and leaned out it. "We're going to escape." She looked back over her shoulder.

Adni slowly nodded. Her bones ached. She was so tired, but if she didn't listen to Julian and go, there was no telling what Solipher would do. "Let's go."

Julian nodded and hoisted her legs over the windowsill as she crawled out. She perched just outside it as Adni followed.

Adni's stomach lurched as she gazed into the chasm below. It had to be at least a hundred feet down. There was no way they'd survive a fall like that.

"Careful now!" Julian flashed a teasing smile.

The look warmed Adni's heart. "You too."

Julian climbed downward, allowing Adni space to slip outside the window. She had never been more grateful for pants in her life. She couldn't imagine attempting this in heels and a dress.

Adni wedged her boots into the same holds as Julian had.

"Looking good!" Julian called up.

The Spyre twisted below, harsh and uneven rock. It'd be a nightmare to climb down. Adni sighed. Only Julian could make her attempt this madness.

Slipping her fingers and boots into any hold she could find, Adni made her way down slowly after Julian. They didn't have long before her ceremony. If they were going to get out undetected, they needed to get to the bridge and get out before someone came looking for her.

Whatever way Julian had found out of these mountains, Adni hoped it was easy to get to. They were bound to meet resistance if they weren't quick.

They must have descended several floors by the time Adni's muscles started to weaken and her hands grew slick with sweat. She refused to look down and see how much space remained. It would only entice her limbs to give up.

"We're nearly there!" Julian called. "Hold on!"

Adni nodded, whether Julian could see her head or not. She was too busy catching her breath as her limbs trembled on the rock. Her fingers were cut to hell, but at least her boots were good for climbing.

"Adni?" someone called overhead. Shouts rose from the window up above. Her heart leapt as she looked up.

No. They'd been found out.

Adni threw a desperate glance over her shoulder. Julian was maybe seven feet from the bridge, and Adni wasn't much higher than that. Her breath fled her lungs in a relieved sigh.

She steeled herself. She could do this. She had to.

Inching lower, Adni urged her muscles to cooperate as she eased down to the next set of holds. A soft thump sounded below. She glanced down. Julian waved from the bridge.

Thank the blue skies.

As the shouts grew louder, Adni reached the height of Julian's head, and leapt. Her knees slammed against the ground and her palms pressed into the cold stone. She sucked in a deep breath as pain shot up her legs.

Julian grabbed her arm and hoisted her to her feet. "No time for rest now."

Adni nodded and followed as Julian pulled her across the bridge and down the mountainside.

With every step, the shouts grew louder. Voices echoed in the chasm. Cries of outrage, of irritation, of betrayal.

Adni's pulse pounded in her ears as fear tightened around her heart. What would they do if they caught her? Kill her, most likely. She gulped. She'd be lucky if they only killed her. Whatever Solipher was, he didn't seem like the forgiving type.

A tunnel opened up to their left, and Julian dove inside. The dungeon.

"Why are we back here?" Adni panted.

Julian jogged down the tunnel until the passage widened into a cavern. "Astrid, James!" she called.

Adni perked up. James was here? Did that mean he had recovered?

Astrid peeked from inside a cage, and slid the door open. The lock was burned through. James leaned heavily against her, his head hung as he dragged his feet.

"We're here," Astrid said. "James isn't doing well."

"Give him to me," Julian said. She motioned for Astrid to hand him to her.

"You traitorous little worm!" Kaldar's shout cut through the dungeon and echoed down the tunnel.

They all froze, except Adni, who turned to look over her shoulder.

The perfect picture of a dragon in human form, Kaldar seethed fury, his fists trembling and his teeth bared. This wasn't good.

"Kal–" Adni began.

"Shut up!" he screamed. "You could have been my new sister. You could have been part of this family. Why would you give up your power for *her*?" Kaldar motioned viciously at Julian.

Adni's eyebrows pulled together as she glanced between them. She didn't have an answer for Kaldar, not one that would satisfy him anyway.

"I was a fool to think you'd truly given in." Kaldar shook his head. "But no matter, I'll kill you myself."

Adni's eyes widened as Kaldar leapt. Darkness bunched around his fists as he flew right at her. Adni ducked, rolling across the stone floor, just out of reach of his darkness.

He spun on his heels, faster than she'd ever seen him, and threw blackness at her. Adni twisted from reach, and a yowl of rage echoed inside the dungeon. Kaldar always hated how she did that.

Instead of throwing more of his magic, Kaldar pounced, slamming into her shoulders and knocking her onto the ground. Air exploded from her lungs as her back cracked against the stone floor. His weight pinned her down, and his fingers closed on her throat.

Adni choked as Kaldar squeezed. Her nails scraped along the backs of his hands in an attempt to dislodge them, but she couldn't get a grip. Pain rushed through her neck, and clenched around her chest as she fought for air.

"K-Kal!" she gasped.

His fingers tightened and stars danced across her vision.

"Get off her!" Julian shouted.

Kaldar didn't budge.

Black speckles encroached on her vision as her limbs grew weaker and weaker. Her mind went in all directions, unable to figure out how to get herself out of this.

Heat exploded across her skin, and Kaldar yelped as he leapt back. Flames burned the fur of his coat. He slapped out the sparks before twisting toward Julian.

Fire circled Julian's closed fist. She narrowed her eyes at Kaldar. "Leave her alone." Something between a hiss and a snarl rumbled between Julian's teeth.

Adni coughed as she sucked in air while looking between them. Her throat hurt and her lungs burned, but she could breathe. She stared at the fire wrapping Julian's fist. *Magic?*

Kaldar's eyes widened as he stared into the flames. "B-but you're a human."

Julian smirked. "Not quite." She whipped a fist out, and flames burned through the air. Kaldar leapt out of reach as fire licked his heels.

Confusion twisted his brow as he looked between them. He had no idea what to do, that much was obvious. "I can't sense your magic," he mumbled beneath his breath. "What are you?"

Julian put her hands together. Flames turned into a small sun between her hands before she launched it at Kaldar.

Kaldar threw his arms up, creating a shield of darkness. The sun burned and sizzled against the blackness, tearing through it. Kaldar leapt out of the way as the flame flew past where he stood moments before.

"That's impossible!" he shouted. His fists trembled.

Was he afraid?

"Go, before I burn you alive." Julian narrowed her eyes.

Kaldar fled for the tunnel, disappearing into the black.

Adni sat on the stone, her mind racing with possibilities as she looked between Julian and Astrid. While Astrid didn't seem surprised, her mouth set in a grim line; Adni's heart was ready to leap from her chest.

If even Kaldar was afraid of Julian, and had no idea what she was, could it mean Julian was ashen?

Or worse, was she a beast like Solipher?

Could dragons be real?

TWELVE

"It's time to go." Julian pulled Adni to her feet. The flames around her hands had disappeared.

Adni swayed, her mind spinning as she looked between Julian's hands and face. What was she supposed to think? What was she supposed to do? Was she fleeing one set of demons for another?

"Come on." Julian took over care of James, slinging his arm around her shoulder and holding up his waist. She led the way to the back of the dungeon, where darkness reigned.

Astrid plucked a torch from the wall and glanced at Adni, fear welling in her wide eyes. "Are you coming?"

Adni gulped and nodded. Did she really have a choice?

Julian led the retreat to the back of the dungeon, Adni and Astrid on her heels. Flames flickered over the walls, casting eerie shadows in every direction. The cavern narrowed into a tunnel.

Howls of pursuit echoed all around, mingled with an angry rumble. No one called her name again, but the meaning behind the sounds was clear. If they caught Adni, she'd be lucky to get out alive.

Adni shook her head, concentrating on pumping her legs as she raced after Julian, who nearly carried James down the long corridor.

Branches curved off the main path. Left. Right. Left. Julian flew through them all as if she knew exactly where they were going. And maybe she did. For all Adni knew, Julian had lived there in the past. Maybe she was a rogue ashen who'd escaped Izenfir. Maybe she was one of the dragons.

Her brows furrowed. She'd never seen a female dragon. Ashen, sure, but not one beast like Solipher. Were there female ones?

Adni shook her head. Though the thoughts were a lovely distraction, and something she'd definitely be taking up with Julian later, she needed to concentrate on their flight. The howls hadn't disappeared yet. Someone was following. Whether it be Solipher, Kaldar, or any of the others, they'd be fast, unhurt and most of all, not carrying a sick man.

She glanced at James, who dragged his feet with every step. Julian held his waist, nearly lifting him off the ground as she moved.

Her heart raced as they twisted through passages, fleeing deeper and deeper into the mountains. Her body ached and her legs burned, but still they ran. Even as Astrid tripped, she pulled herself back up, determination in her gaze. Julian's pace didn't falter. She didn't slow. Even after being caged for days, with most likely little food, the woman led the pack like a warrior.

Adni's cheeks warmed as she watched the curve of Julian's hips while she ran. Julian was an impressive woman, whatever she was. Her stomach twisted. Though Julian had saved her, Adni wasn't sure of Julian's motives.

The sounds of their pursuit slowly faded as minutes turned into hours. Her breaths grew ragged, and their pace slowed, only so Astrid and Adni could keep up, she was sure. Her chest burned along with every other muscle in her body. She needed water. She needed rest. They all did.

But the distant calls kept her moving. They couldn't stop to rest, not if the mountain-dwellers were still on their tail.

"Everyone all right back there?" Julian called over her shoulder. Her blue eyes flashed with concern as she met Adni's gaze.

Adni could only nod. Her throat was tight from breathing hard. All of her concentration needed to stay on the ground in front of her.

"Yes," Astrid gasped between breaths. She wheezed and stumbled next to Adni. The flames of her torch shook with her limbs. Astrid's eyes drooped with fatigue. After being stuck in a cage for years, Adni thought she was holding up quite well.

More long minutes ticked by until the only sound in the darkness was their breathing and the slap of their boots on the stone floor.

Julian slowed to a stop and leaned James up against the wall. He slid down to sit, where Astrid collapsed at his side.

"We'll rest for a while," Julian said. She wiped the sweat from her brow and took the torch from Astrid before she too sat against the wall.

Adni fell to her knees and leaned against the cold stone. It soothed the warmth of her sweaty forehead and cooled the burning inside her. Every inch of her ached, begging for a week of sleep.

Julian met her gaze. They couldn't stay long, and they both knew it.

"You know where we're going?" Adni asked as she caught her breath.

"Yes." Julian nodded.

"How?"

"I know these mountains."

She didn't elaborate.

James chuckled, drawing the attention of all three women. He breathed hard, but some color had returned to his face. His eyes locked with Astrid's, half drooped and beyond exhausted, but filled with love.

"This reminds me of the first time we explored the mountains," he said.

Astrid smiled and leaned her forehead against his. "We aren't fighting any beasts this time."

"Not yet." He raised his eyebrows comically before he kissed her forehead.

The couple curled up together, leaning against each other for support.

Adni's heart clenched. She'd only ever seen one other couple look at each other that way; her grandparents. Though she'd been young when they passed, she still remembered the way they danced around the tavern when the night was done and the drunks had left. Her grandfather would dip his wife, and kiss her as she howled with laughter.

Astrid closed her eyes, and so did James. They fell asleep, looks of calm relief on both of their faces. How long had they been kept apart? How long had it been since they'd held each other?

Adni's eyes burned. She blinked quickly to push back the tears.

"You should rest too." Julian gently nudged Adni's boot with her foot.

"So should you." Adni looked up.

Julian shook her head. "I'll keep watch and listen just in case."

Adni nodded and leaned her head back against the stone wall. Though it was rough and uncomfortable, poking into her every limb, she fell asleep in minutes.

* * *

GENTLE HANDS SHOOK HER SHOULDERS, pulling her from sleep. Adni opened her eyes slowly, her head fuzzy and her body aching.

"It's time to go," Julian whispered. Her breath fogged the cold air.

Adni slowly sat up. At some point she must have sprawled out on the tunnel floor. She was fairly certain she'd been sitting up when she'd fallen asleep.

Julian stood and moved to the other pair. She shook them gently, cooing softly for them to wake up. Astrid groaned loudly, and James blinked with heavy lids.

After a few minutes they were all up and moving, this time at a much slower pace. Julian held James up again, while Astrid led the way, flame in hand. No one spoke, except for Julian to give directions to Astrid. Adni brought up the rear, wincing as her throat ached with every inhale.

Kaldar must have strangled her much harder than she'd thought, or she'd been too busy to notice how much it hurt before. Maybe adrenaline had kept the pain at bay. But with it gone, her body was a giant painful sore on par with her mind.

Her family could be dead. Though Solipher had shown her a vision of the act itself, she still struggled to believe it. Her mother couldn't be gone. Her siblings had to be okay. She'd seen enough magic in the last week to know the visions could have been conjured. But she hesitated her thought process. They'd been *so real*. She'd smelled the burning of the fire, and the copper of her mother's blood. Could Solipher fake that?

She wasn't sure. She had no idea to what extent his magic stretched.

Whether they were alive or not, Adni had to return to her mountain town and find out. Her stomach twisted and her heart tightened. She had to know. She would know. Even if the thought of returning to the dark mountains again soured her stomach, she needed to return, for her family.

The clap of their boots echoed in the tunnel as they continued mindlessly through the mountain. Every step became mechanical. One step closer to freedom. They had to keep going. Had to keep moving. If they didn't, someone might catch up to them.

But where were they going? How did Julian keep track of all these passages? There were so many twists, so many turns. It all looked the same. Dark jagged rock, uneven floors. One cross road, two. After dozens of forks in the road, she'd never be able to find her way back— not that she wanted to.

Her stomach growled, clawing at her insides. It was long passed suppertime, and she'd barely had any breakfast alone with Daniella in her chambers. She couldn't complain though. How much had James or Astrid eaten in months? Years? Yet they were still alive.

She sucked in a sharp breath. She had to suck it up, had to be strong. They'd get out of this.

* * *

WHEN ADNI WAS sure they trudged long into the night, Julian finally stopped at a wide, curved cavern where the ground wasn't quite so rough.

The embers of their torch were dying, leaving hardly anything to be seen but the outlines of their bodies.

Adni trailed her fingers along the wall to keep herself straight. The sharp sting of rock through her fingertips had kept her awake, and kept her moving, but the sting had grown dull.

"We'll camp here," Julian said. She lowered James to the ground. He flopped onto his side and collapsed into sleep.

Astrid trembled as she lowered herself onto the cold earth. Though she wore a coat, it was thin and torn, and her limbs were so skinny. Julian took the torch from her fingers and lay it in a dip in the earth.

Flames burst through the darkness, startling Adni. She stepped back as Julian lit the torch anew, fire licking the air hungrily. Julian sat beside it and crossed her legs. She brushed back her hair with one quick swipe. Even Julian was exhausted.

Adni looked between the flames, and Julian's worn out expression. She twisted her lip between her teeth. The fire had startled life back into her. She still had so many questions. Who was Julian? *What* was she? And why had she hidden her true identity this whole time? If Julian had just told her who she was, maybe Adni would have listened. Maybe she'd have come out of the darkness sooner, or maybe she wouldn't have given in at all.

She took a seat against the wall, opposite Julian. Astrid inched closer to the fire, laying her head on James's lap. She was out cold in moments.

Silence lapsed, only the crackle of flames between them.

Adni's chest ached. She wanted to ask Julian so many things, but fear settled inside her gut. She liked Julian, maybe more than liked her, but had she lied to Adni? Something wasn't right. She had to know.

"What are you?" Adni's voice was hardly a whisper.

Julian looked up; her eyes round and dark even in the light of the torch. Her carefree smirk was gone, as was her metal shoulder plate and bracer. Julian was left in a leather coat and pants, no sword or shield in sight. She looked strange without them, vulnerable.

"It's complicated." Julian looked down at the flames. The light danced in her eyes. "I don't want you to hate me."

Adni's eyebrows furrowed. She wanted to say she could never hate Julian, that she enjoyed their time together far too much, and was beyond grateful for Julian's insistence on rescuing her. Without Julian, Adni might have never returned to who she was. Though pain stole her breath every time she thought of her family, and whether they were dead or alive, that didn't mean she had to lose herself to it.

Julian sighed. "I'm a daughter of the Holy Fire, a dragon like the rest of them."

Adni raised her brows. So dragons did exist?

"My great-grandmother created the first Holy Fire. My mother was the last female dragon they know of." Julian motioned back the way they'd come. "They kept her in slavery for hundreds of years, forcing her to bear child after child. All males. The lines of dragons would die without more females, and so when my mother had twins, she hid me away to escape a fate like hers and sent my brother, Dareys, to Izenfir while I lived in the mountains alone."

Adni's eyes widened. She couldn't imagine being subjugated for hundreds of years, let alone the few James and Astrid must have endured. Having children on top of that? Was her mother even allowed to see the children after she bore them? Adni shook her head. The dragons were crueler than she thought.

Not only that, but Lord Dareys, the carefree, cruel-eyed father of Valeria, was Julian's brother. He looked far older than Julian, but his familiar smile suddenly made sense.

"When it became clear another female might not be born, that's when they started seeking humans with magical abilities. Dragons are proud creatures, and they desperately wanted a way to continue their lines, even if they didn't remain pure. It helped that they could already sense magical humans, crave them even." Julian gulped. "So high-breeds like Solipher began mating with the magical humans he found. Thus, the *ashen* were born."

"And Kadia was one?" She needed to hear it from someone other than Kaldar and Solipher. She needed to hear that the same blood that once ran through the veins of the only woman to ever conquer the six kingdoms, also ran threw her.

"Yes." Julian nodded grimly. "Kadia was one of Solipher's first children."

"But why did he let her go to the six kingdoms? Why let her destroy them?"

"They don't care about anyone, Adni. Most of them have given into the darkness residing in all things. Once they give into it, they don't feel love, or sadness, or joy. They only hunger for power."

Adni's eyebrows furrowed. "So, you don't feel joy, or sadness or... love?" Her cheeks warmed.

"I do." Julian reached across the space between them and squeezed Adni's fingers. "My mother taught me that there was another way. It's a constant battle to fight off my darker self, but I don't need to give in to her. I have my own power, and that's all I need."

Adni nodded. "Why did you show up that day at the river?"

Julian looked away. She bit her lip, a long silence drifting between them. "I've been looking for you for a long time."

"Why?"

"My mother could sense you. Her grandmother, my great grand-mother, was one of the ancients, the first dragons to flee the fire beneath the earth. Her power was far greater than even Solipher's." She smiled. "She told me to find you, that you were the key to bringing down Izenfir, destroying the Holy Fire and dooming the remaining dragons to life in human form. Adni, she could feel your magic from the day you were born. You have a great gift."

Her stomach twisted with uncertainty. Though she wanted to

believe everything Julian said, she had still lied to Adni. She wasn't just a traveler adventuring across the six kingdoms. And now she wanted Adni to believe she was some sort of great magical creature? Her mother didn't have magic, not that Adni had ever seen. She wanted to believe she knew her mother well enough to know that.

Julian sighed. Her smile faded. "I know it's a lot to take in."

Adni pulled her hands away and leaned back against the tunnel wall.

"You can ask me anything. I won't lie to you," Julian said.

But how could Adni trust someone who'd already lied?

Adni looked at the two lovers lying nearby. Suddenly she remembered the slaves, and the mine they dug at the bottom of the chasm. "What are the slaves digging for at the bottom of Izenfir?"

Julian's eyes darkened, and her jaw set. "He's looking for more ancients."

Adni gasped, surprise slamming into her chest. "*What?*"

"I told you about how the dragons burst from the flames inside the earth." Julian raised her eyebrows until Adni nodded. "Well the first ancients came from the chasm. It wasn't always a valley. Thousands of years ago it was a volcano."

Adni tilted her head. "A volcano?" She'd never heard of such a thing.

"A hollow mountain filled with molten rock and fire."

"And that's where the ancient dragons came from?"

"Yes."

"And Solipher is trying to… dig out more of them?" Her pulse pounded in her ears, and her breath quickened.

"Yes."

"What happened the last time the ancients emerged?" Adni asked. Dread swelled inside her stomach.

Julian's lips thinned. "They rained hellfire upon the land beyond the mountains for a hundred years before my great grandmother united them."

Cold fear wrapped around her heart and clenched like a serpent.

This was impossible. This was madness. Solipher would destroy Warshard if he unleashed another generation of dragons.

"This is why we need to stop them, Adni." Julian's gaze hardened to blue steel. "I won't let him destroy all of those people."

Adni swallowed hard. She couldn't wrap her mind around it. Images of her home in Salander, burning by Kadia's hand, were still seared into her mind. But this would be worse. *So* much worse.

"You should rest."

Adni looked up. How could she rest after what Julian had just told her?

"We can talk later." Julian smiled faintly, even as chaos flew through the depths of her eyes.

Adni nodded slowly. She stared at the flickering flames on the floor. Smoke rose from the rag. So many thoughts ran through her head, but none she could catch. Her entire body slumped against the wall. She rested her head back. She was so tired she could hardly think. Her legs ached, and her head swam. She could figure out whether to trust Julian later. For now, she needed to regain her strength for tomorrow when their flight continued, and the real war began.

Flames warmed her toes as she wiggled her boots closer to the torch. She closed her eyes, taking a deep, calming breath, and embraced the bliss of darkness.

THIRTEEN

*D*arkness met her gaze when she opened her eyes the next day. Was she still asleep? Adni blinked slowly. Or had she gone blind? Pure nothingness lie around her. Hard rock pressed into her shoulder and her face lay in the crook of her arm. She stretched out her muscles. A dull ache remained, but most of her soreness was gone.

She should still be hurting. Did the dragon part of her help her heal? Being ashen explained how she'd survived her little tumble off the waterfall.

Adni pressed her fingertips together. Yesterday they'd been bloody by the time she fell asleep. Now they hardly tingled.

She sat up, pressing her back to the wall. A shiver worked its way up her spine. The torch, their one bit of warmth, was out. No wonder she was staring into blackness. They were trapped deep in the mountains, with no skylight, no torch, no fire to light their way.

"Are you awake?" Julian whispered.

Adni jumped, and looked around as if she could find Julian's face. She cleared her throat. "Yes."

Julian snapped her fingers. The sound echoed down the tunnel as flames burst through the black.

Adni shielded her eyes as harsh firelight blossomed before her eyes. "A little warning next time, please." She rubbed her eyes and lowered her hands, blinking back the white dots dancing across her vision.

"Sure." Julian chuckled half-heartedly as she lit the torch with her hand.

Her heart leapt as the flames caught and the torch returned to its dull blaze. Julian rose, the red flickers disappearing from her palm.

Astrid and James lay curled up against the wall, wrapped in each other's arms, shivering in the cold. They both looked ready for a bath, a meal, and a month's worth of rest. After all they'd been through, they deserved it.

Julian shook them gently, awakening them from their slumber. Astrid wiped her eyes, and James blinked up at Julian, still half-asleep.

After a few minutes of quiet shuffling and grumbles about the hour, they all stood and began their trek again, deeper into the unknown.

* * *

Silence stretched like the hours. They kept a steady pace, but didn't care to jog or run. James couldn't take much more, and continued to slump against Julian. His face had grown pale again and his eyes hollow. If they didn't get out of these mountains and get some food soon, he might not make it.

Adni twisted her lip between her teeth as she followed Julian and her keen sense of direction. Astrid led the way, torch in hand, but she looked over her shoulder every minute of two, checking to make sure James hadn't slipped into death's embrace without her knowing.

Tears brimmed in Astrid's big eyes. While it was clear she'd been at least somewhat cared for in the dungeon, the same couldn't be said for James. Was that guilt behind her eyes? Worry? Desperation? Adni had a feeling it was all three.

When silence had finally become too much, Adni sighed and stepped up to join Astrid at the head of the pack. Julian gave her a curious glance as she passed.

"How did you survive in that dungeon for so long?" Adni asked.

Astrid looked at her with wide eyes. Adni winced. She hadn't realized it might be insensitive to ask.

"I don't know really," Astrid said. She twisted her fingers around the thick branch of the torch. "I drew in the dirt, counted the minutes, spent hours imagining what was going on in the rest of the world." Her lips quirked slightly. "There were others in the cell next to me, before Julian." She glanced over her shoulder. Adni did too. "I spoke with them when no one was around, learned what I could about the outside world. I kept picturing the day when my sister would arrive and slay them all."

Adni smiled.

"They call her the Immortal Queen. Slayer of Kadia, and Freer of Slaves. They say she has the biggest army in the six kingdoms." Astrid shook her head. "I honestly can't believe it. Haven never enjoyed swordplay."

Adni snorted. "Who doesn't enjoy swordplay?"

Astrid shrugged. "I never did. I prefer a bow. It's a much more elegant weapon."

"I suppose." Adni paused. "Do you miss her?"

"With every moment that passes." Her sigh fogged the chill air. "Everyone thinks I'm dead. They had a funeral for me. My sister grieved my absence." Astrid sucked in a sharp breath. "I can't believe I let her think she's all alone in the world, especially after our parents and brothers."

Adni's heart clenched and her eyes burned. What if the same thing had happened to her? What if her entire family was truly gone?

"We were never close," Astrid continued. "But my brother, Marcel, and Haven were as thick as thieves."

"I'm sure she misses you, too." Adni bit her tongue to halt the quake in her voice.

Astrid smiled. "That's kind of you to say."

"Why did they keep you all this time?"

Astrid's shoulders rose and her fists tightened. Fear clouded her eyes. "Solipher intended to use me in some plot again my sister. He used to visit me, telling me stories about Haven and how he couldn't wait to test her immortality. He spent hours detailing how he'd tear her apart." Tears dripped down her chin.

Adni reached for Astrid's hand and squeezed her fingers. "I'm so sorry." She couldn't think of anything else to say. Solipher was a monster. How could she ever have wanted him as her family?

* * *

ANOTHER DAY WENT by inside the darkness of the Cinder Mountains. They rested periodically, whenever they found the tiniest drip of water off the damp, jagged rocks. James wheezed constantly, and hardly opened his eyes any longer. Adni assisted Julian in carrying him, while Astrid led the way, determination in her eyes.

On the afternoon of their third day scouring tunnels, cold pre-winter light dusted the rock ahead. Could it be daylight?

Astrid spun to face them, a gasp on her lips and hope flashing in her eyes. If they'd finally found the outside world, they could save James. Or so she hoped.

While Julian and Adni picked up the pace, Astrid ran for the light, having found strength in her hope.

They emerged into blinding light. Adni covered her eyes and blinked rapidly to rid the white dots from her vision. She squinted at the river below, a small wooden bridge arching over it.

"We did it!" Astrid squealed her delight and danced in a circle, her arms open to the sky above. She flopped to the ground, lush grass bending to embrace her.

Adni closed her eyes, her head tilted to the sun. She'd lived most of her life in darkness, and after being in the light for only a few days before Solipher took her, she wasn't willing to give it up again.

But her heart ached and home called. She had to know whether

her family was dead or alive. She had to know if Solipher murdered them in cold blood before the whole world went to hell.

Fire burned through her veins, and her fists tightened.

Julian looked at her, a question in her eyes, but she said nothing.

"I suppose this is where we part ways," Adni said. Her stomach flipped at the thought. She wanted to see them all to safety, but she *needed* to know her family's fate.

"What are you talking about?" Astrid flipped onto her stomach. Her pale skin glowed in the sun. The olive tone beneath her flesh told Adni, Astrid wasn't typically a pale girl. Most of Rythern's people weren't.

"I need to know if Solipher killed my family."

Julian lowered James to the ground. He blinked awake, looking around in awe at the field of grass sloping down to the river. Beyond the river, tall pine and oak trees rose from the ground for miles. Smoke curled in the distance. A town.

"Where is your family?" Astrid asked.

"The mountains…" Adni glanced back at the tall slabs of rock at her back. She shivered at the thought.

"The ones inside Salander," Julian added. "Outside Elmhurst."

Astrid's eyes widened. "It'd take you a week to travel there on foot. Maybe longer."

"I'll find a way." Adni's jaw hardened. She had to find a way. She wasn't sure she could last a week. Her stomach ached, splinters of hunger shooting through her gut.

"Come with us to Palmyra." Astrid stood, stepping closer to Adni. "We're already in Rythern territory."

Adni glanced around, unsure how she could tell. All the trees looked the same to her, and with no towns or structures to identify, she wasn't sure how Astrid knew where they were.

"I can't," Adni said.

"Please, Adni." Astrid took her hands. Adni's cheeks burned. "You've already helped us escape that foul place, and you must be starving. Come with us to Palmyra. It's only a few days journey. As soon as we arrive we can send word to Salander and get someone to check on your family."

Astrid's words were tempting, as was the genuine kindness in her eyes and wide smile lighting her face. Though her eyes were sunken and dull, her hair mussed and greasy, Astrid was still lovely.

Adni shifted from foot to foot, glancing between Astrid, James and Julian. She was right. It would take her a week to get home, maybe more, especially in her state. What if she couldn't find food? She could try and steal something, but people were bound to aid the Princess of Rythern. And if they didn't, Julian always had her charms.

She looked at Julian. Her gaze was hard, conveying a thousand things, most of all, the words they'd exchanged at night in the tunnels about dragons, ashen, and the coming war.

Adni shook her head. She couldn't believe she was about to say this. "Fine. I'll come with you."

Astrid grinned and wrapped her arms around Adni's shoulders. Her arms were thin, her body mere skin and bones. Adni's chest ached as she hugged Astrid back. "Thank you."

Adni nodded and released the princess. Though it was strange to think of this frail woman she'd first found in a cage as a princess, she was royalty. "Should I be calling you My Lady, or something?" Her cheeks flushed. She hardly remembered her childhood lessons on Warshard royals anymore. The customs hadn't been important when she lived in the mountains.

Astrid laughed, tears welling in her eyes. "Adni, after all we've been through, I think you can just call me Astrid."

Her cheeks burned with embarrassment. "All right."

Astrid shook her head, the amusement fading from her eyes as her gaze fell on James. "We should get going." A leadership quality Adni hadn't heard from the small woman flashed in her tone.

"Agreed." Julian hoisted James back off the ground.

"Time to go already?" He shook his head. "You ladies run me ragged."

Julian grinned, the first true smile Adni had seen from her in days. "A man could never handle three ladies at once."

They all laughed as they made their way down the hillside to the river below. Palmyra was only a few days north, so Astrid had said. The quicker Adni got food in her belly, the better.

FOURTEEN

They reached the small cottage of a woodcutter a few hours later. Tall trees lay on their sides, stacked neatly several yards from the small log cabin. The surrounding land was stripped of trees, the grass lying bare, with only a few pine needles remaining. Stumps stuck from the ground at the edge, but most were already dug from the ground, leaving piles of overturned earth at their sides.

A tall man with greying blond hair and a thick beard slammed an axe against the trunk of an oak tree. Sweat beaded on his forehead and his breath fogged the cold afternoon air.

James shivered against Adni as they stepped from the forest into the clearing. Julian had already given up her coat for the man, but it wasn't enough to keep him from trembling with every step.

Astrid wasn't fairing much better. Her shoulders slumped and her eyes had gone dull. She glanced at them, as if wondering why they'd stopped, until Julian nodded in the direction of the woodcutter.

Her gasp cut the air. Crows cawed and took flight, rustling the surrounding trees. Finally, they'd found somewhere to rest.

The woodcutter paused, his thick brow wrinkling as he looked over at the small group. His eyes flew wide, most likely at the sight of James, though the rest of them weren't looking much better.

"Hello there," the woodcutter said. His voice was rough like the edge of his axe. He lowered the weapon to the ground as he hurried over. "Are you all, all right?"

His sincere concern for a stranger's well being made Adni smile.

"Not too bad, but we could use a bit of help," Julian said. Though she sounded like her usual self, sweat beaded on her forehead. Even she was exhausted.

"Come with me." The woodcutter turned back toward the cottage. Thin smoke rose from a chimney. It wouldn't take much to turn the smoke dark grey and billowy. With it, they'd finally get some warmth.

The man led the way to the log cabin. Julian and Adni followed quickly, towing James along with them, while Astrid stumbled behind. None of them had eaten in days. She couldn't imagine how hungry Astrid and James must be after so long. At least Adni had been fed in the mountain, even if she had shared most of her meals.

"There isn't a town around for miles," the woodcutter said as they mounted the steps of the cabin to the porch. "Where did you come from?" He glanced over his shoulder as he threw the door wide open. He ushered them in first, his brows cinched with concern.

"The mountains," Adni said.

The small cabin was a large room, with a single bed, a small table and two wooden chairs, a fireplace, a worn-out sofa and a kitchen cut from the same wood as the log walls.

"The mountains?" the man gaped as Julian and Adni lowered James onto the bed. He passed out before his head hit the pillow.

Adni exchanged a look with Julian. They couldn't very well tell this man the truth. He'd think them mad and throw them out.

"We were exploring the tunnels when we got lost. Our rations were eaten up in days. I don't know how long we were stuck in there." Julian edged her voice with desperation, as if recalling the memory. Though they had been stuck in the mountains for some time, Julian had always known the way out.

Adni shifted uncomfortably. Julian's ease with a lie wasn't helping Adni decide if Julian was trustworthy.

The man scratched his head. "That wasn't a smart idea, kids."

"We know that now." Julian sighed. Her shoulders slumped.

The woodcutter bought their story without any further details. He busied himself flitting around the kitchen and the fireplace, lighting the dying coals before plucking dried meat from a rack. He handed them each a piece before grabbing some water. Julian and Adni took a seat at the small kitchen table while Astrid sat on the edge of the bed, her fingers laced with James's.

"Sorry I don't have much besides this." He motioned at the salted meat. "It's reaching the end of the season and I'll be headed back into town soon."

"It's plenty." Julian flashed one of her dazzling smiles.

Adni's heart fluttered.

"What happened to him?" The man's cheeks reddened at the sight of Julian's smile. He cleared his throat and scratched his long hair again.

"He took a bad fall." Julian didn't miss a beat. "He hasn't been able to eat much since he's been in and out of consciousness."

"That must have been some fall." The woodcutter boiled water over the fire and fetched herbs from the counter for tea.

Adni dug into the meat, ripping off pieces with her teeth. Salt blossomed on her tongue. It took everything she had not to moan in delight. Food had never tasted so good. She ripped off pieces as Julian chatted with the woodcutter. Several minutes later they had steaming cups of tea in hand. Her hunger pains ebbed away. Now all she needed was a good night's sleep on something other than the hard ground.

"Is your friend still asleep?" The woodcutter nodded at James.

Astrid looked up; her eyes glazed with worry. "Yes."

"Hm." The man rubbed his beard with his thumb and index finger. "He might need a healer." Astrid's eyes widened. "I don't mean to worry you, dear," he rushed to add.

Astrid squeezed James's fingers and kissed the back of his hand. "He'll be all right. I know he will."

"You mentioned you were heading into town soon?" Julian asked.

"Yes." He nodded. "I always leave before the first snowfall. A friend will arrive in a few days to pick me up."

Adni's eyebrows cinched. "What do you do in case of an emergency?" Did he really have no other way out of the forest?

"I have a horse, lass. The old boy is reaching the end of his years, but he's good in a pinch."

She hadn't seen a stable, but then again, she'd never seen a woodcutter's home before either. Maybe the horse was tethered somewhere nearby.

"What are the chances we could borrow your precious steed?" Julian sipped her tea, batting her long eyelashes over the steaming liquid.

The man stuttered. "Well, I don't know about that, lass."

"I don't know if our friend will last until someone comes to retrieve you from the woods. We only need a way to town." Her brows turned up. "We could find your friend and give him your horse to bring back to you."

It sounded reasonable, though a bit over zealous considering they didn't know this man. Adni looked at the woodcutter. His cheeks were reddened again. He was completely taken in by Julian's pout. Again, Adni's stomach flipped with unease. Julian manipulated this man as if she'd spent her whole life caught up in deception. Though Adni would never describe Julian as a damsel, she was all too good at acting like one.

"I suppose I could part with Martin for a few days…" the man said.

"You are too kind!" Julian's eyes lit with gratitude. Her whole face glowed.

"It's nothing." The man coughed and returned to handing out tea before setting the kettle on the stove. He leaned against it and sipped the contents of his own cup. His brow lowered over his eyes as if wondering what he'd just agreed to.

* * *

By morning, the group set out for the nearest town, a small village called Randsa. It was a fair distance, but with energy coursing through Adni's limbs, and a desperation to reach Palmyra, the trip didn't daunt her.

Roots stuck from the pine needle covered earth, threatening to trip her with every step. Adni kept her eye on them while trying to keep up with the horse. Astrid rose behind the slumped over James. She cast glances over her shoulder at Adni and Julian, clearly worried James wouldn't make it to Randsa, but kept the brown horse, Martin, at a steady pace all the same. Though his white snout was graying, he trotted like a newborn, happy to be free of his pen in the woods.

Astrid led the way through the forest, Adni and Julian racing to keep up. They leapt over branches, fallen trees, skirted thick bushes and dodged roots the best they could. Adni's heart pounded in her ears. She hadn't felt so alive in some time. With the scent of sap in the air, and sunlight heating her cheeks, she was all too happy at their pace. It sent her pulse racing and her chest aflame with each breath.

In the forest, she was wild and free. She could soar through the trees and jump any hurdles. Julian wasn't far off, flashing her adrenaline filled grins between trees.

Was this the endless energy and power of the ashen? She had had this power her whole life, but never gotten the chance to use it. In the mountains everything was cramped and close quarters. She could hardly throw an arm out without hitting one of her siblings—or a stone wall. But in the world beyond the mountains, space was endless. Why would anyone want to be stuck in such darkness?

By noon, they reached the town, covered in sweat, and a smile stuck to her face as they entered along the main road.

Chatter rose on the wind, along with the smell of burning wood. Randsa wasn't quite the size of Elmhurst. It had half the amount of homes, none of which were two stories, and half the people. Few children roamed the streets between wood and cobblestone homes. She was sure there had to be more cattle than people. But still the people that were there they smiled in the warm sun and went about their days.

Astrid slowed the horse to let Adni and Julian catch up. Adni breathed heavily as she leaned against Martin's hindquarters. Though her heart was full and her chest light, Astrid's face was grim.

Adni squashed her smile and squeezed the princess's fingers. She couldn't tell the princess that her lover would be all right. She didn't know if he'd survive his time in Izenfir or not, but she prayed to whatever gods were listening that he would.

Julian took up the lead. The woodcutter had told her where to go, a barn at the end of the lane, with a wooden fence and a small cottage next to it. There'd be a white horse in the outside pen, and an elderly couple with kind faces working in the yard, tending their chickens, feeding the horses, and doing whatever else they did in retirement.

The lane wasn't long. Hardly any time passed before they reached the other end of town, and there the barn sat, just as the woodcutter had described.

A white-haired woman with wrinkles around her eyes and a straw hat kneeled next to the pen on the right side of the short barn. She held out a hand to a small white and black spotted foal. The tiny horse nuzzled the woman's hand, and the woman giggled.

"Ma'am?" Julian approached the elderly woman first, while the rest of them stopped a few feet away.

The woman looked up, curiosity in her bright hazel eyes. Her olive skin was tanned from the sun, and her smile was sincere. "Hello," she said. "What can I do for you?"

"Samuel, the woodcutter lent us his horse." Julian looked back at Martin, who grazed lazily at the grass sticking out of the lawn.

"Oh my! Has something happened?" The woman's eyes flew wide as she approached Martin. The horse raised his head in greeting. "We weren't supposed to see you for another few days." She ran her hands over his snout and ears, petting him gently. The horse chuffed and banged his nose against her chin.

"Your friend was kind enough to help us out," Adni said. She had never known so many kind people in all her life.

"He's fine, but he lent us Martin to get us here as quickly as possible," Julian explained.

The woman looked up, seeming to notice for the first time that two people sat atop the horse. She gasped at the sight of them. "Blue skies! What has happened?"

Julian explained while Astrid dismounted and led Martin to the barn. The woman listened with wide eyes, her smile fleeing all too quickly.

"I'll get my husband. He's the town healer," the woman said.

It seemed they were definitely in the right place.

The woman ran off inside the house while Julian and Adni eased James out of the saddle. Once he was firmly on the ground, his eyes opened for the first time in hours.

"What's going on?" he asked.

Astrid smiled and placed her hand on his cheek. "We're just getting you some help." Tears formed in the corners of her eyes.

Adni exchanged a look with Julian. She hoped more than anything that these people could help them. Astrid might be strong now, but Adni knew what it felt like to think you'd lost everything. Her chest burned at the memory. Her mother crawling across the floor, her brother lifeless against the wall. She shook her head. She couldn't think about that now. Not yet.

The woman returned with her husband, a tall clean-shaven man with dark eyes and gray hair pulled back into a low ponytail. While Julian filled him in on their edited version of events, they led James and Astrid back into the two bedroom home. Once James was set up in the second bedroom, with a small wooden bed that had once been a child's, the healer rushed them all out of the room, only allowing Astrid to stay.

Adni and Julian returned with the healer's wife to the kitchen, a small room with a pinewood table and four chairs. The woman sat them down, made them tea and sliced thin pieces of ham for sand-wiches. She asked them about their journey as she buttered fluffy slices of bread and cut up tomatoes.

Julian went through every question as if her answers weren't a bunch of lies. Adni's chest twinged with every word. Julian lied *so* easily. Could she not be doing the same thing to Adni?

Though Adni wanted to believe she couldn't, she had no way to be sure. Julian had come into her life suddenly, and besides what Julian had told her, she didn't know much about the woman. She might know the taste of her kiss, and the way her breath deepened when she slept, but she didn't know if this Julian, the flirty, carefree one, was real, or made up to sway her.

Adni shook her head. She ate and drank her tea. Her muscles grew heavy, weighed down with exhaustion.

Long hours passed as the healer's wife flitted between rooms, cleaned up, and continued her chores. Adni and Julian helped where they could, keeping their minds busy with dishes, feeding the chickens, collecting eggs, and delivering fresh hay to the three steeds inside the barn.

When the sun had set for ages, the healer finally left the spare room and returned with an update.

"James should be fine," he said.

Adni exhaled loudly. "Thank the blue skies."

"That's good news," Julian said. She beamed, her eyes shining like beacons even in the low light of the hearth.

"He's extremely emaciated, dehydrated, and might have a concussion, but once he's rested up and gotten some food into him, he should be all right." The healer sat at the kitchen table with them. He ran a hand through his silver hair. The bags below his eyes were dark with fatigue, but at least he didn't seem worried.

"That's good, dear." His wife held his hand.

The man nodded before slipping off to bed. It had been a long day for all of them.

"I'm sorry but we only have the one extra bed," the woman said. Her brows turned up. She truly hated to inconvenience them in any small way.

"The floor will be fine." Adni smiled half-heartedly. She was ready for sleep, even if it meant lying on the ground for another night.

"Well, there is always the barn. It's very warm at night, and the hay is soft." The woman brought two blankets from a small closet. She handed them to Julian. "But it's up to you."

Julian looked at her, and Adni shrugged. "The barn sounds good."

The woman said goodnight and welcomed them to come back inside if they got cold. Once she'd excused herself to her bedroom, Adni and Julian fled outside to the confines of the barn.

The pungent odor of dung lay just beneath the overpowering stale smell of hay. Adni wrinkled her nose as Julian led the way to the back of the barn, where a large pile of loose hay sat next to ten bales or so. Julian handed her a blanket smelling of lavender, and Adni buried her face against it. Her eyelids were heavy as Julian spread out the hay, almost like a mattress, before laying one of the blankets on top of it.

Adni nearly collapsed on top of the pile, her limbs weary and her head fuzzy. It wasn't as comfortable as her bed in Izenfir had been, but it wasn't nearly as bad as the stone floor of a tunnel.

Julian lay next to her, draping the second blanket over them both.

"It's been a long day, huh?" Julian asked.

Her hot breath brushed Adni's cheeks. Dim starlight filtered in from the windows of the barn. Though they'd closed the door behind them, it was nice to have the smell of pine trees brush her nose every now and then.

"It has," Adni agreed. She closed her eyes and nestled into the blankets, fully expecting sleep to pull her into its dark embrace immediately.

But after several long moments of silence, she was still awake.

Adni opened her eyes. Pale blue light brushed the side of Julian's face and hair. It turned her eyes to the night sky, small stars winking within her irises. Adni blinked in surprise as she realized Julian was staring back at her. Her whole body heated and the haze of nearby sleep fled like birds from the trees.

The last time they'd slept side by side seemed like eons ago. So much had happened, but the same heat still burned through every inch of her.

Julian shifted slightly. Adni wished she could see her better. She wanted to know if Julian blushed too, or was she far too collected for that? Did her insides melt and her stomach flip?

Adni took a deep, calming breath. There was a lot she wanted to ask Julian. Maybe talking about something would push away her embarrassment.

"So how did you find me anyway?" Adni asked. She bit down on her lip, hoping to tame her stomach. Maybe a bit of pain would break through whatever spell she was under.

Julian shifted once again. "An amulet a witch gave me."

Adni raised her eyebrows. "A witch?"

Julian's lips quirked. "Yes, they do exist."

"Huh."

"I could sense you back then, but had one hell of a time getting to you," Julian continued. "By the time I'd found your trail, my sense of you disappeared."

"The amulet helped you get it back?"

Julian nodded. She reached down her shirt and pulled out a long dark cord with a large red jewel embedded in dark steel.

Adni's eyes widened. It was nearly the same one her mother had given her. But instead of being fashioned with a careful hand, the steel was harshly cut, and not carved with any beautiful loops like hers had been.

"You recognize it, don't you?" Julian returned it to her shirt.

"I had a similar one." Her brows pulled together.

"Your mother got it from the same witch that made mine," Julian said. "It's how your mother hid you for so long, and how I hide my magic from the dragons."

Adni's eyes widened and her pulse pounded in her head. "It is?"

"It is. The magic in the amulet suppressed your gifts, hiding your magic from anyone who might be looking for it. I lost your trail when your mother gave it to you." Julian paused, letting Adni digest that.

She'd always thought the amulet had been passed down from her grandmother, and one day she'd pass it down to her children. She wrinkled her nose at the thought. She'd never been a fan of kids.

"I found the witch who'd made the amulet. She still had some of your blood left, the blood she infused in yours." Julian shifted. Her breath brushed Adni's cheeks as she inched closer. "I asked her to make me one so I could find you, and she did, after a quest of my own." She smiled at a memory, but didn't share it with Adni. "Once I got the jewel, I learned the magic of the amulet liked to play tricks. It took me all over the six kingdoms for years until I learned how to interpret it."

If she was telling the truth, Julian had been searching for Adni for over ten years. Her mother had given her the jewel when she was seven years old, just before they fled to the Cinder Mountains after Ithrendel went up in flames.

How old was Julian?

"I finally found you in the river, half drowned," Julian finished.

Adni nodded slowly. Her mind worked to figure out a thousand things at once. "That explains why my mother never let me take the amulet off."

Julian reached out. Her fingers brushed a strand of hair from Adni's face.

Adni's heart leapt as she locked eyes with Julian. Though a small smile played on Julian's lips, her gaze was serious. It swirled like storm clouds before rain.

Before Adni could do or say anything, Julian let her hand fall limp on the blanket next to her head. Disappointment stabbed her chest. Adni bit her tongue so she wouldn't suck in a sharp breath.

She had no idea what these feelings meant. She'd never *liked* a person before, not like this. There'd been handsome boys in her village, and prettier girls, but she'd never cared for any of them. They were a distraction keeping her from her dreams, keeping her from Salander. But now Salander seemed like a far off dream, one she wasn't even sure she wanted anymore.

Adni's fingers twitched against the soft cotton. They inched across the blanket until they brushed Julian's warm skin. Her fingers tingled as warmth shot up her arm. Julian's gaze softened and her smile spread as she took Adni's hand, interlocking their fingers.

Heat burned across her cheeks as Julian traced circles with her thumb along the back of Adni's hand. She swallowed, her heart suddenly in her throat.

"You should get some sleep," Julian said. Her blue eyes danced with mischief.

Adni nodded. She lay still, though every inch of her was on fire. How was she supposed to get any sleep with her pulse racing in her ears?

But eventually she did, as the next morning cawing crows woke her from sleep, and her fingers were still locked with Julian's.

FIFTEEN

Four castle towers came into view before the spires of the dark stone palace beyond. Like Ithrendel, the city was spread out around the main castle walls on every side, stretching for miles in every direction. Two and three story stone homes stood atop cobblestone streets in blocks, with long roads between them. Smoke rose from the stone brick chimneys as the sun dipped for the snow-topped mountains in the distance.

Adni stood in awe of Palmyra, Rythern's capitol city. Hundreds of people roamed the streets, people from all over the Kingdoms, and beyond. Men, women, and children with blonde, black, brown, and even red hair, and eyes just the same. Foreigners like the new Queen of Salander, marched by in numbers, their swords clanging against their metal armor.

"Queen Haven brought hundreds of Seaburn warriors with her across the sea during the Great War," Julian whispered. She leaned in close, her breath tickling Adni's ear.

She shivered and glanced at the tall woman, who slid her a sly smile.

"I can't believe we've finally returned." Tears brimmed in Astrid's wide eyes. James stood at her side, much better off.

After they'd spent a day and a half in Randsa, they caught a trolley to Palmyra, all thanks to the kind healer and his wife. Just like they'd promised, it only took a few days travel to arrive at the great city.

Adni's heart raced as they descended the streets, with new sights and smells in every direction.

Astrid led the way at a brisk pace; practically racing from the market they'd been dropped off in towards the castle walls. Her newly clean brown curls bounced against her shoulders as she towed James behind her. The man laughed and shook his head, keeping a good hold on her hand as she pulled him faster and faster.

They continued up the street as long shadows descended between the buildings. Cheers from a local tavern roared out the door as a couple came and went. The fresh smell of bread wafted up her nostrils. It was all almost enough for her to forget her sore feet and growling belly. Though they'd been fed well the last two days, it had been hours since they parted from Randsa.

The castle walls rose from the earth at the top of a small slope. The thick dark bricks blocked out most of the sky the closer they drew.

Adni wiped her sweat-slicked palms on her trousers. Though she was happy to be clean, every hour that passed was another she went on not knowing what happened to her family. And it was another hour Solipher went on scheming. Her blood boiled at the thought of him. Even if he hadn't killed her family, he'd made her believe he had, and his plans to resurrect ancient dragons weren't ones she'd let him go through with.

She shot Julian a look, but Julian was staring wide eyed at the castle gates. Adni looked away quickly. She still wasn't sure if Julian was telling the truth about dragons, ashen, or any of it, even if her heart told her she was.

The gates remained open, two thick wooden slabs braced in iron leaning against either side of the walls.

Half a dozen guards stood by the large doors, swords at their hips and shields at their backs. Two were foreigners with tawny-yellow skin and dark hair, and the other four were of Rythern. All of their faces were stern, their backs straight and their armor pristine, like immovable statues.

Astrid slowed, and glanced over her shoulder at Adni. Her brows were furrowed, her lips set in a thin line.

Everyone thought the princess was dead. What were they supposed to say to the gatekeepers?

"Halt," one of the guards snapped. His eyes were dark beneath his helmet. "What business have you in the castle?"

Each of their small group exchanged a look.

"We're here to see someone," Astrid began. She cleared her throat. "I'm here to see the Queen." That bite of leadership returned to her tone, making Adni smile.

"Your names," the guard said. Another appeared at his shoulders with a long scroll. With the sun shining on the back of the parchment, Adni could see a list hundreds long of names permitted entrance to the castle.

Before Adni could jump in and deliver a fake name, Astrid spoke.

"Astrid Brienne Fyre."

Silence rested at the gate front. Even the trolleys moving by seemed to hush as the guards slowly exchanged raised eyebrows.

"The missing Princess of Rythern?" the guard asked.

Astrid raised her chin. "Yes."

After a long moment, the guard's mask cracked, a smile pulling at his lips. "You can't be serious, ma'am. The princess is long dead. You really expect us to believe you're her?"

Astrid's jaw hardened.

"My apologies, but I'm going to have to ask you to leave."

"I will not."

James shifted at Astrid's side. He used to be a Rythern guard. He should have been the one to lead the conversation. Astrid would be lucky not to be sent to an asylum making claims like that.

"If you won't leave, we will be forced to escort you away." The guard narrowed his eyes, regarding each of them with a suspicious glare.

Great.

"Please fetch my sister, and she will confirm my identity." Astrid crossed her arms defiantly.

"I will not bother the Queen with your slander."

"Slander?"

James stepped forward. "How about Blythe? Is she still in the Queen's Guard?"

The guard rolled his eyes. "You expect me to interrupt the Captain of the Queen's Guard now?"

A growl of irritation rushed through Astrid's teeth. "If not Blythe, then one of the Queen's other personal guards. Lareina, or Malka. They know who I am."

The guard sighed and motioned forward with two fingers. The guards at his back advanced, stepping around their superior and in front of Astrid and James.

"There's no need for that!" Julian stepped forward, taking hold of James's elbow. Adni did the same with Astrid.

"Let's be going you two," Adni said. Her heart thumped faster. If they were imprisoned it could be days before they got word to Salander to search for her family, and even longer before they devised a plan to stop her father.

"Apologies, we weren't aware they were crazy when we agreed to travel with them." Julian smiled and bowed as she pulled James back. "My deepest apologies, sir."

"Making such claims will get her in trouble." The head guard nodded at Astrid. "I suggest you seek help for her."

"Excuse me!" Astrid yanked out of Adni's grip. "I've had just about enough of this! I've been trapped, imprisoned, starved, and threatened for years. I will not put up with this behavior in my own kingdom!"

Adni's eyes widened as she reached for Astrid's arm again.

"What is going on here?" the voice of a woman boomed above the others, sharp and authoritative.

Adni looked behind the guards crowding them. A tall woman, taller than any she'd ever seen, stood with crossed arms at their backs. Her brown hair was short and spiky, her eyes narrowed and dark. Her armor held the Rythern crest at her breast. If Adni remembered correctly, that meant this woman was part of the Queen's Guard.

"Captain," the head guard snapped to attention, his eyes widening in surprise as he spun to bow. "These miscreants are trying to worm their way into the palace. We were just about to send them away. Apologies for the disruption."

The woman's hard gaze roamed the group. Her wide jaw stiffened as it landed on Astrid and James. Her mouth twitched and her eyes flashed wide, breaking her otherwise stern expression. She pushed passed the other guards to stand in front of the princess. "Lady Princess?"

Adni breathed a sigh of relief. This had to be Captain Blythe.

"Blythe! It's so good to see you." Tears flooded Astrid's eyes. Her raised shoulders finally relaxed as Blythe folded the princess in her arms.

Though it had to be uncomfortable to be hugged so hard by someone in armor, Astrid hung on to the guard woman for several long minutes.

"You're alive," Blythe whispered. She released Astrid and straightened. Tears welled in her eyes as well. It was startling to see such a quick change, from the hard faced captain to a relieved friend.

Astrid nodded and wiped the tears from her face.

"You've been gone for *years*." Blythe's dark brown gaze trailed over Astrid's thin arms and protruding collarbone. Her eyes darkened with worry.

"I know." Astrid sniffed. "I'm sorry."

Blythe shook her head, and again wrapped her arms around Astrid. "You don't need to be sorry." It was clear the Queen's Guard understood something terrible had happened. She held Astrid for a long while until the princess gathered herself enough to speak.

"Can I see my sister?" Astrid asked. Her fingers shook. She'd been so strong up until this point, it was about time she let go.

"Of course." Blythe turned to the other guards, her stern face back on, and flicked her fingers at them. "Out of the way. The Princess of Rythern has returned to us."

The gate guards looked at each other with wide eyes as they parted to let the small group through. Blythe led the way past them. Julian flashed a smug smile and Adni forced herself to hold back a smirk. It felt all too good to prove the gate guards wrong after they'd threatened to throw them out.

"Where have you been?" Blythe asked as they walked. "You're so thin."

While Astrid filled her in on some of the details, leaving out much about Izenfir and everything about the dragons and ashen, Adni glanced around the courtyard.

The cobblestone street turned to smooth stone inside. The road to the castle was lined with colorful flowers and white bricks. The courtyard widened as they marched up a few steps, curving into a wide oval with a fountain at the center. On the other side, it narrowed again to lead up to the castle steps, which wound on either side up to a pair of large metal doors.

Her heart leapt. The doors were all too similar to the ones in the Spyre. Steel carved in intricate patterns.

Tall stained glass windows occupied the front of the castle, some three stories high. The thick dark bricks rose into columns with large towers at every corner, similar to the outer walls.

Blythe led them up the steps and through the main doors. Guards nodded to the captain as they passed. Maids, squires, and other civilians ran by in the main lobby. Two sets of stairs curved from the entrance to the second floor. A large crystal chandelier hung from the curved ceiling two stories up. Colored light filtered in through the stained glass windows, casting dazzling patterns across the smooth floor.

The chatter and bustling of people had been overwhelming at times in the city, but inside the castle it all paled in comparison. People flew by in every direction, desperately preparing for something.

"Apologies, the King is returning soon, and there are preparations being made for a grand ball," Blythe explained.

At the top of the steps, a small party moved down the hall, a woman in black leather pants and a grey coat led the pack, a curved sword on either hip. Red waves bounced at her collarbone as she motioned in the air, flicking her fingers around to demonstrate a point to the blonde walking beside her.

Something tingled inside her head. Heat twisted around Adni's heart.

Blythe looked up the steps, and smiled slightly, as if she couldn't tame her excitement any longer. "My Queen!"

Adni's eyes widened. The woman with red hair turned to face them, a smile on her lips, and dazzling hazel eyes. Thick jewels lay against her throat, rubies in every shape and size, surrounded by gold. Adni had never seen a queen before, aside from the Salander King's bride. She'd always assumed all queens wore elaborate gowns along with their crown. Was this the Immortal Queen? She couldn't be more than twenty-three years old—but if Adni remembered correctly, the Queen should be around thirty.

"Captain Blythe," Queen Haven called back.

"Come here, please," Blythe continued.

Haven nodded to the procession following her, and descended with the blonde woman trailing behind her. Her wide hips swayed and her heeled boots clicked as she reached the main floor.

Adni wasn't sure she'd ever seen someone with hair so red, or eyes so bright. The heat in her chest tightened the closer Haven drew.

Haven's smile dropped suddenly, and she gasped as if all air had flown from the room. "*Astrid?*" Her eyes widened in disbelief and her hands trembled as she reached forward.

Adni shifted from foot to foot. The heat inside her burned through her chest and into her arms. She suddenly understood what the warmth was. She was sensing Haven's magic.

Astrid threw herself into the Queen's arms. Either one of them or both of them must have lost their balance, as they both fell to their knees, embracing one another on the floor.

"Astrid, is it really you?" Haven whispered. Tears flooded her eyes as Astrid's spilled down her cheeks. She held Astrid's face in her hands, looking over her thin face and wide eyes.

Astrid could only nod as she cried.

Adni exchanged a look with Julian. Her brows cinched together and her eyes burned. The sisters had been apart for over ten years.

Yet through all that time and much suffering, they'd both survived. If these two royals could deal with the separation of death for ten years, maybe she could wait a few more days to find out if her family was okay.

WHEN THE TEARS FINALLY STOPPED, and both Haven and Astrid returned to their feet, the Queen led them all from the main hall to the second floor where they entered a large study. Haven introduced the blonde woman she'd been with, Lareina, a castle healer and her personal guard.

Astrid glanced at the rest of them, worry in her eyes, and a question on her lips. How was she to explain who Julian and Adni were? If she told Haven the truth, she'd be giving them up for what they were.

Would the Immortal Queen, slayer of the Evil Queen Kadia, be so kind to creatures just like her?

Adni gulped. She forced herself to stay rigid and not flee for the door. She had nothing to be ashamed of. Though she didn't fully understand who or what she was, she was still Adni, the daughter of a treasure hunter and resident to the six kingdoms. Julian on the other hand, what lie would she come up with this time?

Julian sat beside her on top of a wooden desk closest to the door. Their legs brushed, and Adni blushed. If she weren't so busy combating the growing fear inside her chest, she might take more time to think about Julian's closeness.

"These are my new friends." Astrid looked at them, flashing a small smile. "Adni and Julian."

"Well met." Haven nodded in greeting.

"Well met," Adni and Julian said in unison.

"They saved my life." Astrid beamed.

Haven's eyes widened, as did Adni's and Julian's. There it was, Astrid was about to tell the tale of how they met. This could end it all.

A soft rap on the door broke through her turmoil. Blythe straightened from where she leaned against the wall, and opened the door.

"Lady Nina," Blythe said. "Come in." She opened the door wider, and stepped aside to let a small, thin woman with dark beige skin and curly blonde hair to step through. She couldn't be much older than Adni.

"Good evening," Nina said. "You know you needn't call me *Lady*, Blythe." Her blue eyes flashed with amusement as she narrowed her eyes at Blythe.

Blythe cleared her throat. "Apologies."

Julian stiffened and grabbed Adni's hand. Adni nearly leapt in surprise as she looked at Julian. What on earth had possessed her so suddenly? Julian squeezed Adni's hand, not saying a word as Nina stepped inside and Blythe closed the door.

Adni met Nina's eyes across the room for the briefest of moments. Fire squeezed her insides, forcing the breath from her lungs. Though she'd been able to feel Haven's magic faintly, Nina's was overwhelming.

"Astrid, this is Nina." Haven rose from her seat at the windowsill.

"A pleasure to meet you." Astrid stood.

Nina smiled shyly. Though Astrid made a move to hug her, Nina took a small step back. "Astrid, Haven has spoken about you at length. I'm so happy you're all right."

"Nina is my new head advisor. She's from across the sea," Haven explained.

"Seaburn?" Astrid's eyes widened.

Adni raised a brow. The people she'd seen from the foreign country across the sea had so far been dark-haired and eyed, with either tawny yellow or black skin. Upon further inspection, she realized Nina did have some of those markers. Beautiful sandy skin, and large hooded eyes. Her curls were tight and fell around her face like a golden mane.

"Yes." Haven sat back down. Astrid and Nina joined her on the windowsill bench.

Adni took a deep breath to right herself. She exchanged a look with Julian.

"Are you sure..." Astrid trailed off as she glanced at Adni and Julian.

"She is my most trusted advisor." Haven squeezed Astrid's hand.

Astrid nodded, but her lips pressed into a firm line. Though the princess was clearly familiar with Blythe and Lareina, Nina seemed to be a new addition.

"Now please, tell me where you've been all this time," Haven said. "It's been *so* long."

Astrid smiled ruefully. "You don't know the half of it, sister."

"Then tell me. What has happened?"

Astrid again sought the approval of Adni and Julian.

The girls exchanged long looks. None of them were sure how to explain it all, if any of them would believe it, or if Adni and Julian would be sentenced to prison or worse for their relation to Queen Kadia and her kind.

After a long moment, Astrid began. She explained everything; where she'd been, who she'd been with, what happened to her in Izenfir, and how she'd been freed. She glazed over how she knew Adni and Julian, claiming they were captives as well. One night they'd gotten a hold of the keys, got James, and fled as fast as they could.

With each passing moment, Adni's heart beat louder, and Queen Haven's eyes grew darker. Nina glanced between the sisters, holding on to Haven's other hand when Haven cast her gaze to the stone floor. Nina's brows rose and Haven's mouth twisted as if she might be sick.

When Astrid finally finished, Haven's hands shook.

Julian squeezed Adni's hand. It was all right. Astrid hadn't revealed anything damning about them. But something still worried her friend.

"What's wrong?" Astrid asked.

Haven shook her head, closing her eyes tightly.

Nina shifted uncomfortably on the bench. "Before Haven defeated Kadia, I had a look into her mind. All there was, was darkness, and it all came from a place beyond the mountains. A place called Izenfir, full of beasts just like Kadia."

Adni suppressed a gasp. Julian again squeezed her fingers. This is what Julian was trying to tell her. Nina wasn't a normal human, she was magical like them, and Julian could sense it just like Adni could. But how far did the young woman's powers go? If she could access someone's mind, could she see inside Adni and Julian's?

Sweat slicked her palms and cold fear descended on her skin. Goosebumps ran up her arms.

"A few years after the battle, Haven became obsessed with finding Izenfir." Nina's brows pulled together sympathetically.

Haven cleared her throat. "I wanted to find it and stop another Kadia from rising up and destroying Warshard, but…" The strength in her voice faltered.

"But it turned into an obsession," Nina continued for her.

"It's taken a long time to get my head on straight." Haven tucked her hair behind her ear.

Cold silence lay over the room like a blanket made of fear. They knew better than anyone else what Izenfir was capable of, but only Julian really knew how to find it.

Adni looked at Julian. The woman's eyes held a hurricane. Her expression was slack and worried. This wasn't the Julian she'd come to know.

"I'm so sorry," Astrid said.

Haven shook her head. Her lips twisted. "I'm the one who's sorry. I should have looked for you longer. I should never have given up."

Astrid shook her head. "Don't be ridiculous." Astrid folded Haven in her arms, and together they clung to each other. Tears again streamed down their cheeks while the rest of them sat in silence.

Julian was right. They needed to destroy Izenfir. Adni wasn't sure how she could help, but she'd do her damndest. These people didn't deserve any of what had happened to them. So many lives had been destroyed by Solipher and his kin. Adni wasn't about to let that continue.

SIXTEEN

Once it was clear they all needed time to rest and recover, Haven called in maids to show them to their quarters. They'd be sent hot water to bathe in, and food from the palace kitchens. Whatever they wanted, it was theirs—for saving the princess's life.

Adni and Julian thanked the Queen before following a small maid from the study. Though her feet ached in her tight leather boots, her mind was on fire.

If the Queen had spent so long searching for Izenfir, it meant she was ready to go to war. All of them were. And Adni and Julian were about to be part of it. No one was leaving them behind to sit and wait for word of how things had gone. Julian claimed Adni was the key to destroying Izenfir. Whether the rest of them knew it or not, they needed Adni, and Adni needed Julian.

A few long hallways later, the maid stopped at a pair of large double doors with iron clasps and handles.

"Here we are," she said. "Miss Julian, I can lead you to your room next."

"I'll stay with Adni," Julian said gruffly. Her tone conveyed there would be no arguing. The petite woman opened the door before bowing and excusing herself.

Adni shook her head as the maid retreated down the hall. "You don't need to stay with me. I'll be fine."

Julian's jaw hardened. "You need my protection, Adni. Without your magic, you won't be able to fight Solipher or any of the ashen off if they come for you."

Adni's eyes widened. The hair on the back of her neck rose. "You think they will?"

"It's a possibility I want to be prepared for." Julian shrugged.

After a moment's pause, Adni agreed, and they entered the room— or what turned out to be *rooms*, together.

The sitting room was small; with a fireplace a single sofa, and a long wooden table. Beyond was another set of twin doors, opened to reveal a large bedroom with a king sized bed of dark oak wood and a thick velvet comforter.

"Wow." Julian whistled. "Talk about the royal treatment."

Adni smiled. That was the Julian she knew. "I've never seen so much red in all my life." From the walls, to the comforter and the cushioning of the sofa, everything was shades of dark red.

Julian waltzed around the sofa, trailing her fingers along the fireplace mantel as she toured the sitting room.

Adni passed to the bedroom, where yet another doorway led to a bathing room. She shook her head as she looked around. A dark oak armoire, vanity, two chairs, and a bench nestled into a small alcove by the windows, some of the few not made of stained glass from what she'd seen.

Though her water hadn't arrived for a bath yet, she yanked off her boots and coat, leaving them in a pile on the plush carpet by the bed. She wiggled her toes against the thick strands of carpet. The tensed muscles in her feet relaxed.

She could do with a whole week of relaxing, but she didn't see that coming any time soon, not with an inevitable fight on its way. But how could she help the Queen's army defeat Izenfir?

Her brows furrowed as she looked at Julian, who inspected a large painting of the mountains over the mantel. Adni's nostrils flared. She'd had enough of the mountains. But still, they were everywhere and everything she'd ever known.

"Julian, you said I have some sort of magic that'll help defeat Izenfir, but you never said what it was." Adni fidgeted with the hem of her shirt. It desperately needed washing.

Julian turned to face her, her mouth set in a grim line. Her lips parted to answer, then closed. She inspected Adni's face until Adni's cheeks were red. "Adni, you can control dragons."

Adni's eyes went wide. A humorless laugh bubbled from her chest. "Julian, you're kidding."

Julian shook her head. She wasn't kidding.

"What does that even mean?" Adni threw up her hands. "How can I control them? I haven't had magic all my life. I didn't even know magic existed until Solipher showed me." Did Julian expect her to defeat her father? This was madness. Pure, utter madness.

"Believe it or not, it's the truth." Julian left the sitting room and joined her in the bedroom. She glanced down at Adni's bare toes and smiled for the briefest of moments.

"How?"

Julian looked up. "I don't know how your magic works, I just know that it does. My mother told me so, and I believe her."

Adni groaned. "And she didn't pass on the knowledge of this so called dragon controlling magic? That seems terribly convenient."

Julian chuckled. "Magic comes from all different places, Adni. You need to find it within yourself."

Adni sat back on the bed. It drooped beneath her. She wanted so badly to sink into it and never get back up and face this lunacy. "How do I do that?"

"You remember the feel of magic, don't you?" Julian raised an eyebrow.

Adni froze. Of course she did. How could she forget the burning in her fingers or surge of power through her limbs? Her fingers itched on her thighs. She missed that power. She missed the magic in her hands and fire in her belly every time she used it.

"How did you feel when you summoned it?" Julian stepped closer.

"Angry, afraid, powerful, fearless." Adni looked up as she thought. She'd felt so many things. None of them good.

"Then start with that. Call those emotions into you and pour them out of your skin. Feel it inside your chest, your body, your *soul*." Fire lit Julian's eyes as she approached Adni.

Adni's cheeks heated as she grew closer. The passion in her voice was something she'd only ever heard in her father when he spoke of finding riches. "I-I don't know if I can do that."

Julian took her hands. "You can."

"But how do I practice controlling..." She still couldn't say dragon. "Your kind?"

Julian stepped back, pulling away her hands. Adni instantly missed their warmth. Julian held her hands up at her sides, her palms cupped to the air. Flames burst to life.

Adni gasped, her eyes widening. Red, orange, and yellow danced inside her palms, competing with the warmth of the fireplace.

"Control these." Julian held one hand out to her.

It warmed Adni's fingertips as she reached for it. "But..."

"You can do it." Julian smiled. Adni met her gaze. "I know you. You can do this."

Adni gulped and nodded. She held out her own palm and called back everything she remembered of her dark power. The rage, the fear, the freedom.

Julian dropped the flames into Adni's outstretched hand.

The flames didn't burn her. They sizzled in her grasp. Adni's eyes widened as she stretched her hand open. The fire didn't burn.

Maybe she was half dragon after all.

* * *

THE NEXT DAY, a meeting was to be held. A maid brought Adni and Julian breakfast, which they scarfed down hungrily, even after a large meal the night before. She just couldn't get used to having good food for every meal. She'd never be able to go back to eating dried fish every day.

After breakfast, Adni and Julian returned to Haven's study, where the maid said the meeting would take place. A long night of practicing magic hadn't left her as tired as she thought it would. Instead, her limbs tingled and her heart raced at the thought of fire in her hands.

She'd gotten good at holding it, tossing it back and forth with Julian. But when her excitement became too great, overwhelming her lust for power, the fire burned her hands. By morning the burns were gone, but the memory was heavy on her mind.

Adni needed to get better. She needed to practice as much as she could to control dragon magic. Even if she couldn't create it herself, she'd still be able to defend against Solipher and Kaldar, or whoever else may stand in her way.

Her fingers itched at her sides as they entered the study.

Warm morning light fell over Queen Haven's red hair, turning the crimson waves to fire. Adni's cheeks warmed as the doors closed behind them.

"Good morning." Haven turned from the window and stood. Again, she wore leather pants and a simple strappy coat. The swords at her hips bumped the bench as she stood.

"Good morning, Lady Queen." Julian bowed slightly, as did Adni.

She was again reminded how much of Warshard's customs she was unfamiliar with.

Adni and Julian greeted Haven's guards, Lareina, and the two they hadn't yet met: Malka, a skilled archer with blazing green eyes and a stony expression, and Aura, a beautiful tawny-skinned foreigner with thick braids and a permanent scowl.

"How did you sleep?" Haven asked.

Julian made polite conversation, taking a seat on a desk top near the window. While she led the conversation, Adni sat beside her, rubbing her sweaty palms on her new trousers. The maid had also been kind enough to bring them clean clothes this morning. Though the leather pants were tight, her blouse was loose and comfortable, and her jacket right for the season.

What Adni really wanted to discuss was her family. But how did she approach the subject with *the* Queen? She should have asked Blythe, or someone else before they left yesterday, but her mind had been spinning and her stomach growling.

"Lady Queen?" Adni had to be brave, or she might be waiting weeks for any news.

"Please, call me Haven." The Queen shook her head as if calling her by her title were ridiculous. And maybe it was, Adni had no idea.

"May I ask you something?" Adni's fingers twisted around her sleeves. She'd never been a shy girl, but under the weighted gaze of a queen, her heart raced.

"Of course." Haven turned her full attention on Adni, only increasing her heart rate further.

"My family... I'm afraid something terrible has happened to them in my absence." Adni gulped. She couldn't tell the Queen exactly why she feared it. "Is there a way to send word to someone in Salander, maybe even Elmhurst outside the mountains? They live in a small village inside the mountain colonies. My mother is Galia Seren."

Haven's eyebrows pulled together. "Of course. I can send a letter to King Emeril's royal advisers myself. They'll be able to send someone."

Adni exhaled loudly. She closed her eyes as a thousand pounds lifted from her shoulders. "Thank you. I would be so grateful."

"Anything for my sister's saviors." Haven smiled.

Not long after, the rest of the meeting's attendants arrived. Haven's five advisers, plus her head adviser, Nina. Her two other personal guards, Lareina and Blythe, and of course Astrid and James. Once the group was settled around the tables and chairs, Haven stood to take control of the room.

"With Astrid's return, we've learned much about Izenfir, and as I'm sure you've all suspected, I plan to go to war." Haven tilted her chin up. "You all know I do not take war lightly, but I won't have this one dragged out over a decade. If I can help it, this will be one swift battle, a culling if you will."

Adni shifted uncomfortably. She knew they'd plan on killing or imprisoning all the ashen as well as the dragons, but to call it a culling put it in a darker perspective.

"I've already sent word to the other kingdoms kings and ministers. I'm sure each of them will want to be involved so we can deal with this problem before another Kadia arises." Haven paused. "We'll convene a war summit here in Palmyra to decide on the best course of action."

"Ministers?" Adni whispered to Julian. Her brows cinched. She'd been in the mountains a long time, but she didn't recall tale of any ministers in Warshard.

"After the Great War, the King of Eris was killed along with his whole family. Instead of finding someone to take the throne, a minister was elected and a council was put into place to govern the Kingdom. Dagan did the same after Kadia was defeated," Julian explained as quietly as she could.

Adni nodded. That made sense. She wouldn't want another evil queen ruling her kingdom.

"Before the officials arrive, I'd like to be prepared with a possible plan of action," Haven continued. She paced the room, her hands held behind her back. Adni felt as if the Queen were a military general instead of a monarch. "I'd like to hear from all of you, but especially the four of you." Haven stopped and faced Adni, Julian, Astrid and James. They sat near each other on two desks.

"Us?" James raised an eyebrow. His cheeks were still sunken, but color was returning to his pale skin.

"What do you want to know?" Astrid asked. Her eyes widened. She had to be afraid Haven would ask her more about Adni and Julian.

Adni silently thanked her for being such a loyal friend, even in the face of her own blood.

"How can we get inside Izenfir?" the Queen asked.

The group of four exchanged glances.

Julian cleared her throat. "Lady Queen, may I?"

Haven nodded, and Julian stood to face the room. She was far braver than Adni would have been in front of so many unfamiliar people, especially in the face of war.

"I used to be a slave in Izenfir. I was kept there for years, and explored many of the tunnels," Julian began. She kept her voice even, powerful, and sure of herself. Adni smiled. Even though Julian was lying, it was a good lie. "There are hundreds of tunnels in those mountains. It's a huge maze. But I can navigate them well and get us inside."

Haven raised an eyebrow. Julian was fit, with healthy skin and hair, very unlike James and even Astrid. They'd have a hard time believing Julian was indeed a slave in Izenfir. That wasn't good.

"What do you propose then?" Haven asked.

Julian placed her hands on her hips. "Go in by night, even early morning if we can. Everyone will be asleep, and it'll be easiest to get an army in unseen."

"I think we're getting ahead of ourselves here." Blythe stepped up to join them from her spot leaning against the wall. "How many of them are there? What are they? How do we defeat them? What kind of numbers do we need to go in with?"

Adni's head spun. She didn't have the mind of a strategist, but she was glad someone did.

Julian exchanged a look with Adni. What were they? How were they supposed to explain that without sounding like crazy people?

"Well?" Haven prompted.

"They're dragons." All eyes turned on Astrid.

"Not all of them," James interjected. "Some are half-breeds, like Kadia."

Julian nodded. "They call them *ashen*."

Haven's eyes widened as she looked around at the others. Whispers rose through the room.

"They're telling the truth," Nina said.

"You're sure?" Haven turned to her adviser.

That's right, Nina could read minds. Though Adni wasn't sure to what extent. She shifted uncomfortably once again. Could Nina read her mind?

"I'm sure." Nina nodded solemnly.

"That's madness," Aura piped in. "Dragons are creatures of myth."

"Not anymore," Julian said.

"How are we supposed to kill *dragons?*" Blythe sat down hard next to the archer, Malka.

Julian cleared her throat to gather their attention. "There's one simple way. Trap them in human form."

Adni raised her eyebrows. Though she'd never seen Solipher or the others in dragon form, she still found it hard to believe that was true. Even so, how were they supposed to lock them in human form?

"How?" Haven asked sharply.

"Inside the Spyre at the center of Izenfir is a glass orb holding what they call the Holy Fire. It's the source of dragon magic. Without it, they'll either be stuck in human form, with only their magic to defend them, or they'll be trapped as a slayable beast."

"So we'll either be dealing with a bunch of Kadias, or monsters." Aura shook her head. "Wonderful."

"It's doable." Haven crossed her arms. "At least if they're one or the other and can't change at any second, we'll be able to deal with them. Our priority has to be to take out that orb."

Adni nodded. If that was the only way, that's what they had to do. At least in their human forms, Adni could control their magic. She would do her best to keep everyone safe while the army did what they had to. In the end, they'd be taking down dozens of enemies to the six kingdoms, freeing hundreds of slaves, and preventing another Kadia from ever arising.

She looked at Julian, who's brow was low, and her eyes dark. She would really give up her own people to save the six kingdoms. What had Warshard ever done for her? Adni made a mental note to ask.

SEVENTEEN

After the meeting, Adni and Julian slipped into the hall after the others, who left with white faces and grim frowns. They'd taken the news much better than she'd expected, all things considered.

"That wasn't so bad," Julian said.

"Do you think we can do it?" Adni slid Julian a sideways glance. Even with a large battle as a distraction, taking down the Spyre would be difficult. It would be well guarded in case of an attack.

"I do." Julian nodded, her jaw set.

"Adni?" Astrid's fingers brushed Adni's elbow.

She turned and stopped to face the princess. "Astrid. Is everything all right?"

Astrid smiled. "Yes, I was just wondering if we could speak privately for a moment?"

Adni glanced at Julian. She didn't see why not. "Of course."

Julian said her goodbyes and continued down the hall, while Astrid wrapped her arm around Adni's elbow, locking them together.

"Thank you for keeping our secret," Adni whispered.

Astrid led the way down the hall and descended to the first floor. The castle wasn't nearly as busy today. Haven must have cancelled the ball in wake of the coming battle.

"It's nothing." Astrid waved her off. "You and Julian saved me and my James. I know you aren't like the others."

Adni's skin chilled. The other ashen didn't have to be evil, but after their chosen path, there was no denying their cruelty. Had it been because of visions like Solipher showed her? Or had they all chosen power over being human? Her stomach twisted.

"It must be difficult to keep that from your sister," Adni said.

Astrid tilted her head as they walked the hall. "It is, and it isn't. Haven is a lot different than she used to be. I'm not sure I could trust her not to do something drastic with the news."

Stone arches passed overhead as they headed down a long hall cast with ruby light. Stained glass windows bathed the corridor in color, making the golden frames of portraits flash, and the metal of pots shine.

Astrid steered them inside a corridor where she loosened her grip on Adni. A few steps led down to a courtyard lined with windows, trees casting shadows inside. Shields and swords lined the walls on either end of the room. It must be used as a training field for practice sessions. Since the Queen wore two swords on her hips, Adni imagined the men and women of Rythern must be well trained. Why not have indoor battlefields for practice?

"It must be strange being back." Adni descended the stairs, admiring the afternoon sun and the flowers just outside the lower half of the windows. The bushes would lose their leaves soon, and the flowers would wilt. She was surprised they hadn't already.

"It is, made all the stranger by these dark times."

"I can't even imagine." Adni couldn't imagine a lot of things, from being held in Izenfir for years, cold and alone in a cell, to living in such a castle with hundreds of rooms, and even more people.

"No, you can't."

Adni's eyebrows furrowed as she turned to face Astrid.

Something hard slammed into her back, forcing her to the ground.

Her forehead cracked against the smooth stone floor. Pain shot through her shoulder as a knife slid through her shirt, deep into her skin.

Her breath hissed out between her teeth and her head spun.

"You can't imagine any of it," Astrid snapped. "You're betraying your own father for these people you don't even know! I can't let you destroy the Holy Fire!" Another stab pierced her back.

Adni's sense returned to her with the shock of red-hot pain. She twisted sharply, knocking Astrid off her. The princess tumbled to the ground, rolled, and leapt to her feet, a bloody dagger in hand.

"Astrid, what in blue skies are you doing?" Adni gasped. Her heart raced as blood dripped down her shoulder blades to her spine. Her skin throbbed as she backed away.

"Solipher made me promise if you ever turned on him, to kill you." Astrid smirked. The crazed widening of her eyes seemed out of place on such a pretty face.

"*What?*"

Astrid laughed, her voice high and feminine, edged with madness Adni'd never experienced. The princess lunged, slicing her dagger at Adni's chest.

Adni leapt back, her pulse pounding in her skull, her head aching from having been smacked off the floor. She jumped left and right as Astrid advanced, slicing wildly for her every limb.

"Astrid, stop!" Adni's voice caught. Her mind raced.

Something was wrong with Astrid. She wasn't nearly as well put together as Adni had thought. Her time in Izenfir must have rendered her insane. Whatever Solipher did to her, she was his pawn now. She was working for Adni's father, and he'd sent Astrid to kill his own daughter.

Adni leapt back from another stab. The blade sliced a long line across her cheek. Pain flared through her face. She winced.

"Astrid!" she tried again.

But if Solipher had prepared her for Adni's departure, had he known Adni would escape? Was this all some sort of trap?

Adni's back hit the wall. *Damn.* She hadn't been paying close enough attention. Astrid's blade cut through her jacket into her shoulder. Her pained cry echoed in the hollow room as black dots preyed on her vision.

Astrid laughed and pressed the blade deeper.

Adni pushed her with every bit of strength she had. Astrid flew back while Adni rushed for the exit. Of course she'd end up on the side with the swords. She needed something to defend herself—anything. But with every movement of her arms, heat coursed through her limbs and chest. Pain sucked the air from her lungs and spilled it into the chilled air.

"Traitorous little brat!" Astrid leapt to her feet.

Astrid's boots slapped against the floor behind her until she leapt through the air. Astrid slammed into her back. Adni's chest hit the stairs into the courtyard, knocking all the wind from her lungs.

"Adni!" Julian's voice cut through the panic in her mind.

Heat flared through the air. Astrid yelped and jumped away.

Adni's limbs trembled as she flipped onto her back. Astrid narrowed her eyes at Julian, a snarl on her lips as she crouched in the middle of the floor.

Julian got between them, her nostrils flaring and her teeth bared. She pointed a sword at the princess. The flames disappeared in her palm. "I don't know what's come over you Astrid, but you need to calm down *now*."

Shouts rang in the hall and guards flooded the courtyard. For a brief moment they paused, most likely confused at the sight before them. A crazy-eyed princess with a bloody dagger, a girl bleeding out on the floor, and another pointing a sword in her defense.

Adni was surprised when the guards immediately went for Astrid. They knocked the dagger from her hand, even as the princess screamed bloody murder. They pinned her to the ground, as Adni's head spun, threatening to send her into unconsciousness.

Julian kneeled beside her, dropping the sword as her hands flew for Adni's cheeks. Her thumb wiped the blood from Adni's cheekbone. "You're going to be all right." She smiled. "Ashen heal fast." She whispered the last part, just loud enough for Adni to hear as her eyelids drooped.

Wet slicked her back and chest. How much blood was she losing? It had to be a lot for the pain to drift away.

Adni squeezed her eyes shut for a moment before opening them. She had to stay awake and make sure everything was all right.

* * *

WHEN SHE OPENED HER EYES, she wasn't in the courtyard anymore. She'd been transported to a small room with white curtains and sunlight streaming in through two tall, arched windows. Adni lay on a small cot with Julian sitting by her side.

Her eyebrows furrowed. She'd closed her eyes for a mere second. Where was she?

"You're in the infirmary," Julian explained. She squeezed Adni's fingers.

How had they gotten her here without her waking up? Adni shifted onto her elbows. Her coat was gone, as was her shirt. Thick bandages wrapped her chest and upper abdomen. Her pants remained, as did her socks. Her boots sat on the floor next to the door.

"What happened?" Adni asked.

Julian's smile fell. She looked away, her eyebrows pulled together. "Astrid… she must have been manipulated, or brainwashed, or something." She seemed hesitant to say anymore, as if confirming Adni's father was a brainwashing lunatic would make him any worse in her eyes.

Adni's nostrils flared. Cold descended on her skin. It wasn't so hard to believe. Astrid had been in Izenfir for years, giving Solipher plenty of time to play with the princess's mind.

A soft rap on the door sent her heart racing.

The door cracked open, and Queen Haven peeked inside, her brows pulled up and her hazel eyes wide with guilt.

"May I come in?" Haven asked.

Adni glanced at Julian and back at Haven, then nodded. "Of course."

Haven slipped inside and closed the door gently behind her. Her fingers twisted around each other as she inspected the room, clearly uncertain about what to say.

Adni wouldn't be sure what to say either, especially if her sister had just tried to kill someone. She sat up against the thick pillows at her back. Julian looked between Adni's bandages and the Queen, as if weighing how good this encounter was for Adni's wellbeing.

"My deepest apologies." Haven hovered beside Adni's bed. She clasped her hands in front of her as if preparing to bow. "I had no idea my sister was… changed."

Adni's heart fluttered with gratitude. "It's no one's fault but theirs." She nodded at the window. The mountains stained the horizon.

Haven tucked her hair behind her ear and sighed. "You're right."

Adni had seen the Queen as a general since the moment they'd met. Seeing the same woman embarrassed made her shift uncomfortably.

"All the same, my sister is clearly not herself. I hope you can forgive her." Haven met Adni's eyes. Their hazel depths swirled with uncertainty.

"Of course." The corners of Adni's lips twitched into a tiny smile. "I hope she recovers quickly."

"I hope you do as well." Haven looked at the bandages wrapping her chest.

Adni's fingers twitched on the cotton sheet covering her abdomen and legs. She pulled the piece of fabric up to cover herself. Her cheeks heated. She wasn't clear on a lot of Warshard customs, but being half-naked in front of someone she hardly knew certainly wasn't one of them.

"Thank you," Adni said.

"I'll leave you to rest." Haven excused herself, fleeing the infirmary, only leaving the briefest whiff of vanilla in her wake.

Once she was gone, Adni leaned her head back against the pillows. Her back throbbed and her chest ached. She hadn't realized it until now. She might have dragon blood, but she still needed time to heal.

"How long will it take?" Adni asked.

Julian shrugged. "A few days."

Her brows shot up. "Only a few days?" Adni had never been stabbed before, but she was sure it'd take weeks for most to fully heal from such wounds.

"I told you, ashen heal quickly." Julian winked.

Adni shook her head. She still found it hard to believe. "So I'll be healed enough for the coming battle."

Julian stiffened. "Yes."

They hadn't had the chance to talk about the coming war yet, or what their parts would be in it. They both needed to be on the team headed to bring down the Spyre and destroy the Holy Fire. But how would they get past the dozens of ashen and dragons to find the flames? How were they supposed to destroy centuries old magic?

"Good. How will we do it?" Adni looked at Julian.

"We?" Julian raised an eyebrow. "It'll be easy for *me* to bring down the Spyre."

Adni narrowed her eyes. "If you think you're doing this alone, you're mad."

Julian chuckled. "Adni, I know what must be done. I'll transform into my dragon form and destroy the tower."

Adni's eyebrows furrowed. "But I thought you said destroying the Holy Fire would get all the dragons stuck in whichever form they're in when it happens."

Julian's gaze hardened. "It will."

Adni sat up quickly. Pain shot through her back. She winced. "Then you'll be stuck in your dragon form forever?"

Julian nodded stiffly.

"No. You can't!"

"It's the only way to bring down the entire tower before one of the others gets wind of our plan," Julian said.

"There has to be another way."

"It has to be done, Adni."

Panic flickered through her chest. "We can figure something else out. We can scale the tower again."

"We'll be seen."

"Not if we do it at night," Adni snapped.

"We'll slip and fall to our deaths if we try it in the dark." Julian smiled ruefully, as if this were the only option. This couldn't be the only way to stop them—it just couldn't.

"Julian–"

"Adni, it's all right." Julian squeezed her fingers.

Tears burned the back of her eyes. "But–"

The door creaked open. Nina appeared in the doorway, a small smile on her face. Her blonde curls were pinned to the top of her head, but some still managed to fall around her cheeks.

"I hope I'm not interrupting," Nina said.

Adni sucked in a sharp breath to get a hold of herself. She blinked quickly to push back the coming tears. She hated letting anyone see her weak, especially someone she hardly knew.

"Not at all," Julian said. She smoothed her expression easily, as if they hadn't just been debating her fate.

Adni forced herself not to glare at Julian. This conversation wasn't over.

"How are you feeling?" Nina sat on the edge of the bed, inches from Adni's leg, and Julian's arm. Julian sat back, releasing Adni's hand, putting some distance between Nina and herself.

"Fine, all things considered," Adni said. She smoothed the sheet over her lap.

"That's good to hear." Nina's smile remained as she glanced between them. It was clear the young woman knew she was interrupting something, but still she remained, having even went far enough to make herself comfortable.

Adni shifted, suddenly reminded of what she'd learned of the young adviser. Nina could read minds. Was she doing it now? Could Nina hear her every thought?

"I know you both aren't telling the others everything," Nina said.

Adni froze, and so did Julian. They both stared at Nina with wide eyes. There it was, Nina knew their secret. What were they going to do? Flee?

"But I don't want you to worry, I'm not going to tell anyone."

Her heart leapt. *What?*

"Telling the others, especially the Queen, will only upset the delicate balance we've finally established," Nina continued. Adni had to assume she meant the balance Haven had found since her obsession had ceased. Having Izenfir back in her life couldn't be easy. "I met Kadia. I saw inside her mind."

That they knew.

"I saw inside her heart, and it was an ocean of darkness, an entire sky of nothing but black." Nina shivered. "I can see inside the two of you, and I see the same spot of darkness, but it is only a small ship at sea. Whatever power you have, I know you aren't here to use it against us."

Adni leaned back against her pillows. Shock ran through every inch of her, sweet relief relaxing her shoulders.

"Thank you," Julian said. A small smile graced her face.

Nina shook her head. "There's no need to thank me. I just wanted you to know, so you know I'm going to help you take down the Spyre once and for all."

Adni nodded, her jaw set.

Julian wasn't going to be the one to bring down the Spyre. Adni wouldn't let her. But with Nina, and the Immortal Queen by her side, maybe they didn't need a dragon's power to win the war.

She could only hope.

EIGHTEEN

A week passed before the other royals and ministers arrived from the six kingdoms. The calm that had settled over the castle quickly disappeared as more and more guards flooded the halls. Advisers, council members, and warriors roamed the castle corridors, hushed whispers about the coming war around every corner.

After the majority of the week had gone by, the castle doctor allowed Adni to leave the infirmary, as long as she promised to keep her wounds cleaned and check back if she had any problems.

Adni had been all too ready to escape the confines of the small space; especially once her wounds sealed a few days later and the last of her pain ebbed.

Julian brushed her elbow as they turned into the dining hall, an enormous room with a long wooden table surrounded by dozens of chairs. On another day maybe a dozen men and women would occupy the chamber, but today the first war council would convene, and there was standing room only left to the two women.

Unfamiliar men and women occupied twenty seats or so. Guards stood at the backs of monarchs and ministers, while even more lined the walls. The Queen had yet to arrive, leaving a seat at the head of the table empty, along with another at the right side. Perhaps that of her husband?

"There are so many," Adni whispered to Julian.

"The kings, queens, and ministers of the six kingdoms." Julian motioned to the table as if displaying them all.

Accompanying the unfamiliar faces was Nina at the left side of where the Queen would sit. Blythe stood nearby, speaking in hushed tones with Malka, and a few other guards. Haven's other advisers weren't present today, but Adni couldn't be sure if it was to save space or not.

"Who are they all?" Adni nodded at the others.

Julian stopped near a group of guards at the Queen's end of the table, giving them a good view of all those present. "The elderly one there–" Julian motioned at a man with a graying beard and clear blue eyes. "–is King Evander of Calisa." She looked to another somewhat familiar pair. "King Emeril of Salander and his wife, Queen Rona."

Adni's eyebrows rose. She had seen the pair once in Salander. They didn't don royal robes or crowns this time. Instead the young king wore a simple coat and trousers. He held his queen's hand. Her hair was twisted in intricate braids and tied back from her angular face. Her dark gaze hardened like a warriors.

"Lady Hilren, Minister of Eris." Julian nodded at a tall woman with short blonde hair slicked back atop her head. Her robes were fine, and the jewels at her throat glowed in the soft light filtering through the tall windows on either side of the hall. "And the Minister of Dagan, Lord Grant." A short, clean-shaven man with tan skin, wide nostrils and wrinkles around his eyes. "The rest are most likely their advisers or spouses."

"All right." Adni might be able to remember all of their names as long as they stayed at separate ends of the table and didn't move around too much. There were so many people, so many unfamiliar faces, that one after another seemed to blend into each other.

The front doors of the dining hall cracked open. The words of the officials were silenced as the Queen entered, her hazel gaze harsh and her jaw sharp in the afternoon light. She held the arm of a tall man with dirty-blond hair, freckles, and deep blue eyes. His gaze warmed as he looked at Haven and squeezed her hand. Everyone at the table stood respectfully.

The couple parted as they weaved through the guards to the head of the table. They nodded greetings to the other royals, the ministers, and their advisers before motioning for everyone to take a seat.

The Queen and her King exchanged a long look, unseen conversation passing between them.

A jealous pang flashed through Adni chest. They moved so easily with one another, like two halves of a whole.

"King Corrin of Wakefin, and husband of Queen Haven," Julian whispered.

Adni looked at Julian from the corner of her eye. Heat built in her chest. Would Adni ever have a relationship like Haven and Corrin? Would something between her and Julian ever be? Though two women in a relationship wasn't completely unheard of, it was still taboo in the mountains. Was it the same in Warshard?

She glanced from Julian to Blythe and Malka, who stood close together. Her heart warmed and her fists unclenched. If two of Haven's personal guards could openly be together, maybe there was hope yet. If they survived the coming battle that is.

"Welcome, my friends." Haven remained standing at the head of the table. "I wish it were under better circumstances." Her gaze roamed the dining hall. "But desperate times have once again united us."

"A similar council hasn't been held since the Great War," Julian whispered. Her breath was hot on Adni's neck.

Adni shivered.

"As I stated in my letters to each of you, it has been confirmed that Izenfir, the land the Evil Queen originated from, is very much real, and worse than we thought." Haven went on to explain what she'd learned from her sister, James, Adni and Julian before she addressed the issue of how to best proceed.

"This is madness!" Lord Grant stood abruptly, his hands slamming against the table. "Dragons do not exist!"

"Then what better explanation do you have for Kadia's magic?" Haven snapped. She narrowed her eyes at the minister.

"Magic is one thing, but the creatures you speak of are of legend. Fairy tales made up for children. Would you have us believe trolls and goblins are real as well?" the minister countered.

Adni shifted and glanced at Julian. Julian had told stories of trolls. For all Adni knew, the beasts were real as well.

"That is beside the point." King Evander stood. He looked around the table, calling silence with his stern gaze. "You may not remember the tyranny of the Evil Queen, but the rest of us do."

Haven stiffened and her gaze hardened. She had been the one to bring down Kadia all those years ago. She would know better than anyone what the Mad Queen was capable of.

"Of course I remember," Lord Grant argued. His cheeks flushed bright red. "But no one knows where this magic came from any more than we know where Queen Haven's comes from." He pointed an accusatory finger at Haven.

Corrin stood abruptly, the legs of his chair scraping across the floor. "If you were listening to my wife, then we *know* where Kadia's magic comes from now."

"And who's to say Queen Haven's doesn't come from the same place?" Lord Grant shouted.

Adni's eyes flew wide as she exchanged a look with Julian. No one knew where Haven's magic came from, but that didn't mean she was an ashen like Kadia. Adni could feel the tingle of Haven's magic. It wasn't strong like the ashen's and Nina's, or like fire, like the dragons'. It was small, a warm gust through Adni's mind when Haven was near.

"That's pure slander," Evander barked.

Lord Grant shook his head and took a breath. "Apologies, I didn't mean it like that. All I'm saying is we know nothing."

Haven nodded. "We might not understand how my healing works, but we know where the darkness of Kadia came from. We can't let another like her rise again."

That, they could all agree on. No one wanted to see another five-year war, especially one that ravaged the Kingdoms and left thousands dead.

"What exactly are you proposing, Lady Queen?" Lady Hilren stood, her fingers intertwined, her hands held in front of her. Her back straightened as she addressed the Queen.

"One last battle." Haven tilted her chin up. "We create a plan, one final assault to wipe out every being like Kadia, and these dragons. We'll infiltrate Izenfir and launch a surprise attack. There's no way they'll see it coming."

The quiet rumble of discussion brushed through the room, startling the quiet left by Haven's statement. Ministers spoke with their advisers, as did the other kings and queens. Haven watched and waited, as did the rest of the Rythern court. Though Julian had said Haven had the largest army in all the six kingdoms, Adni couldn't imagine she wanted to go to war alone. This meeting would decide who would follow, and who might flee.

Evander stood once more. "When do we leave?"

A smile broke Haven's mask. "As soon as we can."

Evander nodded. "What's your plan?"

"Those who've escaped Izenfir–" Haven glanced at Julian and Adni. "Have described it as a chasm with tunnels throughout and a Spyre at the center. Inside the Spyre is an orb that controls the magic of these beasts. If we can destroy it, we can trap them in human form. I propose we lead an army into the bottom of the chasm as a distraction while a small team moves to take out this orb."

"A fine plan," Evander said.

King Emeril stood. "Who will be on this small team?" His eyes flashed like he already knew.

"I will, of course," Haven said. "It'll be just like old times." She smiled as she exchanged a look with her guards. They didn't seem quite as amused as the Queen, but Nina laughed as she stood.

"I'll be joining as well," Nina said.

"So will I," Julian said. "I can lead the way."

"Julian was one of the slaves who escaped," Haven explained.

The others nodded their approval.

"We should escape with few casualties," Haven continued. "I'd like to move as soon as possible. Who will lend their aid?" Her gaze roamed the table.

"I will," Evander said.

"And I." Emeril held his fist to his heart.

"You already know I will." Corrin smiled.

Haven squeezed his hand.

"I don't have the resources to spare," Lord Grant huffed. "Not after the last war." His lips twisted into a frown, further wrinkling his face.

"I'll lend whatever I can," Lady Hilren said.

"Then it's settled." Evander clapped his hands together. "We go to war."

"Again," Haven said.

"Again," Evander agreed.

* * *

AFTER THE MEETING was over and the officials dispersed to send word to their kingdoms, Haven invited Adni and Julian to join her in her chambers.

Adni exchanged a look with Julian. Fear spiked through her heart. Had Haven figured out what they were? Or was there some other reason to speak to them in private?

Haven led the way to her chambers alongside Corrin. They walked arm in arm ahead of the two women, who trailed a few steps behind.

Cold sweat slicked Adni's skin beneath her jacket. They could still run. There was plenty of time to escape. They could feign illness, or Adni could pretend her long gone injuries were acting up.

A few corridors passed before they came to a halt before two large oak doors. Two guards standing on either side of them opened the chamber doors for the Queen and King.

"Come in." Haven looked back at the pair.

Adni swallowed the lump in her throat. It was now or never. She looked at Julian. Should they run?

Julian shook her head, just barely. Adni's eyebrows furrowed. Julian wasn't worried at all. How could that be? Even if Nina had confronted them a mere week ago, she could still have given them up to the Queen. But why now?

Adni took a deep breath. She needed to get a hold of herself.

They stepped into a large sitting room with a stone fireplace, two plush red sofas and thick drapes hanging from the back wall. Fleur-de-lis covered the walls in shades of red and gold. A painting of a castle hung over the fireplace mantel, sand and sea in the distance. Adni wasn't sure which kingdom it was, be it Dagan or Wakefin. Both bordered the sea, and both had cities on the water.

"Mum!" the tiny voice of a little girl rang from the bedchambers beyond the drapes hanging over another set of double doors.

A little girl with blazing red hair and wide blue eyes appeared in the doorway. Her skin glowed with sun and freckles, and her tiny hands sought her mother's skirts.

"Marian." Haven beamed as she kneeled beside her daughter.

Adni's heart warmed as the two embraced.

Marian gasped as she looked over Haven's shoulder. "Papa!" She leapt into her father's arms next. Corrin lifted her up and spun her in a circle, chuckling as Marian squealed with delight.

"I'm finally home," Corrin said. He stopped their spin, and held Marian on his hip. His blue eyes glowed with warmth as he stared at the four-year-old.

Marian wrapped her arms around her father's neck and clung to him while Corrin took a seat on one of the sofas. Haven sat next to him, motioning for the other two girls to have a seat.

"You have a beautiful daughter," Julian said.

Adni sat beside her and shifted awkwardly. She was terrible at small talk.

"Thank you." Haven's general-like sharpness was gone, softening into a motherly smile.

Marian blinked out from under her father's chin, her wide eyes inspecting the newcomers with interest.

"A wonderful name as well." Julian winked at Marian, who grinned and shifted to look at the woman bathing her in compliments.

Haven's smile twisted sadly. "Marian Astrid Fyre. We named her after my siblings; Marcel, Lucian, and Astrid."

Adni looked up, her brows pulling together. She'd forgotten Haven only had her throne because of the deaths of her family. The young queen had been the only one left after the Evil Queen killed her parents and two older brothers.

"Who are you?" Marian asked.

"Julian," she said. "And this is Adni."

Marian looked between the two of them. Though Marian clearly inherited many traits from both of her parents, did she also inherit her mother's magic?

While Julian made small talk, Adni searched her mind for that familiar tingle. It brushed her consciousness, telling her something was nearby, but Adni couldn't tell if it was simply Haven, or if Marian factored into her feeling. She made a mental note to ask Julian about it later.

"I'm sure you're wondering why I asked you both here," Haven said.

Adni blinked clear of her thoughts and focused on the Queen. Marian slid from her father's lap and returned to the bedchambers. Corrin followed, casting a glance over his shoulder as he disappeared into the other room.

"It crossed my mind," Julian said.

Haven smiled. "After my sister's attack it's clear these dragons planned to use Astrid against me for some time. Once the armies of the six kingdoms have amassed, I need you both to lead us to Izenfir personally."

Adni's stomach twisted. She still hadn't come to terms with returning to those mountains. Darkness edged in every corner and cold seeped into her skin. She didn't miss the mountains, even though she did think of them as home.

"Of course we will," Julian said. Her jaw set with determination.

"I need you to pick the most direct route, but one that will get as many soldiers in unseen as possible to amass in the bottom of that chasm," Haven continued. "Do you think it's possible?"

Julian nodded. "I do. We can come up through the slave quarters at the base of Izenfir and amass around the mines."

"Excellent." Haven nodded. Her mouth set in a grim line. "And is there an easy way to get unseen to this Spyre?"

Julian shoulders stiffened. Adni glanced between them. There wasn't one that Adni knew, as she was sure Julian knew as well.

"Not without some resistance," Julian said after a long pause.

"What kind of resistance should we expect?"

"If we breach in the early morning like I've suggested than several ashen guards will be posted on the Spyre, while others patrol the ledges surrounding the chasm." Julian's eyebrows furrowed as she thought. "We can avoid some of the patrols, but the ones at the Spyre will be unavoidable."

"How many are posted at the Spyre?"

"Two at the main doors, and several throughout."

"Two like Kadia?" The color drained from Haven's face and her eyes widened.

Corrin leaned on the doorframe between rooms. His eyebrows furrowed as he watched his wife tuck her hair behind her ear.

Julian's lips thinned. "Yes."

"Then we'll need a fair sized group to infiltrate won't we?" Adni asked.

"If we have too many we run the risk of being found out," Julian said.

"And with too few we'll all be killed." Haven's fingers shook in her lap.

They both agreed.

"Who do we have so far?" Julian asked.

Haven glanced at Corrin, who smiled sheepishly. "Besides the three of us, my husband insists on coming. Nina will and so will my four personal guards."

Would nine be enough?

"I'd suggest bringing a few extra guards, My Lady." Julian crossed her arms and leaned back against the sofa. "If we keep our group under fifteen, we should be able to handle the guards and get inside."

Haven nodded. "I'll do as you suggest." She glanced between them. "Do either of you know how to fight?"

Adni stiffened, while Julian put on an amused smile.

"Yes, of course," Julian said.

Haven smiled slightly. "Excellent. And you?" She looked at Adni.

Adni looked between them. She had to assume Haven wasn't referring to any magical abilities. Though she'd only seen Julian fight with magic, when she'd first met Julian, the woman carried a sword and shield. "Not much," Adni admitted.

"You can join my classes in the courtyard this week. It'll help to prepare you."

Though Haven's words suggested it was optional, her tone conveyed the opposite.

"Gladly," Adni said. She'd seize any opportunity she could to learn how to fight, especially if they were about to head into war. There was much more at stake than even the Queen realized.

"I have one last question for you." Haven looked pointedly at Adni. "You've seen the orb, correct?"

Adni started. "Y-yes." How did she know that?

"Nina told me," Haven said, as if reading her thoughts. "You were stationed inside the Spyre recently weren't you?"

Adni took a deep breath. So Nina had told Haven that Adni was a slave as well. "Yes."

"Did you learn of any way to destroy the Holy Fire?"

Adni looked at Julian, reminded that Julian planned on sacrificing herself to bring down the entire Spyre and the Holy Fire along with it. Adni twisted her lip between her teeth. She couldn't allow it, even if she couldn't think of another way.

"None specifically." Adni paused. "But from what I saw, the exterior of the orb was made of glass."

"Glass we can break." Haven straightened.

"The chasm is very deep," Adni continued. "If we can't break it with our weapons, we could try dropping it into the ravine." She hadn't a clue if that would work, or if it was possible, but anything was better than letting Julian go.

Haven nodded. "At least we have a backup plan then."

A high-pitched cry rang from the other room. Corrin spun for the door to their bedchambers and Haven leapt to her feet.

"Marian!" Haven rushed to the other room, while Adni and Julian followed.

The royal bedchambers was similar to the sitting room, the same wallpaper and dark furnishing, but much wider, and three other doors leading to separate rooms.

A large fireplace glowed against one wall. Flames licked the charred remains of wood inside. Marian sat beside it, her eyes filled with tears. She held one of her hands gingerly, the skin reddened.

"Marian, are you all right?" Corrin plucked her from the ground and into his arms.

Haven hovered at his shoulder, brushing Marian's hair from her red cheeks. Tears streamed down her face. "What happened?"

Marian glanced down at the fire. A small doll with black hair and buttons for eyes lay beside the embers. Small flames at its legs and arms. "My doll," she whimpered.

Both parents visibly relaxed.

"It's all right, honey." Haven smiled and took Marian's hand gently. She kissed her fingers. "We'll make you a new doll."

Marian nodded, though the tears continued to fall.

Adni looked at Marian's burned fingers. The redness didn't leave, didn't heal away like she'd expect of the daughter of the Immortal Queen. So Marian didn't have her mother's magic after all.

Haven turned to Adni and Julian, a small smile still on her lips. "Thank you for your advisement." Haven nodded. "I should attend to my family now."

"Of course." Julian bowed, and Adni mimicked her, the movement much more awkward than intended. "Have a good evening, Lady Queen."

"You two as well." Haven turned back to Marian, cooing softly as Adni and Julian took their leave.

NINETEEN

The *shing* of swords scraping against each other rang through the hollow courtyard over and over. Several days after the first war council was held, Adni was beginning to understand the weight of her sword and arc of the blade.

Dozens of men and women shuffled through the large space, blades slamming against swords and shields, the sounds echoing off the high ceiling.

Lareina led the beginner class on the far side of the room while Blythe instructed a more advanced group near the tall windows overlooking a large garden. While the head of the Queen's Guard paced the floor between the pairs facing off, Adni and Julian stood opposite one another, blades at the ready and chests heaving.

Adni took a deep breath to steady her shaking hands. They'd already been practicing for several hours, leaving her mind sharp but her body aching. The heavy metal blade was familiar in her hands, stretched in front of her as if she might slice it at her opponent.

Julian waited with a devious smile plastered to her pretty face and her blade ready. Though Blythe had taught Adni a proper stance,

Julian's was different, one foot far in front of the other, her blade behind her, but pointed outward, and one hand in front of her.

Adni imagined flames licking Julian's palm, or a shield firmly in her grasp. She pictured the thick piece of wood with the faded red paint of a serpent. It had been lost when they were brought to Izenfir by her father. Would Julian ever get it back?

"Adni, Julian. Begin on my count!" Blythe barked over the sounds of scuffles on every side.

Julian's eyes flashed with mischief as Adni shifted her feet, stepping into her ready stance. Her knuckles went white around the hilt of her blade. She shouldn't be holding it so tight, but Julian had a habit of slapping it out of her hands.

"Three, two, one, begin!"

Adni flashed forward, on the offensive this time.

Her heart raced and her pulse pounded in her ears as she swiped at Julian's extended arm.

Julian stepped back faster than Adni could blink, catching Adni's blade with her own. Her smile spread into a toothy grin. A flash of irritation bit Adni's heart. This was all so easy to Julian. Though she'd finally begun breathing heavily, Julian wasn't covered in sweat like Adni.

Adni pushed hard against Julian's blade. Julian pushed back.

Once Julian's breath brushed her cheeks, Adni leapt back. Julian pitched forward and Adni sliced for her head.

Julian ducked and rolled underneath Adni's blade.

Her heart leapt into her throat as she fought her momentum, trying to spin and face her opponent.

Cold metal pressed against the base of her neck. She'd lost.

"Nice try," Julian said.

Adni narrowed her eyes over her shoulder.

"Nice work, Julian." Blythe stopped nearby. "Reset your positions and begin again. This time, I want you to attack first." She raised her brows at the blonde woman.

Julian nodded. "Yes ma'am."

Blythe rolled her eyes. Julian had been jokingly calling the Queen's

Guard ma'am ever since she realized it bothered the Captain. Adni had only ever called older women ma'am, and she assumed the custom must be the same in Rythern. Every time Julian said it, Blythe made a face like it made her feel old.

Adni returned to her starting point, as did Julian. The woman's stance didn't change, even as Adni moved on the defensive. She wasn't very good at taking Julian when on the offensive. Julian was far too quick, and easily overpowered Adni.

She gulped. Adni had wanted this her whole life. She wanted to train, to learn how to fight. She wouldn't give up now.

"On my mark." Blythe continued her pacing. "Three, two, one, begin!"

Julian leapt before the last word tumbled off Blythe's tongue. Her blade slammed against Adni's, pushing her back across the floor.

Adni's boots skidded back and she gritted her teeth. Julian's strength was nearly enough to pitch her backwards, but Adni couldn't let her get the advantage so easily.

"Come on, Adni," Julian taunted.

She glared, a growl on her lips. Adni stepped back, righting her stance to push Julian back without falling over. Julian leapt from their locked blades and spun to swipe at Adni's shin.

Adni jumped instinctively, Julian's blade inches from her boots. Before she landed, Julian drove her shoulder into Adni's chest.

Air exploded from her lungs, sending her gasping as she fell backward. Julian dove, her forearm slamming Adni against the smooth stone floor. Her arm pressed against Adni's collarbone, while her hand pinned Adni's wrist above her head.

Julian's breath bathed her cheeks and her blonde waves tickled her ears.

Adni's eyes widened. Julian's fingers were hot against her skin, and her thick lips twisted in the flirtatious smile Adni knew all too well. Her thighs pressed against her hips, her knee gently pinning Adni's other wrist.

Flames of desire tore across her skin, lighting her from head to toe. Her pulse quickened, hammering inside her head as she stared at

Julian's smile, remembering the warmth of her lips against her mouth, and sweet taste of her tongue.

"Good work, Julian," Blythe said.

The gruff voice broke them apart. Julian flew to her feet, leaving Adni's cheeks on fire. Her mind raced, unsure what to think, or feel.

"Adni, that was quick thinking, but you exposed your abdomen too easily." Blythe crossed her arms over her chest.

Julian offered Adni a hand. Adni accepted it, letting Julian pull her to her feet while she fought to stop her head from spinning.

"Keep your sword up next time instead of flinging your arm out."

Adni took a deep breath, and nodded. "I'll keep that in mind."

"Good." Blythe stepped to the head of the class. "That'll be all for today!" she called to the rest of the class.

The familiar clang of swords and shields stopped, and hushed voices resumed. Each of Lareina and Blythe's students shook hands and congratulated each other on a job well done.

"That really was a good move," Julian said. "Good instincts."

Adni's cheeks heated once more. "Thanks."

"Don't mention it." Julian returned her blade to its sheath. They'd each been given a sword and sheath to keep, allowing them plenty of time to get used to their new weapons before they returned to the mountains.

Though more and more warriors flooded Palmyra every day, filling the castle and the streets, Adni wasn't sure it'd be enough. They'd be up against *dragons*, and *ashen*. Last time the six kingdoms faced a single ashen, thousands died.

Adni shook her head and wiped the sweat from her forehead. She returned her sword to the leather sheath at her hip. Later, they'd clean their blades, but for now it was nearly dinnertime.

The courtyard emptied out, students returning to their homes and their duties, just like their teachers. Blythe met with Malka at the entry. The stony expression they both wore cracked as their eyes glowed with warmth. The two women exchanged smiles and nods, so simple, yet intimate in its own way.

"Ready to go?" Julian asked.

Adni nodded and together they left the courtyard.

"Adni, Julian?"

Both of them paused by the arched entry. Adni looked over her shoulder. Haven approached from the main hall, her foreign guard Aura at her shoulder.

"Lady Queen." Julian bowed. Adni copied her.

"How was practice?" Haven stood next to them. Something dark shadowed her normally bright eyes. Where had the young queen been?

"Good," Julian said. "This one is going to spear me any day." She grinned and nudged Adni's arm playfully.

Adni rolled her eyes. "Hardly."

"Well, that's good to hear." Haven's lips twitched as if she might smile, but the expression never formed.

"May I ask how your sister is doing?" Julian asked.

Adni's heart skipped as she looked at Julian. It wasn't exactly impolite to ask, but she doubted the Queen wanted to talk about it.

Haven sighed. "Astrid is being guarded and cared for. I'm afraid they did a number on her mind. Even James doesn't seem to be able to talk her out of the state she's in."

"I hope she'll be all right." Adni's eyebrows furrowed.

"I'm sure she will be with time." Haven shook her head. "I do hope you can forgive her, Adni. This isn't like Astrid at all. When we were girls she never would have harmed a fly, let alone stab someone."

"I understand." Adni's heart clenched. She wished the two sisters would have had a happier reunion. Though they had to be blessed by the blue skies to be reunited at all, they both deserved to have a real relationship without the influence of Solipher.

"Thank you." Haven smiled. "I should meet King Emeril and his men."

"Of course." Adni stepped aside to let the Queen go. They said their goodbyes and Haven disappeared back down the corridor, taking her shadow with her.

* * *

AFTER DINNER in the grand hall, Adni and Julian returned to Adni's chambers to continue her training. While by day they practiced with swords, by night magic burned across her fingers and lust filled her heart.

Her pulse beat behind her eyes as Julian stood across from her, sparks flaring across her palm.

"Are you ready?" Julian asked.

Adni gulped. Anticipation ran through her arms to her fingers. Her skin prickled with goose bumps, and her chest lurched with excitement. "Ready."

Julian nodded. Flames burst on her palm. Adni's heart leapt into her throat, stealing her breath. She fought to calm herself, to pull out the familiar darkness in the back of her mind, calling out her desire for power, her hunger for the flames.

The flicker of fire twisted into a ball twice the size of Julian's outstretched hand. The orange glow brushed Julian's high cheekbones and brightened her blue eyes. She didn't smile, didn't wink or flirt like she might any other day. They both took this magic seriously. They both took Adni's training seriously.

If Adni was going to fight ashen or dragons, they needed to.

Julian leaned forward and tossed the fireball. Adni reached for it with her mind, heart, and body. Her fingers caught it, turning it over in her hand. Warmth burst across her skin, sending a shiver up her spine. But it didn't hurt. It didn't burn.

Adni took a deep breath and focused. She pictured the flames in her mind. She imagined them growing and twisting into a blazing bird. A phoenix of legend.

She closed her eyes and saw the long feathered tail, the curved beak and claws, the wide wings smoking through the air.

A gasp broke the quiet.

Adni opened her eyes. The bird was just how she imagined. Big, beautiful and on fire. Her heart skipped with excitement. Pride rushed through her chest, pulling a grin to her face. She'd done it. She'd created something from Julian's fire—something besides sticks and stones. Something real. Something *alive*.

Pain burst across her palm. Adni yelped and dropped the flames.

The phoenix disappeared into a whisper of smoke.

"Damn!" Adni spat. She'd let her excitement overcome her *again*. She thought she was passed this.

"That was good," Julian said. Her eyes glowed with pride. "Really good."

Adni looked at her hand. Red flared across her skin. She was lucky she didn't have welts again.

Julian stepped closer. "How bad is it?" She didn't wait for an answer. Julian took her hand. Her fingers were warm.

"It's fine." Adni yanked her hand back. Her cheeks burned with embarrassment over feelings she wasn't ready to express.

Julian arched an eyebrow. "Are you okay?"

Adni held her hand to her chest. Her palm throbbed and her fingers ached, but it was bearable. What wasn't bearable, and kept bothering Adni, no matter how hard she pushed it away, was Julian's need to save them all. She hadn't forgotten Julian planned on giving up her freedom to save Warshard.

She turned to the bathing room to cool her hand. Before their training had begun, they'd gone over the plan to take down the Spyre again. They were leaving in two days when the last of the reinforcements arrived. They'd suffer a week of travel across Rythern and through the mountains before they arrived in Izenfir.

A week. That's all she had left with Julian if Julian had her way.

Adni shook her head. Her heart clenched painfully. She entered the bathing room and found the clean water waiting in the tub. It was long chilled. She was supposed to use it before dinner, but she'd been far too hungry to pause for a bath.

"Adni, what are you doing?" Julian sighed.

"Cooling my hand," Adni replied gruffly. She sat on the edge of the tub, carved from stone, an interesting piece that reminded her of bathing in the mountain rivers.

"Then why so grumpy?"

Adni glared, and Julian flashed a small smile. "You know why."

Julian's smile fell. "This again?" Adni said nothing. "Adni you know

I'm doing this for all of you. I can't let Solipher or any of them get away with abducting children, and turning them into evil monsters. I won't let them enslave them, or me, and especially not you."

Adni sighed. It did nothing to dissuade cold chilling her limbs. She hadn't felt this helpless since she woke up in Izenfir.

"But why *you*? Why can't we scale the Spyre and destroy the Holy Fire together?"

"You know why," Julian countered. "If we do that we'll be found out in minutes. All of the dragons will sense us tampering with the Holy Fire. They'll know what we're up to before we've even reached it."

"There has to be another way!"

"There isn't! If I don't knock down the Spyre in one hit, this war will be for nothing!" Julian flung her arms out, as if the drama of flinging her limbs somehow added to the gravity of her words.

Adni stood quickly, a growl rumbling from her throat. "It isn't fair! You're going to give up your entire life destroying that thing."

"It's my choice." Julian's voice quieted. Darkness settled in her gaze, just like it had before. She was shutting Adni out. She was done talking about this.

"You're being a martyr, that's all you're doing," Adni snapped. Her fists clenched, her nails digging into her palms. She winced as her burn flared painfully. "You know there's another way, but you won't give it a shot."

Julian sighed. "You're young. You're an optimist. I'm just being realistic, Adni."

Adni's eyes widened. It was the first time Julian ever mentioned her age. Though Adni was much younger than Julian, she'd never used it against her.

"Please understand why I'm doing this." Julian stepped up in front of her. Her fingers brushed Adni's fists.

Adni pulled away. "No. I won't. Not as long as you insist on sacrificing yourself." She returned to her bedchambers, leaving Julian in silence.

TWENTY

An ocean of soldiers set out from Palmyra, spreading like waves over the surrounding hills to settle in the forests. Somehow they all had to fit in the mountain tunnels. Somehow they'd all spread out over the chasm floor.

Adni shook her head as the massive parade crested the first hill. Palmyra disappeared behind them, a dark gray spot between the trees.

The further they rode on horseback, the further her mind wandered. She shouldn't have left before receiving word of her family. She should have gone herself, rode off to Salander, and then to Elmhurst. It'd take her some time, but at least she'd know by now whether her mother and siblings were alive or dead.

A cool breeze brushed the bare nape of her neck. She pulled her hood closer as a shiver ran up her spine.

The Cinder Mountains towered in the distance, snowy peaks growing larger by the day. Winter was on the horizon. The first snowfall would come before they returned to Palmyra. *If* they returned to Palmyra.

This quest could very well be the end of her journey. Solipher would kill her if he got his hands on her. Kaldar would too. Her own brother would slay her in cold blood for her betrayal. She wasn't sure she'd blame him.

Guilt clenched around her heart. She knew she shouldn't feel guilty. They were monsters, but Kaldar was the product of Solipher's evil influence, and if the Rythern Queen thought he needed to die along with all the other ashen, Adni wasn't sure she could stand by.

Days passed as they drew closer to the mountains. Julian led the way up the steep cliff side into a valley of dead trees. The distant rumble of a river mingled with the rumble of hooves. Not all rode horses, but most at the front of the pack did. They led the way to the war. They'd be the first to enter this final battle.

The chill of the mountain descended on her shoulders. Adni dismounted her white stallion alongside Julian and the others. The mouth of a cave was carved from the base of the cliff.

Julian steered toward it.

"Is this it?" Haven slipped from her horse's back, landing a few feet behind Julian. Her husband and guards descended behind her.

"It is," Julian said. Her lips thinned as she glanced between the shadows of the cavern and the army. Though the cave mouth was wide, Adni was sure it would narrow once they entered. They'd be lucky to fit three wide.

"Then let's get started. We have a long trek ahead of us." Haven looked back at the others and signaled for her men to advance.

Six of the Rythern Queen's Guard lit torches before leading the way inside. Haven's personal guards followed alongside a few Wakefin soldiers. The young queen was quick to follow, her King following accompanying her, the same determined set to his brow.

Julian looked back at Adni. The cliff side blocked the sun, shadowing her tanned cheeks. Once they entered that tunnel there was no turning back. This was Adni's last chance to run home.

Adni bit the inside of her cheek. Copper filled her mouth. She might want to find out what happened to her family more than anything, but she also had a duty. She couldn't let Julian do this alone.

She couldn't let Solipher dig another generation of ancient dragons from the earth.

Adjusting her rucksack, Adni trudged past Julian to the cave mouth. Julian flashed a brief smile as she stepped up to join her.

Adni had made her choice. She hoped she wouldn't regret it.

* * *

THE TUNNELS WERE JUST how she remembered them—an endless maze no one would dare follow. No one but the most desperate of people.

While they walked, Julian explained to the Warshard royals why slaves rarely attempted to flee. Though Izenfir kept hundreds of them, few had ever tried the tunnels, even if they were readily available. The mountains were a maze with few exits.

Adni was surprised they hadn't come across any skeletons, but if Julian was right there were thousands of tunnels. It was unlikely they'd come across one that someone perished inside.

The days drew long, and her limbs weary. The guards surrounding Adni and Julian joked and nudged each other. They were far enough that they wouldn't receive a reprimand from the King and Queen.

"They really want us to believe there are *dragons* at the end of these tunnels?" a Wakefin guard asked. His voice was edged with humor.

Adni and Julian exchanged a glance. There was nothing funny about this mission or the hundreds of lives that might be lost.

"I can't believe the King is humoring his wife like this." Another soldier sighed and shook his head. Metal scraped against rock as someone shoved him into the wall.

"Respect your leaders," a Rythern soldier snapped. Her voice hissed between her bared teeth. She was a foreigner like Aura. Her dark gaze sliced through the Wakefin soldiers. The woman hurried forward to join the other Rythern guards ahead of Adni and Julian.

Once she was gone, the Wakefin guards' muffled laughs filled Adni's ears. Her fists clenched and her skin prickled with irritation.

"They're all mad!" one said. Their laughter continued, but they didn't dare insult Queen Haven directly again.

Night had to be drawing near as the army slowed. Julian glanced left and right at the shadows dancing along the walls. Adni wasn't sure she'd ever seen her worried before. Then again, they were descending into the bowels of Izenfir where hundreds of dragons and ashen awaited them. If they weren't successful in taking down the Holy Fire, they'd be lucky to escape alive.

Adni sighed, her breath fogging the chill air. "We're almost there, aren't we?"

Julian looked at her from the corner of her eye. Her lips thinned and she nodded curtly.

The tingle of magic hadn't left Adni's skin, not with Nina nearby, so she'd never be able to tell when they arrived in Izenfir without Julian's help. She had to learn to decipher her feelings, how to tell when other magical beings were nearby even when beside one. Maybe Julian would give her a lesson before dawn and the war began.

"Halt!" a gruff voice called from ahead.

Adni stopped in her tracks. The rumble of boots slowed before stopping completely. The laughs, whispers and chatter behind them petered out.

"We camp here for the night," the voice called again. Adni thought it might be Blythe, but she couldn't be sure. The Captain was leading the way after Julian gave instructions. The path was mostly straight, with only a few turns in the road. "Tomorrow we fight."

Her words pressed against Adni's shoulders. She gulped. Warm fingers squeezed her hand. Adni looked up into Julian's dark blue gaze. The look told Adni not to worry, that everything would be fine. Julian's touch left her hand, leaving her skin cold.

Chatter and the bustle of night time returned. Several tunnels led from the main one. Some narrow, some wide. A cavern opened up at the front of the pack, where the Queen and King made their beds alongside their guards. A fire was lit at the center, the warm light mingling with the dim light of torches.

Adni and Julian joined the group at the edge of the cavern. They slipped their bedrolls from the packs on their backs and lay them out alongside Nina.

The heat of flames brushed her skin, and the scent of smoke filled her nostrils. It was welcome after days in cold. Only by night did she fully regain the feeling in her toes.

Adni sat back on her bedroll, propping her rucksack against the rough cavern wall alongside her sheathed sword. Her fingers lingered on the hilt. The Queen had given it to her as a personal gift. Though it was a simple straight blade, with a leather wrapped hilt, it was sharp and would shine in the firelight if she drew it.

A smile ghosted across her face as she crossed her legs.

Dread-filled whispers filled the chamber. While some remained quiet, others exchanged hurried words. Some laughter drifted further down the tunnel, but their cavern was sullen.

Haven and her husband leaned close together on the opposite side, exchanging quiet words that furrowed both of their brows. Adni could only guess what they were saying. Something about the plan for tomorrow, or worry over the mission.

The rest of the guards leaned against their own bedrolls or prepared stew over the fire. Lareina stirred the boiling contents, the thick scent wafting up Adni's nostrils and pulling at the growling beast inside her belly. She licked her lips. Hopefully Lareina would be done soon. The last few nights she'd been quick with a spoon and quicker with a ladle, dispensing as much stew to the troops as she could before sitting back herself, joined by her fellow guards Blythe, Malka and Aura.

How long had the guards been together? From the way they spoke it had to be about a decade. Of all the stories that were told of the Immortal Queen, not many mentioned the four guard women who had such great influence over their queen.

Adni hoped she would one day be like them, joined with a group of powerful women ready to take on the world and defend their home-land to their last breath.

Nina slipped off to help Lareina, kneeling beside the low flames. Adni looked at Julian who twiddled her thumbs and stared down at her hands.

"Do you think we'll get in a last practice tonight?" Adni whispered.

Though they'd been unable to get away the last few nights, her fingers itched to feel the warmth of Julian's flames. She had to be ready to control the magic of whoever came for them.

Julian looked up. "I don't know if that's best."

If they were caught, Adni could only imagine what would happen to them. They could be branded traitors and killed on sight.

Adni twisted her lip between her teeth. But if she couldn't practice, she couldn't defend against Solipher and the others either. They were bound to find out what she was eventually.

"Be patient," Julian mumbled. "We'll slip off once the others fall asleep."

Her heart jumped against her ribs. She nodded and settled back against the wall as Lareina passed bowls of stew out to the troops.

Adni sipped at her soup, enjoying the welcome heartiness of beef and potatoes. Even after being with these people for nearly two weeks, she still wasn't used to the good food. She might be able to stay with them forever if it meant no more dried fish and stale bread.

Chatter continued through the cavern as the soldiers finished dinner. The guards ahead, beyond the cavern, laughed uproariously, their voices echoing through the wide cavern.

Soon the others would settle down for the night and they'd slip off. Soon the burn of magic would grace her fingers, and her hunger would be sated.

A burst of air, like a long warm breath rushed through the tunnel, pulling at her ponytail and brushing her cheeks. Her eyebrows furrowed as the torchlight flickered out. The blazing fire at the center of the room shifted and swayed as if it might go out. The embers burned bright at the base of it, illuminating the concerned and confused faces of the others.

"What was that?" someone asked.

"Wind in the mountains?" another said.

Adni slowly stood. The chatter and laughter stopped abruptly. The earth rumbled around them, the distant scrape of rock suddenly audible. Pebbles fell from the ceiling, clicking against the ground.

She looked around at the others as another gust rushed through.

Nina and Lareina dove to cover the flames, while the others leapt to their feet.

Julian grabbed her sword, but froze as she stared wide-eyed at the tunnel ahead: the tunnel leading to Izenfir.

"What is it?" Adni whispered. Her voice carried further than she meant it to. It echoed, carrying her fear back to her ears again and again.

Julian looked at her. "They've come."

Goosebumps burst across her skin. Adni's eyes widened as she finally understood what the sounds and the wind was.

Dragons.

"Run," Adni said. Her heart pounded in her ears as she spun for the tunnel. "Run!"

Heat flared through the far tunnel. Screams filled the air. Soldiers leapt for their swords, and the Queen's Guard twisted to leap in front of their queen.

Julian leapt at Adni, knocking them both to the floor. Air exploded from her lungs as her back slammed against the stone floor. Heat grazed her boots and light filled the cavern as fire flared past Julian's shoulder and down the tunnel.

Her heart raced faster, even as the flames disappeared and the surrounding rumble filled her ears. The cavern quaked and the scrape of something sharp against stone drew closer.

Scorched but alive, the Queen's Guard yanked Haven and Corrin to their feet. Blythe scooped Nina right off the ground. The blonde yelped as they leapt for the tunnel leading back the way they'd come.

"RUN!" Blythe roared.

While some remained frozen, Julian lurched to her feet, pulling Adni with her. She was pushed and pulled forward by dozens of hands as soldiers scrambled back down the tunnel.

"There's a fork back this way! Take it!" Julian shouted above the rush of boots.

This wasn't how it was supposed to go. This wasn't the fight they were supposed to have. Adni's mind flew with her feet as they tore through the tunnels, leaping over charred bodies, discarded rucksacks and bedrolls set aflame.

They had a plan. They were supposed to assemble in the chasm and distract the enemy while a small group of them went to destroy the Holy Fire. It was a good plan. One that might get a lot of them killed, but would save the most lives in the long run.

Ash crunched beneath her boots. Screams rose at her back. That wasn't the plan. That was chaos.

Julian grabbed her arm and tore her sideways into an open tunnel where the flames hadn't touched.

"This way!" Julian called.

A roar of a beast she'd never truly believed existed drove spikes through her skull. The rumble was the rush of feet. The scraping was scales on rock. Dragons were after them. Dragons would burn them alive.

Heat licked the skin on the back of her neck, singeing the short hairs as flames flew through the tunnel. Julian pulled her forward, out of reach of the fire. Her heart rammed against her ribs as she looked over her shoulder.

Fire dissipated at the tunnel mouth, leaving long black scorch marks across the dark stone.

"Come on!" Julian pulled her arm, tearing her gaze from the scaled arm that appeared by the tunnel.

Adni ran, the fire of adrenaline pushing her faster than she'd ever run.

Someone shouted orders over the screams at their backs. Someone knew what they were doing. Adni could hardly think over the fear sending her heart racing faster than her feet. If it beat any harder, it might break out of her ribs.

Her lungs burned as they rocketed through tunnels, twisting through passages and forks in the road.

"We've got to continue the mission!" someone yelled, possibly the Queen.

"Forget the mission!" another female voice barked.

"No, she's right," the King snapped.

"We can still bring down the Spyre!" Julian panted. "I can get us up through the dungeon tunnels and we can finish the job." What she didn't say was the price of their job. The cost of the mission might be all of their lives.

"Let's do it," Haven said. "Julian, up here. Lead the way!"

The group ahead of them slowed now that the rumble grew distant. Julian didn't release her arm, pulling Adni along to the head of the group.

"This way!" Julian motioned for them to follow.

They all took off running, screams still ringing in her ears and the beat of her heart still hammering inside her head. How many had been killed back there? How many would still die?

Adni shook her head as frustrated tears burned the back of her eyes. It didn't matter now. They had to bring down the Spyre or their lost lives would be for nothing.

TWENTY-ONE

sh, sulphur, and blood flooded her nostrils and tore sense from her brain. They'd left the army to their deaths. Hundreds—no—thousands of people. Fire would burn them alive if they were lucky, but if they weren't, the teeth and claws of mythical beasts would shred through their skin until they bled to death.

A shiver ran up her spine. Her skin chilled even as sweat coated her forehead. Adni had the sense of mind to keep her hand on her sword, but not much else. Her head swirled with images of beasts and fire, of the death and chaos in the tunnels below.

They were leaving them all behind to whatever fate had planned for them. If they didn't succeed, every death would be for nothing, and the ashen would eventually come for Warshard again.

Adni squeezed her eyes shut. She had to get a hold of herself. There wasn't time to dwell on the lives of those she could do nothing for. The faster they took down the Holy Fire, the faster they'd stop the bloodshed. Though the dragons would be stuck in their beast form, their power would be lessened. Maybe that would give the armies a fighting chance.

The narrow tunnel widened as they reached the dungeon. No one occupied the cells. Only empty shadows and barred cages lined the walls.

"What is this place?" Haven asked.

Julian glanced over her shoulder. "It's where they kept your sister and I."

Haven's nostrils flared and her brows descended over her eyes. Her fists clenched by her hips. Adni couldn't blame her for her anger. She'd been shocked the moment she found Julian and Astrid in the cages.

The group continued in silence, the squeak of their boots on the damp stone the only sound.

Cold sweat slid down Adni's spine as they passed the dungeon to the tunnel leading to the chasm. Soon they'd be at the Spyre. From the determined set of Julian's jaw, it was clear she still planned on sacrificing herself.

Her heartbeat sped as she pictured Julian turning into a dragon, only to knock down the Spyre and forever be stuck as a scaled beast. Adni would never feel her hand in hers, Julian's warm lips on her skin, or her fingers in her hair.

With each beat of her heart, Adni desperately reached for an idea, some way to stop Julian. She could lock her in the dungeon, or race into the Spyre as fast as she could. If Adni was inside, she was sure Julian wouldn't topple it. But Julian was fast. Could Adni be faster?

Wiping the sweat from her palms on her trousers, Adni glanced at Julian. The blonde didn't even glance her way, her gaze riveted on the pale cold light filtering in at the end of the tunnel.

"Leave the torches," Julian said. She released Adni's arm. "The stars will be enough to guide us."

The others propped their torches against the wall. There was no way to douse them, and it'd be best to keep a few for later in case they did survive and needed to flee the way they'd come.

Fresh air brushed the loose strands of hair from her cheeks. Winter light dusted Julian's blonde curls and steely eyes. Adni swallowed the lump in her throat as they emerged at the edge of the chasm. Stairs etched from stone ascended on one side, and descended into darkness on the other.

A demonic cry echoed from below, somewhere distant inside the earth. It rumbled and shook the ground as if the earth might split open.

Adni inspected the ledge around the chasm. There wasn't an ashen, human, or dragon in sight. She took a deep breath to calm her rattled nerves. That wouldn't last long. There was bound to be someone left to stop them.

"This way." Julian turned right, taking the steps up one at a time.

Adni followed, her feet leaden as they walked side by side. Her fingers tapped her thigh. She wanted to draw her sword. She needed something to hold, but she didn't want to appear foolish in front of the others.

Julian looked at her. Her lips turned down in a frown. Was this it? The last moments she'd have with Julian as she was?

Adni's eyebrows furrowed. She had to think of something. There had to be a way to keep Julian from sacrificing herself.

They reached the wide ledge of the chasm where the castle was carved from the mountainside and a bridge led to the Spyre.

Her heart raced as they gathered in the shadows. Pre-dawn light split the mountains at the far side. The sun would rise soon, on the day that was supposed to be theirs for the taking.

Julian turned to Adni. Her lips parted to speak.

Adni's heart leapt with panic. She couldn't let Julian say goodbye. She couldn't let this be it. Adni spun to the others. "Julian isn't who you think!" The words tumbled from her lips. What was she doing? What was she saying? "She's one of them."

Eyes widened all around her. Soldiers drew their swords as Julian's mouth dropped open.

"She's betrayed us all."

Adni's heart slowed. She'd said the words before she realized what she was doing, but now she knew. If the others knew what Julian was, they'd detain her. They'd stop her from transforming and hold her back while the others got inside the Spyre. Even if Julian could get away, they'd get inside first.

Julian stepped back as the others surrounded her.

"I won't let you give yourself up to save us," Adni whispered before they descended upon Julian.

Blythe and Malka grabbed Julian's arms, twisting them behind her back. Aura pointed her curved blade at Julian's throat, and Haven advanced with fury in her eyes.

"Is this true?" Haven snapped.

Julian didn't even glance at the Queen. Her gaze remained riveted on Adni. Flames licked her irises, and her nostrils flared with rage. It was the first time Adni might compare Julian to a terrifying beast like a dragon.

"Adni–" Julian started.

"Muzzle her before she gives us away." Haven narrowed her eyes.

A growl rumbled from Julian's throat, but before she could speak, Lareina tore a cloth from her pocket and shoved it between Julian's teeth. She tied it behind the woman's head to keep her from shouting.

"When did you find out about this?" Haven turned to Adni.

Her mind went blank. "I..." Her breath hissed between her teeth. "When we were escaping..." *That's it.* "I wasn't sure at first, but I saw her manipulating the fire." Was that plausible? Adni bit the inside of her cheek. Tears welled in her eyes. Betrayal darkened Julian's eyes, as it did Haven's, but that darkness receded at Adni's explanation.

"All right." Haven looked at the others. "We should hurry. They might not have counted on us getting away." The Queen returned her curved blades to their sheaths and stepped toward the Spyre. Her fingers turned to fists.

"Stay with her." Corrin jabbed a finger at Julian as he exchanged a meaningful look with Blythe. "We'll deal with her later." The Captain of the Queen's Guard nodded. He commanded for three other guards to remain with them, while the rest followed the Queen.

While Blythe and Malka wrestled Julian to the mountainside, Adni turned to the Spyre.

The dark piece of earth twisted from the small pedestal of rock on which it sat. The snake of molten rock that encircled the Spyre glowed in the coming dawn.

Adni gritted her teeth. She took one last look at Julian, who continued to glare daggers at her, before she joined the others. She had to do it. Even if Julian hated her, it was the only way to keep Julian and defeat the dragons too.

Haven led the way across the bridge, stones crunching beneath their boots. The Rythern and Wakefin guards surrounding them glanced back and forth at the mountains surrounding the chasm. Fear and determination clouded the eyes of all. An enemy that could fly from any direction would be a difficult enemy to defend against.

The Queen reached the other side. Though two guards normally stood on either side of the door, none did. She reached for the thick metal rings to open the doors and pulled. The door rattled, but didn't budge.

"Locked." Haven turned to the others.

Corrin joined her, taking the other metal ring and pulling. Again, the metal doors shook, but didn't open.

"We don't have time to find a way to pry them open," Nina said. The small blonde girl hovered beside Adni, shadows heavy in her normally bright eyes. She knew what Adni had done to Julian, but she said nothing. Did that mean Nina understood?

Adni looked up at the Spyre. It was about four stories high. Her last climb down had gone fairly smoothly. Would climbing up be any different? "We can climb," she said.

The others looked at her with raised brows and wide eyes. They might think her crazy, but Adni didn't see another way. If there was no time to find a way to pry the doors open, they had to scale the wall.

"She's right." Haven worked her jaw back and forth. "I don't like it, but it's the only way."

Corrin's brows furrowed as he looked at his wife. "She has as dangerous a mind as you."

Haven quirked a half-smile. "So it seems."

Adni flushed and shifted from foot to foot. Her heart raced as she looked at the windows on the top floor of the Spyre. The only windows on the whole structure. Was that on purpose to keep climbers at bay?

"I'll go first." Haven stepped up onto the stone railing of the bridge. Her fingers probed the stone wall until she found holds big enough to pull herself up.

"You might be immortal, but I doubt anyone could survive that fall." Corrin looked over the edge of the bridge, eyes wide. His half-smile disappeared.

"I've survived being crushed, drowned, and burned alive, my dear." Haven chuckled humorlessly as she hoisted herself up. "I'm not afraid of a little fall."

Adni glanced over the edge of the bridge. Her head spun as she looked into the chasm. It had to be miles deep. How could anyone survive such a fall, even the Queen?

Once Haven was up a few meters, Corrin motioned for Adni to go next. She had to lead the way to the Holy Fire. Corrin lent her his fingers, twining them together for her foot. Adni gulped and pressed her boot between his hands. He hoisted her up the wall as far as he could.

Adni leapt for a hold. Her fingers brushed damp stone before latching onto a rough ledge, part of the hardened molten lava ring. She took a deep breath as her pulse beat against her skin.

She could do this. She had no other choice.

Adni hoisted herself up. Every muscle in her arms quivered in protest. Maybe lifting herself up the side of the Spyre differed from climbing down it.

While Haven worked her way up with ease, Adni gritted her teeth with every move. She pressed her body as close to the Spyre as she could, digging her boots into the jagged stone. Cold, sharp edges nipped her fingertips. Her fingers stung as blood welled in the cuts.

She didn't dare glance down, even as the others grunted below her. Adni glanced up. Haven's boots were a foot above her hands. Her swords clicked against the stone and blood dripped down her fingers, but her brow was set. Adni had never seen a more determined woman in her life.

About a story above her head was the window, the one she'd climbed out of with Julian a few weeks ago.

Her lungs burned as she sucked in cold air. Only a few feet left, she told herself. Once they reached that window she'd never have to climb such a steep ledge again.

Sweat dripped down her back as she hoisted herself up to the next hold. Her muscles tensed and her arms ached. She could do this for Julian. She could do this for the six kingdoms. She could do this for herself and all those who couldn't.

Wind pushed against her shoulders, cold air threatening to tear her from the wall. Adni gripped the stone with all the force she could muster.

A loud swooping sound descended from the sky. Darkness blocked the coming sun. Adni froze, and her eyes widened. Her heart stopped.

What in blue skies was *that?*

A roar pierced the quiet of the chasm and her stomach fell to her boots. Her whole body shook as she looked over her shoulder, right into the ice blue eye of a scaled monster.

TWENTY-TWO

Black scales wrapped the cold blue eye and long snout. Horns curved away from the head and cheeks of its long skull. Its lips drew back, revealing rows and rows of jagged teeth.

A dragon.

Its wings spread to slow its descent, blocking out the entire sky. Finger-like claws curved from the edge of its wings, and a long pointed tail whipped behind it.

The beast dove, its eyes narrowed and its mouth ready to tear them all off the side of the Spyre.

Adni's breath caught in her throat. Her mind went blank. She was a fool to think she could combat a monster. Any second she'd join her family in death. Maybe being eaten alive wouldn't be so bad.

Thunder crashed from the chasm ledge beside the bridge to the Spyre. Heat scorched her skin and slicked her hands with sweat. Her head spun as she looked back; hardly able to believe she was taking her eyes off the creature that was about to be the death of her.

Blythe and Malka lay sprawled several feet from each other, staring up at the most beautiful thing Adni had ever seen.

A white and silver scaled dragon with a golden tongue and dark blue eyes leapt from where Julian once stood. Her screech tore through Adni's skull, digging into her mind and making her dizzy.

The dragons collided mid-air, mere feet from the Spyre. Their clawed hind feet slammed together, their talons wrapping around one another while their teeth snapped at the other dragon's neck.

Julian tumbled below, the other dragon in her grasp, or she in its. It was impossible to tell as they fell to the chasm floor.

The ground beneath them shook at the impact. Two roars, one deep like thunder, and the other sharp like lightning, ascended from below.

Adni shook from head to toe as she stared into the pit. Miles below the beasts rolled back and forth until they disappeared from sight. Julian was down there fighting for her life and theirs. And that eye. That ice cold iris.

Her heart clenched. She knew that color better than any, as it was her own.

Solipher.

Julian was battling her father.

"We've got to keep going!" Haven called.

Adni looked up into the Queen's widened hazel eyes. Though she might be terrified, Haven was handling this situation much better than she. Adni slowly nodded. Her fingers were numb against the stone. She couldn't even feel the bite of sharp rock against them anymore.

"Come on!" Haven continued upward.

Adni could do nothing but follow.

Haven disappeared over the window ledge seconds later. Adni heaved herself up one inch at a time. Her mind swirled and her limbs buzzed with exhaustion. But she had to keep going. There was no stopping now.

Gentle hands wrapped around her wrist.

Adni looked up. She was at the window.

"Let me help you," Haven said. Adni gripped the Queen's hand, and accepted her aid. Haven hauled her inside.

Adni collapsed on the carpet. The fabric was soft between her fingers. While she caught her breath, Haven helped the others inside one by one. First Corrin, then Nina, Lareina and two other Rythern guards. Each of their expressions mirrored the next.

Horror.

She wasn't the only one who doubted the reality of dragons. No one would doubt them now.

Adni stood as the others took a few minutes to gather themselves. Lareina retched in the corner; Haven pulling her hair back while Nina stared with wide eyes at the door out of the room. Her skin was pale and her blonde curls plastered to her forehead.

The room was the same one she'd been primped and bathed in, where she'd nearly given herself to the Holy Fire, but instead accepted her first kiss.

Her cheeks warmed as she remembered Julian's lips.

"Adni," Nina said.

She snapped out of her reverie, her eyes wide as she looked at the small woman.

Nina continued to stare at the metal doors, each carved with dragon heads. Her fingers shook as she pointed at them.

Adni followed her gaze. She didn't see anything out of the ordinary. The room was exactly the same as she'd left it. Something tingled along her skin, something hot that filled her chest with hunger.

Her heartbeat sped as she approached the doors. She hesitated, her fingers over the door handle. A muffled scream rang from beyond the door, hardly audible through the thick slab of metal.

Her pulse quickened, pounding harder and harder until she felt it behind her eyes. Adni's head spun as she wrenched the door open. The scream grew louder.

The group spun for the door, but Adni had already rushed inside.

"Adni!" Nina ran behind her.

She tore the doors open at the end of the hall.

The Holy Fire burned bright, blue fire licking the edges of the orange, white, yellow and red. It twisted and writhed inside the glass like an angry ocean storm. A thick white beam, like curling flames burst from the glass, linked to a man strapped to a thick black board of some kind.

His screams filled the chamber. Adni was surprised they hadn't heard them from outside. But the shutters were closed tight, holding the heat and magic inside.

Heat coursed through her arms to her fingers. Her mouth went dry and her head spun. Power vibrated inside the Holy Fire. Power she craved like she'd never craved anything before.

The cry of the man snapped her out of it. She recognized that voice.

Adni spun to face him. White hair and pale skin behind blue and white flames.

Kaldar. Her brother was being burned alive.

She froze. Kaldar was ashen. Kaldar was one of *them*. Why were they torturing him? *How* were they torturing him? And how was he still *alive*?

"He's not going to die, Adni." Nina narrowed her eyes at the bright light.

Adni spun to face her. She'd almost forgotten Nina could read minds. "How?"

Nina shook her head. "It's trying to tear the dragon magic out of him." She motioned to the glowing flames. "But it can't take the magic he was born with."

"So he's stuck burning alive?" Adni's heart dropped. Though he'd done nothing for her, he was still a person. He was still her half-brother. He wasn't inherently evil. Solipher had made him this way.

Nina nodded grimly.

"Is that it?" Haven appeared at their shoulders.

Adni and Nina exchanged a look.

"What's going on?" the Queen added.

Neither of them answered.

Haven advanced on the Holy Fire. She drew one of her curved blades. "Is he one of them?" Her knuckles went white around the hilt of her weapon, but she didn't point it at him. Instead, she turned to the fire. "Let him burn while I destroy it." She spun her sword in hand so the hilt faced down. Haven raised her arm to slam the butt of the hilt on the glass orb.

Adni leapt forward. She put herself between the Queen and the Holy Fire. Her heart rammed against her ribs. Sweat soaked her back as heat licked her spine. "You can't!"

Haven raised an eyebrow. "What are you talking about? Move."

Cold fear mingled with the heat of the flames. If Adni let Haven destroy the Holy Fire, Julian would be stuck in her dragon form forever. She looked at Kaldar. But if they didn't destroy the fire, her kin would continue to burn.

"I-I can't," Adni stuttered.

She was completely blowing her cover. They already believed she'd been betrayed by Julian. She had no excuse to explain this. They'd kill her to get to the flames. The lives of many were worth more than hers, and yet Adni's boots remained rooted to the floor.

Haven's eyes narrowed and she flipped her sword back into her hand, the tip pointed at Adni's throat. "Get out of my way."

Adni gulped, but she didn't move.

"Haven, wait a minute." Nina stepped up to Adni's side. "There's got to be another way around this."

Haven blanched. "Are you both *mad*? We need to destroy that thing *now*."

Adni shook her head. "If you do, Julian will be trapped inside that beast forever." Her fingers burned and her heart thudded painfully in her chest.

"I've had enough of this!" Haven reached for Adni's shoulder.

Adni ripped her sword from its sheath, forcing Haven to jump back out of the way. Her chest heaved as she pointed her blade at the Queen of Rythern. She couldn't believe she was doing this. She wanted to be *part* of the six kingdoms, not have them all against her. But when it came down to it, she'd rather have Julian than Warshard.

"You can't destroy it," Adni said. "Not yet."

The *shing* of swords filled the room as the others pulled their blades out. The tips faced Adni, even as Nina stepped in between her Queen and Adni.

"Stop this, all of you," Nina snapped. "You're being ridiculous. No one is killing each other here."

Adni glanced at the woman. Someone was thinking about killing her right now. Nina had confirmed it.

"Nina, I command you to move!" Haven growled. She bared her teeth and pulled her second sword from its sheath. The curved blades glinted in the bright light.

"I won't let you spill the blood of innocents, Haven." Nina stood firm, her fists clenched.

Haven snarled, her pretty face twisting into something ugly. "What do you propose then? We wait for the sky to fall and take it out? We wait until Julian *possibly* takes care of that other dragon? We don't have the time for this! Hundreds could be dying inside those tunnels!"

Nina stepped back, startled as if she hadn't considered that.

Haven was right, but still Adni stood in the way. It was the most selfish thing she'd ever done, but how far had being selfless ever gotten her? Pushed off a waterfall, turned into a power hungry monster, and her family killed. She was done putting all these people she didn't know before what mattered to her. If she allowed them to destroy the Holy Fire, she'd be left with nothing in this world.

Nina glanced back with wide eyes, as if begging Adni to reconsider.

Adni shook her head.

"I've had enough of this!" Haven pushed Nina aside. The small woman yelped as she fell to the floor.

Haven slashed a blade at Adni's. The metal clanged loudly against each other, audible even over her brother's scream.

The ground beneath her feet rumbled. Adni looked up over the shoulder of Haven. Through the long hall leading to the preparation chamber, she could see the outside world as it tilted sideways.

Her heart leapt as the ground fell from beneath her feet. The heat of the Holy Fire scorched her shoulder as it rolled by, the tingle of power following it until it left her skin cold with loss.

Everyone fell to the back wall, along with her screaming brother. He slammed against the wall seconds before Adni did. She skidded across the floor, grabbing the wall before she could fall through the hall door. Two of the Rythern guards flew backward into the hall, disappearing with the Holy Fire.

"Hang on!" Corrin gritted his teeth, his hand wrapped around Haven's wrist. He held on tight, Lareina holding onto him to keep him from following his wife out the window.

Haven's blades clattered down the corridor. Nina pulled herself over the doorframe as the Spyre lurched once more, pitching them downward into the chasm.

TWENTY-THREE

Clear air embraced Adni on all sides as the Spyre freefell. She was weightless for several long seconds that felt like hours. Everything moved slowly, each of them suspended in the open air.

The roar of dragons filled her ears as pressure built in her skull. Her head ached as the deafening screams racked the space behind her eyes.

This was it. This was the end. Julian got what she wanted after all. The Spyre was falling, but she was going along with it. That was a twist she hadn't expected.

The falling stopped, and her entire body slammed against the wall of the chamber. Air exploded from her lungs. She sucked in a gasp, pain burning her chest. She lost her grip on her sword as she twisted onto her back, pulling in air with all of her might.

"Is everyone all right?" someone asked.

Adni's head spun. She blinked back white stars encroaching on her vision. She was alive. Really, truly alive. But how?

"I'm fine," Haven said.

Adni looked up. Haven pushed away the hands of Lareina and Corrin, glaring at them as they fussed over her wellbeing.

Nina leaned beside them, blinking slowly as if waking from a deep sleep.

Once she got her breath, Adni rolled onto her belly and looked over the doorway into the tilted corridor below. They landed at a slant, but the missing Rythern guards were nowhere to be found.

The glass of the Holy Fire lay twenty feet below, smashed into a thousand pieces. Black scorched the earth where the flames had exploded.

"Is he all right?" Lareina pointed over Adni's shoulder.

Kaldar lay beside Adni. The flames had disappeared, leaving his skin red instead of white. He was unconscious, the board at his back broken and his hands slipping from his restraints. Through all of that, his chest still rose and fell.

"He's alive," Adni said.

An agony filled cry, like the last sound of a dying animal rumbled through the tower. Adni's eyes flew wide and she leaned over the doorway again. A white scaled wing swung into view.

Julian.

Adni's heart lurched. She flung herself over the edge of the doorway and slid along the hall into the preparation chamber. Shattered glass littered the remains of dark wood furnishings. The stone tub lie upside down at the far end, and the closet doors spilled gorgeous silks in every color.

She braced herself on the stone window frame. "Julian?" she called. Her heart sped as she kneeled against the hard stone. It dug into her knees as she leaned out.

The same pained cry rumbled louder.

Julian had saved them. Though she was sure it was the fight that collapsed the tower in the first place, Julian had stopped its fall to save their lives, even if it meant her own.

Her fingers shook as she looked back up at the hall. Her eyes burned and her legs gave out beneath her. "We need to get out," Adni said. Her voice was hardly a whisper. She cleared her throat, as if that'd stop the sadness building inside her chest. "We need to get out!" she yelled. Her voice cracked as her fingers wrapped around the windowsill. They needed to get out of the Spyre so Julian could let it go and get free of it. She'd hardly have any space to maneuver with the chasm floor so close.

The rustle of the others brushed her ears faintly. She reached down to touch Julian's wing. Her scales were rough, and her wing trembled either at her touch or the sheer strength it took to hold up the entire tower.

"Julian..." What was Adni supposed to say? She was sorry? She should have let her go along with her insane plan? Julian saved her life, even though Adni had betrayed her.

Gentle fingers lie on her shoulder. Nina appeared beside her, warmth and understanding in her big eyes. "We brought... him," she said, careful to avoid calling Kaldar her brother.

Adni silently thanked her. "We need to get out." She coughed to clear the desperate sob threatening to burst from her lungs.

Nina nodded. "She wants us to climb out this window."

Adni gripped the window tightly. "All right." She glanced back at the others. Corrin carried Kaldar, and Haven followed Lareina last down the corridor. Her harsh gaze cut into Adni like knives. The Queen hadn't forgotten what Adni had done.

But there was no time to deal with it now. Adni took a deep breath and slipped through the window. Her arms held her up until her boots brushed Julian's outstretched wing.

The stone Spyre lie directly across Julian's back, crushing the spikes along her spine and tail. Her wing trembled under Adni's feet. It stretched from the window to the chasm ledge where they'd be able to climb down to the chasm stairs. The peak of the tower had crashed against the mountainside, and rubble descended on the path, but it'd be useable.

Dark blue eyes flashed under the mass of stone and scale. Julian blinked at her as Adni walked carefully across Julian's rigid wing.

"Hurry!" Adni looked over her shoulder as Nina followed.

"Come on! Corrin get down here," Nina said.

Corrin slid down next and held out his arms to accept Kaldar.

Once the four of them were on Julian's wing, another rumble shook the cliff side. Julian couldn't hold all of them.

Adni rushed across the curve of her wing and leapt onto the stone steps etched from the chasm wall. Nina joined her, and soon the rest of them had evacuated and stood at the edge of the chasm.

A roar joined the rumble of the stone tower atop Julian's back. She looked up as a dark beast descended from the sky, a long bloody scratch diagonal across his face.

Pride swelled in her chest. Julian had done that. She'd hurt Solipher.

"Get back against the wall!" Nina slammed her outstretched arm against Adni's chest, forcing her back against the stone wall.

The rubble atop Julian lurched sideways and spilled off her back. Julian twisted down, her claws sinking into the wall and her face pressing against it until the remains of the Spyre fell.

They crashed against the chasm floor, echoing in the wide space. Dust rose from the remains, clouding the air with ash. Adni's eyebrows furrowed. She never realized the floor of the chasm was covered in ash.

"Lady Queen!" Blythe called.

The Captain of the Queen's Guard, and Malka descended the steps above them, eyes wide and swords drawn. Malka had her bow drawn and arrow notched. She pointed the tip at Solipher as he sailed passed after Julian.

Julian pushed off the chasm wall. The earth shook beneath them as she lunged away, twisting in midair and expanding her wings. She dove low before soaring high, Solipher on her tail.

"What in blue skies is going on?" Malka snapped.

"Are you all right, Lady Queen?" Blythe picked her way over the rubble against the mountainside. The fall of the Spyre hadn't completely torn away the stairs, but it was about to.

The roars and snaps of beasts filled the air again as Solipher chased Julian. Red dripped down Julian's white-scaled maw, bloodying her teeth and throat.

"She's hurt," Adni cried. Far worse than Adni had thought. She had to help Julian. She had to do *something*.

Blythe and Malka joined them on the ledge; Blythe checking over the Queen while Malka knelt by Kaldar's side, lowering her weapon. Adni had an idea.

Leaping passed them, Adni snatched Malka's bow and quiver from her grasp. Her heart pounded in her ears as she jumped across the rubble on the steps, ascending the stairs wrapping the chasm.

"Adni, wait!" Nina called. The pound of boots followed behind her.

Adni slipped the quiver over her shoulder and fixed an arrow to the bow. She'd always been better with a bow and arrow than a sword. She notched the arrow and took aim at the black dragon snapping at Julian's tail.

There's no way she was letting Solipher take someone else from her. Even if she could never speak with Julian again, she still wanted her to go on living. The fire of her rage stole her breath as Adni shot off arrow after arrow at her father.

Each sailed right for his belly, his wing, his throat, but the sharp metal point clinked off his scales to descend into the pit below. They were useless. She was useless.

How had Julian ever expected her to control dragons?

They were *beasts*, hundreds of times larger than she, and far more powerful than she could ever hope to be. But she had to do something. So Adni continued to shoot, looking for a weak spot between his scales, his teeth, and his claws.

Adni stopped running, gasping for air. She'd reached the ledge where the bridge to the Spyre remained. Her chest heaved and her hands shook as she took aim again. She followed his movements, the spin of his shoulders and trail of his wings as he arched to follow Julian's quick movements.

Solipher slammed against Julian, throwing her into the pedestal of earth where the Spyre had once been.

"Solipher!" Adni screamed. Her fingers trembled as his icy gaze whipped in her direction. Ash poured from his nostrils.

She shot.

His scream sent her to her knees as the tip of her arrow pierced his eye. The glowing orb exploded and Adni covered her ears. The others collapsed beside her, writhing on the ground. Stars flew across her vision, black, and calling her into unconsciousness.

Adni blinked them back as quickly as she could. She wouldn't let Solipher win. Not this time. The fire of magic flew across her skin. Her heart leapt as she looked up.

Shadows writhed in Solipher's open maw, like black fire amassing between his teeth.

Adni got one foot beneath her. She wouldn't let Solipher destroy all of these people. She couldn't let him kill Julian either.

Darkness blasted from his mouth. Adni threw her hands out, letting all the power hungry hate she could muster pour from her fingers. His shadows crested over them like a wave, flying above her fingers and crashing into the chasm wall.

Earth and stone exploded outward, sending shrapnel in every direction.

Adni threw herself to the earth, her hands over her head. Rocks pelted the ground all around her. Dust filled her nose.

She'd done it. She'd controlled her father's magic.

She coughed up the dust filling her lungs. But in doing so she'd given herself up. Adni glanced under her arm. She caught the widened gazes and dropped jaws of the Queen and her guards. Even of Nina, and her brother, who opened his eyes at last. Confusion flashed through his eyes as he looked between Adni and their father.

Pride and dread swelled inside her chest. She may have saved their lives, but her cover was blown.

TWENTY-FOUR

All eyes were on Adni as she pulled herself to her feet. Her limbs were sore, and her body weary, but her smile wouldn't be tamed. Magic burned along her fingers, tempting her to use it again. Taunting her to.

Adni faced her father. Even in his dragon form, she could feel his shock. His one eye widened and his mouth was half open, hesitant in what to do.

White flashed behind him. Adni gasped. "Julian, wait!"

Julian sunk her teeth into Solipher's neck. He cried out and twisted midair, slapping Julian off him, and back into the Spyre's pedestal. She lay immobile beside the bridge, her eyes half closed and her golden tongue lolled onto the ground.

"No!" Adni froze. Her eyes widened.

Over his shock, Solipher spun toward her, wings flared outward, blocking the red dawn at his back.

"Damn you." Adni hissed between her teeth.

Fire boiled along her arms and into her clenched fists. Let him come at her. Let him throw more shadows at her. Adni would end him before the sun crested the distant mountain peaks.

Solipher dove, his mouth wide open as if he wanted to eat her.

Adni dove to the side. Solipher crashed against the ledge. Stone fell away into the chasm. His teeth sunk into rock. He twisted his head, throwing a mouthful over his shoulder.

She leapt to her feet, eyes widened as he turned his one-eyed gaze back on her. Clouded slime dripped down the other side of his face where his eye had once been. His nostrils flared, ash pouring from within.

He dove again, snapping at her heels.

Adni leapt away. A shadow moved in her peripheral. She spun as Kaldar lurched from his spot on the ground. He tore one of Haven's curved blades from its sheath and pointed it at his father.

Surprise quickened her heart. Kaldar was going to fight with her. Whether it be for revenge or to save himself, she didn't care. Adni wasn't alone in this fight.

Kaldar's familiar blue gaze met hers. He nodded curtly. Adni mimicked him before turning to face Solipher's hulking form.

Solipher's eye shifted between them. The slit of his pupil narrowed further. A growl rumbled from his chest. He was angry. But it wasn't Kaldar who betrayed his father. No matter what Kal had done to deserve torture by the Holy Fire, Solipher was the betrayer here.

The dragon pushed away from the mountainside. It shook beneath Adni's feet as Solipher twisted through the air before turning to face them. Blackness dripped from his fangs like blood. His jaw widened and darkness burst forth in a blast like fire.

Adni tensed as she threw her hands out. Magic burned across her fingers as she took his darkness and twisted it back around. It writhed through her hands, around her hips and shot back at Solipher's head.

He plummeted through the air into the chasm to avoid his own magic before returning with a roar and another shadowed blast.

Again, Adni stole his power. The heat curved across her shoulders, curling from her feet, just above her head. It wrapped her arms and waist like a serpent. This shadow was hers. She could use it to combat her father as long as she kept fire in her heart and hunger on her tongue.

Arrows arched through the air at Solipher's head. They bounced off his scaled skull. He swatted them away like flies and dove at the Queen and her guards.

Kaldar lunged across the ledge. Solipher slammed against the wall, the curved claws atop his wings digging into the floor to hold him. He snapped at Nina, but she was fast and leapt from his teeth.

Adni raced across the ledge to aid them, but Kaldar was closer. His blade sliced across Solipher's cheek, cracking bits of his scales. They flaked to the earth with Solipher's scream. The dragon lurched back as Adni threw her hand out.

Shadows burst from the mass wrapping her hips. They crashed against Solipher's wing, tearing through part of the thick leather-like skin.

A smile spread across her face. They could do this. They could defeat a dragon. Never in her wildest dreams could she believe it.

Kaldar shot forward, slicing a clean line through the skin the missing scales revealed.

Solipher roared, the sound driving knives through her ears. Her head spun, and her feet slowed. Something hard and scaled slammed into her back, throwing her across the ledge. Her father's tail. She crashed against the stone wall of the chasm. Pain stole her breath as she collapsed on the floor. Her fingers trembled against the cold stone. The flames of hunger were gone. The darkness wrapping her shoulders was gone.

"Adni!" Nina called. Boots slapped against the rock until they paused by her side. Gentle fingers wrapped her upper arm. "You've got to get up."

Adni winced as pain speared her back. "I lost it," she panted. Warmth flickered over her fingers as Nina hauled her to her feet. Flashes of darkness, of blood, and of her dead family flew across her vision. Nausea roiled through her stomach, and her legs buckled.

"Apologies," Nina whispered. She didn't release Adni, or let her return to her knees. Instead she propped Adni up against the wall before letting her go.

The nausea fled her stomach and the images receded, leaving her dizzy. So that's what happened when a mind reader touched someone.

Kaldar's battle cry rang out as he lunged at Solipher, slicing at the scales on his snout and cheeks. Scales burst from Solipher's thick hide. Blood welled in the cuts both Kaldar and Julian had left.

A rumble like thunder escaped Solipher's jaw. He slammed the side of his snout against Kaldar, sending him rolling across the ledge. Black welled between his teeth and blew from his mouth. Haven and the others leapt aside as the blast was turned from one end of the ledge to the other.

"Your brother needs you," Nina said.

Adni took a deep breath. The pain inside her bones had already lessened. She didn't have any more time to heal. She needed to attack while Solipher was distracted. Pulling back the fire to her fingers and the desire for power into her bones, Adni reached out to the black flames.

Shadows rolled from the main blast, into her grasp. She pushed out, thrusting them at Solipher.

They slammed against his chest, throwing him from the chasm ledge. His pained cry vibrated into her skull. His claws scraped stone as he pulled himself back up over the ledge. His tail flicked back and forth like a cat, threatening to throw anyone nearby into the pit below.

Kaldar got his feet beneath him and stood at her side. He wiped the sweat from his brow and pointed his blade at their father.

Adni pulled the shadows in her hands, molding them into the shape of a blade. She gripped the hilt. It was solid beneath her fingers, even as shadowy flames licked the makeshift blade.

Solipher snarled as he rocketed forward, throwing stone up beneath his claws. Nina dove toward the entrance of the stone castle, while Adni leapt forward. Her heart pounded in her skull as she sliced at his throat. She twisted beneath his large body, ducking low to the ground as she tore the tip of her blade along his underbelly.

He roared and thrashed his head side to side. Kaldar ducked, slamming his chest against the ground as Solipher's spiked skull crashed against the mountain wall. Large stones fell from the castle wall where his head had hit. He twisted to face the mountainside.

Adni raced below his chest, slicing every which way. If he wanted her out from beneath him, he'd have to fly away. Her blade cut through his scales. The thick pieces ticked against her shoulders before falling to the ground. She drove her blade at his exposed skin. Heat seared her shoulders as blood dripped from his open wounds.

Solipher leapt. Her blade sailed through clear air.

Wind thrust her to the ground. It tore at her hair and clothes, throwing her across the ledge with each beat of his wings. Solipher screeched, but Adni could hardly hear it over the pounding of wind on her ears.

She drove her blade into the ground to keep from flying back. Kaldar had already done the same. He looked at her, gritting his teeth. His knuckles were white on the hilt of his sword.

His lips moved to speak. She couldn't hear anything over the whoosh of air against her head.

He repeated himself, moving his mouth slowly so she could read his lips.

Follow. My. Lead.

Adni's eyebrows furrowed, but she nodded. They'd have to work together to defeat Solipher. He was far too large, maybe even too powerful for one of them.

The wind died suddenly. Kaldar leapt to his feet, faster than she'd ever seen a person move.

"Shield!" he shouted. His gaze flashed over to Blythe. The Queen's Guard didn't hesitate in throwing her heavy steel shield.

Kaldar caught it and dropped to one knee by the cliff edge as Solipher dove closer. Adni stood, her legs shaking beneath her. Confusion spiralled through her head. The heat in her fingers flickered. She clenched her fists and focused the hunger in her bones.

Her brother looked back at her as he braced the shield on his back and arms. He dropped his sword and looked at her meaningfully, glancing up at the shield. He pushed it up slightly, a motion as if he might throw someone from the top of his shield.

Understanding blossomed. Adni's eyebrows rose high on her forehead as she looked between Solipher's hulking shape, wings bending outward as he sailed through the sky, and Kaldar, ready to throw her from his shield as high as he could.

Adni gulped. Flames flickered through her chest. This was it. She ran, her boots slapping the damp stone as she raced across the wide ledge. Darkness continued to pour from her fingers in the shape of a sword. She held it tightly as she leapt on top of the shield.

Kaldar pushed upward, throwing her with all of his might. Adni threw a hand down, sending some of the darkness still wrapping her waist in a huge blast. All she had left was her sword. If this didn't work they were all dead.

Wind embraced her on all sides as she flew through the air. Time seemed to slow as she neared Solipher's long snout. His thin lips pulled back and his bright eye flashed. His mouth widened, revealing terrifying rows of sharp teeth.

Adni steeled herself. A battle cry she'd never imagined coming from her own throat flew from between her lips.

Flames of power burned along her skin as she finally landed right on Solipher's tongue. The stench of ash filled her nostrils as hot breath poured across her skin. The ground gave way beneath her, his tongue flicking against her side as he started to slam his mouth shut, ready to eat her alive.

Adni twisted her blade in her hands. Gripping the hilt with all of her strength, she thrust up, driving the tip of her blade through the roof of his mouth, into his brain. His breath stopped. His jaw froze, not even half way closed.

Her heart slammed against her ribs as she twisted her hands, pushing the blade in until only the hilt remained.

Solipher shuddered, and his body went slack.

His jaw fell beneath her. Everything fell. She fell. It was as if she were freefalling inside the Spyre again. But instead of a white and gold room on every side of her, she flew from Solipher's mouth into open air.

Her breath fled her lungs and cold rushed across her skin.

Damp air bit her face as the ledge of the chasm rushed up at her.

She was so high, dozens of feet in the air. If her body hit the ground, she'd die instantly.

Adni shut her eyes. This was it.

She'd stopped Solipher from wreaking havoc on the six kingdoms once more. She'd stopped him from summoning more ancient dragons from the earth. She'd stopped him once and for all.

Something hard and warm wrapped around her shoulders. Strong hands grabbed her arms. Adni slammed against the ground, intertwined with someone. She opened her eyes as the world rolled around her. Her shoulders and legs cracked against the ground over and over, but her head was protected in Kaldar's arms.

They crashed against the castle wall. Hot breath bathed her face as her own breath burst from her lungs.

Pain shot through her chest and blackness flew across her vision.

Adni came gasping back to consciousness, her cheek pressed against cold stone. A hum filled her ears and buzzed through her skull. She looked up, and everything tilted sideways.

She lay still for several long moments, her whole body on fire.

Had she done it? Had she killed Solipher?

Her ears rang and the spinning in her head slowly stopped. She blinked rapidly as someone gently pried Adni and her brother apart. Her entire body ached. Her head ached. Her *mind* ached, strained from concentrating on controlling Solipher's magic.

"Don't move them too much!" Lareina's voice cut through the pounding in her ears. "They might have broken bones."

Kaldar coughed loudly. His arm shook against hers.

"Careful, careful!" Lareina snapped.

"Adni, can you hear me?" Nina's soft voice was close to her face.

The grey sky shone overhead, dark clouds receding to show blue sky. Adni blinked slowly, trying to pull sense back into herself. Everything felt fuzzy and confused.

"Y-yes," Adni said.

A sigh of relief. "Good." Nina's fingers squeezed hers briefly before the touch disappeared.

"Is everyone else all right?" Haven's authoritative voice took over.

Each person said yes one by one. Blythe, Malka, Lareina, Corrin, Aura and the other guards were all fine. Though they were all scraped and bruised, no one would die today. Not even her.

Adni's heart leapt. They might all be okay, but what about Julian?

She sat up quickly. Everything spun. Adni groaned loudly. Warm hands tried to push her back down.

"Don't get up yet!" Lareina gasped.

Adni slapped her fingers aside. "Julian!" A cough exploded from her chest. She propped herself up, pushing her dizziness aside. "Is she all right?"

She sat up. Lareina and Nina stepped out of her line of sight, exchanging concerned glances.

Everyone looked at Julian. The large white dragon had collapsed across the floor of where the Spyre had once been. Her hind legs and tail dangled off the edge, while her chest, long neck, and head remained atop the jagged rock.

Adni's heart raced as she pushed to her feet.

"Adni, wait!" Lareina said.

There was no time to let herself heal. Dragon healing was fast, but not fast enough. She needed to make sure Julian was okay. She needed to make sure she was *alive*.

Adni tripped and stuttered her way across the chasm ledge to the bridge. Her hands slammed against the stone railing. She took several deep breaths. Pain pierced her side. Her ribs might be broken, or bruised. She couldn't tell. She'd never had such a bad injury before.

Forcing her feet forward, Adni limped across the bridge to the other side.

Cold wind pushed her hair back. She reached Julian's large dragon head and collapsed by her side. Her knees slammed against rock. Pain speared her legs, but she ignored it.

Adni lay her hands on Julian's thick scales. Some were torn away. Jagged cuts flared red across her exposed skin. Blood dripped between her teeth, a small pool forming under her pure white maw.

Her heart fluttered as she felt across Julian's scales for a pulse.

"Julian," Adni whispered. Tears stung the back of her eyes. "Julian?"

Julian's scales were chilled. Her skin was cool. Was dragon's skin always this cold? Adni had no idea.

"Julian, please move, or make a noise, or something!" Her voice cracked as her fingers ran over hard, leather-like skin. "Julian, *please!*"

Her heart raced as tears burned her eyes. Heat filled her chest. This wasn't fair. Julian had been through so much. She'd found Adni and saved her. She'd saved her from death more than once. She'd saved her from being a monster. She'd saved her from a long lonely life never knowing what she was.

Julian wasn't allowed to die. She just wasn't.

"If you die, I'll never forgive you." Adni wrapped her arms around what she could of Julian's throat. Something beat against her chest. Her heart leapt. It was faint, but it was there. "Julian!" She felt beside her eye.

The thick eyelids parted to reveal Julian's beautiful dark blue eye.

"Julian, you're alive." Tears burned down her cheeks. Wet pooled against her collarbone.

Julian's eye shut again and her entire body shuddered out one last breath.

TWENTY-FIVE

"Julian?" Her heart hammered louder than the wind rushing against her ears. *"Julian?"* Adni shook her large head. Julian didn't open her eyes. She didn't move. Her heart didn't beat. She didn't make a sound.

Had that been Julian's last breath?

"You *idiot,*" Adni cried. "Why did you have to protect us? Why did you have to save our stupid lives?" Her eyes burned. Her chest burned. Everything burned inside her like a well of fire she couldn't climb out of. "You should have let us fall. You could have killed Solipher yourself! You could have ended all of this and saved yourself if you'd just let us *die!*"

Her fingers trembled on Julian's scales. Her hands balled into fists. She slammed them down on Julian's cheek next to three large horns jutting from her jaw. Adni hit her again and again as the fire inside her burned brighter.

"Julian, you can't leave me. I'll never forgive you if you die!" Adni pressed her forehead against Julian's cold skin. "I'll never forgive you."

Her fists unclenched. She ran her fingers over the curve of her scales and smooth horns. She'd never imagined such a creature existed. She'd never imagined someone like Julian existed. And yet, dragons were real, and she was one of them.

"Please don't go."

Tears fell from her eyes again and again. She couldn't stop them any more than she could stop the tremble in her voice or the flames of despair threatening to swallow her.

"Please! I know why you lied, but you have to live so I can forgive you." Adni squeezed her eyes shut. *"Please..."*

The scales were rough against her face, nipping at her skin. She hardly felt it over the magic burn that ran through her fingers.

She gasped, and her eyes flashed open. Power ran through her chest and down her arms. Julian's large eye flew wide open, her pupil small and narrow.

Julian tensed, her muscles rigid, shaking a few small stones loose. They clattered across the ground as gold welled in the white of Julian's chest as if she were about to breathe fire. It burned bright, rising through her throat. Heat built in the cold air.

Adni sat back, in awe, as Julian opened her mouth. Her hands tingled as a large golden ball with white flames licking its edges slid from Julian's throat, onto the earth. Adni covered her eyes, blinded by the brilliant light. Her whole body shook as the glow died down. Some kind of thick dragon glass circled the ball. White flames writhed inside and out.

The Holy Fire.

Julian's scales glowed brighter than the sun. Again, Adni shielded her eyes as knives pierced her skull. Her heart fluttered as warmth bathed her skin.

And then gentle fingers brushed her arm. "Adni?"

Adni's heart leapt. She lowered her hands. Julian stared back at her, golden hair, and big, brilliant blue eyes. Her lashes were as long as ever, and her smile just as sweet as Adni remembered.

"Julian." Tears welled in her eyes. The burn of despair was replaced with a joy she'd never known. Adni pulled Julian into her arms. Her warmth encircled her. "You're alive." Her fingers wrapped around Julian's arms, clutching the worn fabric.

"Thanks to you." Julian brushed the loose strands of hair from Adni's forehead. Her fingers trembled. "Ow."

"Sorry." Adni sat back, confusion flashing cold through her elation. Dry blood clung to Julian's chin and a large bruise and jagged cut ran across her cheek. "How?" The flames of magic still burned across her mind, but they didn't draw the same hunger she was used to. Instead they spread warmth through her very soul.

"You forced the magic out of me." Julian nodded at the small sun bathing them in warm light. She blinked slowly as if sitting up took all of her energy. "My great-grandmother created the first Holy Fire. I didn't know I could create one too."

Adni glanced between the flames and Julian's beautiful face. Whatever had brought Julian back to her, Adni didn't care. Leaning forward, Adni pressed her lips against Julian's. She wrapped her arms around her, her fingers in her soft hair. Julian tasted like sun, and magic, and fresh rain. She was everything good in the world, and everything Adni ever wanted to have again.

Julian pulled her closer, even though it must hurt to do so, until they weren't kissing anymore, they were crying in each other's arms.

Adni shivered against her, and bit back a sob. She pressed her face into the crook of Julian's shoulder and didn't let go for anything. "You're such an idiot," she mumbled. Tears dripped down her cheeks.

Julian shook as she laughed. "I love you."

Adni pressed her lips to Julian's cheek. She sighed with a relief she didn't know was possible. "I love you too."

TWENTY-SIX

The rumble of an army ascended from the chasm floor. King Emeril and his warrior wife, Rona greeted Haven and the others. Each of them embraced, overjoyed to find one another alive. Emeril filled them in on the happenings in the tunnels. Though hundreds were surely dead, many of them had found shelter in other tunnel systems, finding ways to the surface. Some even sealed the dragons inside the tunnels, using their own brutal force against them.

Though some dragons had to remain, they hadn't made a sound since the Holy Fire was destroyed. Julian explained that without the magic of the original Holy Fire, the one the dragons were bound to, their magic would be weakened, as would the ashen's.

Her gaze lingered on the glowing orb hovering slightly above where the Spyre had once been. Magic fire pulled at her insides, trying to draw her near. Julian squeezed her fingers. She knew the pull Adni would be feeling, but as Julian had said, there wasn't much they could do with the Holy Fire. Adni might be able to move it, but something was different about this one. The flames were pure gold, like a small glowing sun.

Though Adni felt the pull of magic, it wasn't the same dark hunger she remembered of the old one. What would happen if a dragon or ashen bound themselves to this Holy Fire?

Dozens of people Adni scarcely recognized flooded from the great doors of ashen and dragon family dwellings. The half-breeds emerged wide-eyed and confused from the tunnels. Adni started in surprise. She'd forgotten all about them. Did they still have their magic?

Adni looked for Kaldar. He was nowhere to be seen.

Her eyebrows furrowed as she inspected the chasm ledge. Not a flash of white hair in sight.

A scream pierced the silence that had descended over Izenfir.

Several ashen collapsed to their knees in tears. Some screamed at the top of their lungs, while others embraced them.

"Wait!" someone shouted.

A man with blond hair and wide, sightless eyes threw himself over the ledge. Valeria's brother. He fell into the darkness of the pit.

Adni gasped and shot to her feet. Julian joined her, standing precariously at her side. She was still injured, but her eyes widened in confusion all the same.

"Stop them!" Nina pointed at the ashen along the chasm ledge. Rythern and Wakefin guards rushed toward the ashen.

A young woman with dark hair and darker eyes stepped off the ledge next. Another was held back by several of his brethren while he screamed for them to let him go.

"What's happening?" Adni looked at Julian.

"I don't know." Julian shook her head.

Nina stood by the end of the bridge, her eyes wide and filled with tears as she watched the wave of soldiers pin down as many of the remaining ashen as they could.

Adni wrapped her arm around Julian, who leaned heavily against her side. Blood mangled almost her entire back, but still she managed to stand. Dragon healing at work. Together they made it across the stone bridge to Nina's side.

"What's going on?" Adni asked.

Nina turned wide eyes on them both. She trembled terribly. "They're waking up."

Adni's eyebrows furrowed, but understanding blossomed on Julian's face. "They've lost their dragon magic. They have no dark mask left to hide behind," Julian explained.

Cold shock stabbed her chest. She remembered what it had been like coming back from the dark void. It was like cresting the surface of a cold lake. Everything came rushing back in one giant wave.

What had all of these ashen done in the time they'd been here? How many people had they killed or tortured? What atrocities had they committed to make them kill themselves?

Once the ashen were secured, they were rounded up, bound and guarded. Adni recognized Valeria. Her flaming red hair was limp, and dread filled her wide blue eyes. She stared sightless at the ground. None of the fierce fire that Adni remembered was left inside her eyes.

Adni gulped. Would they be held accountable for their actions? After all, no one but them knew what it was like to give up; to give in to the magic hunger. They didn't understand the burning desire, or the anger, the hatred. And to have all of that ripped away suddenly, they'd be back to some state of themselves, something they might not have felt in years. A strange protectiveness washed through her.

"You're right," Nina said.

Adni started. She still wasn't used to having a mind reader around.

"There are bound to be trials for each of them." Nina sighed. "Someone will need to speak on their behalf."

Adni glanced between Nina and Julian. "You can read their thoughts, wouldn't you be able to speak for them?"

Nina shook her head. "Their minds are filled with despair and self-loathing. It will be hard to get through it all and decipher what they think they deserve, versus what they *actually* deserve as punishment."

"They need help to accept what they've done, not a trial." Julian's fists clenched.

Adni had to agree.

"I know, but…" Nina looked back at Haven and the other royals. They stood in a close group with a few of their personal guards. "It won't be easy to sway the others."

Adni's nostrils flared. Someone who had no idea what it was like shouldn't be able to decide the fate of dozens. Even if they had done terrible things, it wasn't *them* who'd done it. It was the power. The hunger. The *beastly* part of them that no longer had control.

"We'll figure it out, Adni." Nina met her gaze.

She sighed. "I suppose we will."

As the ashen were finally set to leave, and the slaves freed from their quarters, the army returned to the chasm floor to find their tunnel to freedom. They left the Holy Fire for now, as there was no way to bring it with them. One day they'd return and see what they could learn from it.

Adni looked to the mines that had once occupied the base of the volcano. The remains of the Spyre blocked the mouth of the cavern leading into the earth. It'd be next to impossible to remove all the stone. Good. Warshard didn't need another war with dragons.

IF IT WAS POSSIBLE, the journey back to Palmyra was longer than the journey to Izenfir had been. Days felt like weeks, maybe even months. Though Adni and Julian had been pardoned by the Queen, dread still sat inside her stomach. With every passing second Adni was left to wonder if her family was still alive. Had Solipher truly killed them? Or was it all a ruse to convince her to turn over her humanity and embrace power?

The closer they drew to Palmyra, the more her heart raced. Once they arrived at the castle, she'd get her answers. Haven had sent word to Salander before they left. Surely a response had to have arrived by now? How long had it been since she left her hometown? How long had it been since she left her family to fend for themselves?

Even if Solipher hadn't killed them, had they died of starvation? Could bandits have taken what little they had left? Terrible thoughts and possibilities circled her mind all day and night. With the rumble of horse hooves in her ears, it was impossible to talk to Julian while they rode. And by night she was far too exhausted for lengthy conversation.

So when the peaks of Palmyra castle finally rose on the horizon almost a week after Solipher's demise, anxiety swarmed her heart and lent sweat to her hands. Her fingers squeezed her leather reins.

Soon she'd find out, whatever the answer might be.

The army descended the hills into the city, narrowing into two horse wide lines to get through the streets to the palace.

Her knuckles went white around her reins and her stomach soured. Was she ready to find out what had happened to her family? Was she ready to face that despair again?

"You're going to worry yourself into oblivion," Julian said.

Adni looked at her. Though Julian's teasing smile usually sent butterflies fluttering through her stomach, the distraction didn't help this time. Her eyebrows pulled together, worry creasing her forehead.

"What if they're all dead?" Adni's heart thudded painfully inside her chest.

Julian smile faltered. "Don't think like that."

With the dying wind, and clop of hooves on cobblestone, finally they could speak. "He showed me, Julian. What else am I supposed to think?"

"Anything but that." Julian sighed.

Adni looked forward. The palace rose in the distance, the highest point of the city. It'd take an hour to reach it at least, and even longer to find someone who could give her answers. She bit the inside of her cheek, frustration burning through her fingers.

She had to be patient. They were almost there, and then she'd have closure, no matter the answer.

* * *

"What do you mean no word has arrived?" Adni snapped.

Haven sighed. She held her hands in her lap. They sat in Adni's sitting room in the same chamber she'd been given before they left. Her heart raced, fury nipping at every inch of her.

"There must have been some confusion in Ithrendel after King Emeril departed. No one has returned word of your family's status yet." Haven had already explained it once, and Adni had forced her to explain it again.

"How could this have happened?" Adni threw her hands up. She'd been beyond patient at this point, waiting weeks to discover the fate of her loved ones. And yet, she was right back where she started. No word. No information. "I need to know if they're all right."

Haven twisted a gold ring around her finger. "I'm sorry, Adni. I don't know what happened."

Adni leaned back against the plush sofa, resting her skull on the hard wooden back. She stared at the vaulted ceiling, tears burning the back of her eyes. She would not allow herself to cry again, not in front of a queen she still felt indebted to for her deception.

"King Emeril will be returning to Salander soon. I'll give him the information myself, and I'm sure he'll personally see to it someone looks for your family," Haven said.

It was so painfully reasonable. Adni raised her head from the back of the sofa. "No, thank you, Lady Queen." She shook her head. "I'll go myself."

Haven froze. "Are you certain?"

There was still so much left to see to, so much left to discuss. Adni was the only ashen that could be trusted, and Palmyra was suddenly flooded with dozens no one knew. There'd be a lengthy trial for each of them, even if none were in the state for one. Half of them had tried to escape on the way back to Palmyra, whether it be by death or by stealing someone's horse. The other half seemed resigned to whatever fate would deliver. They were in no state to be judged by people who didn't understand.

"I'm sure." Adni nodded grimly. "I'll return once I know."

After a long moment, Haven agreed. The Queen stood. Somehow she still seemed as proper as the day Adni had arrived, even after weeks of travel conditions and battle. "If you're certain."

Adni was. She couldn't help anyone until she made sure her family was okay.

Haven stepped toward the door. Adni's heart leapt. She held out a hand to stop her. "Lady Queen, before you go..."

"Haven, please." The Queen smiled.

"Haven," Adni corrected herself. "I wanted to apologize again for lying to you about who I was, but not all ashen are evil like Kadia was."

Haven's jaw hardened, and her gaze turned to steel. She nodded stiffly. "I understand."

Adni was sure Haven would have a hard time accepting it, especially after her time with Kadia all those years ago.

They said their goodbyes and Haven left Adni's chambers. Once the door was softly closed behind the Queen, Adni sighed. Her fingers tingled with anticipation, but exhaustion still pulled at her bones. She turned to her bedchambers to seek rest.

"You can come out now," Adni said.

Julian peeked from the doorway. Haven had wanted to speak with Adni alone, but Julian was already inside. While they spoke, Julian stayed hidden.

"Are you all right?" Julian asked. Her dark eyes flashed in the bright afternoon light.

"I'm fine. I just need to rest awhile and then we can go." Adni collapsed in bed. Silk wrapped her limbs.

"Go, already?"

On the trip back to Palmyra, the one thing they both agreed on was eventually returning to her home, even if word had arrived and her family was dead. Adni wanted to return and collect some of her family's things before they returned to Palmyra for the trials. The Queen already welcomed them to stay, in fact, as was clear from their conversation, she very much expected it.

"Yes," Adni mumbled. She kicked off her boots and turned onto her side.

Julian slid the covers out from under her before kicking her own boots off. She slid beneath the thick comforter, a smile on her face.

"What are you doing?" Adni asked. Her cheeks heated as Julian pressed close by her side. She leaned against the pillows and extended her arms behind Adni's head, welcoming Adni to curl up against her shoulder.

"Come here." Julian's flirty smile returned, dimpling her tan cheeks and setting her skin aglow.

Heat ran across Adni's skin as she glanced between Julian's lips and shoulder. After a long moment she adjusted herself, gently lying her head on Julian's shoulder.

Soft blonde curls tickled her cheek. Warm fingers rested on her arm, pulling her close until Adni was forced to wrap a leg around Julian's.

Her heart beat faster as Julian's warm breath brushed her skin.

"See? Isn't this nice?" Julian teased.

Adni's cheeks flushed all the more. She couldn't deny it. Being in Julian's arms was warm, and pleasant and safe. Her scent, of winter snow and pine trees, filled Adni's nostrils. She closed her eyes.

"If you rest today, I promise we'll leave at first light tomorrow," Julian said. She squeezed Adni's shoulder.

Adni opened her eyes and looked up at Julian. Her dark gaze was warm and far more vulnerable than Adni had ever seen. Julian's cheeks flushed. Adni smiled and entwined her fingers with Julian's, her skin hot beneath Adni's fingers.

"All right," Adni agreed.

Julian nodded and closed her eyes. "Good."

They lay together, in quiet comfort until the sun fell and night began, and sleep consumed them.

TWENTY-SEVEN

When dawn broke the next morning, Adni was already awake. She bathed before Julian woke, dressing in clean clothes left over from before their long journey into battle. The clean leather smelled of tanning oil and wilderness, reminding her of home. Adni breathed it in, a pang of longing flashing through her heart.

She pushed down her thoughts as much as she could. Dwelling on the situation wouldn't get her home any faster. Adni returned to her bedchambers.

Julian yawned and rolled over. Her blonde waves were a mess, but her skin glowed in the morning sun, illuminating her long eyelashes and delicate curve of her nose. In sleep Julian wasn't a flirty warrior or a dragon knight, she was just a beautiful woman.

Adni's cheeks heated. She turned from Julian, slinking around the chamber as quietly as she could to gather their things.

"What are you doing?" Julian stretched like a sleepy house cat, another yawn nearly concealing her words.

"Getting ready." Adni didn't bother hiding her amused smile. She shook her head as she sat their rucksacks on the bench at the end of the bed. The comforter was half draped over it, and she pushed it aside.

"Is it dawn already?" Julian rubbed her eyes as she looked at the tall windows lining the corner of the room.

"Yes."

"Damn." Julian rolled over. "Just give me a few more minutes." She closed her eyes and snuggled into the covers.

Adni quirked a brow and yanked back the comforter.

Julian's legs recoiled toward her sternum and her eyes flashed open. "Hey!"

"You promised we'd leave at first light." Adni pointed at the window. The sun crested the horizon over the distant mountains.

Julian narrowed her eyes. "I did, didn't I?"

"Yes." Adni placed her hands on her hips. "So get up."

Julian sighed dramatically. "*Fine.*"

With a flare only Julian could pull off, she slipped from bed, flicking her messy hair over her shoulder before trudging into the bathing room.

Adni chuckled and shook her head before returning to preparing their things for the next leg of their journey.

A soft rap at the door broke the quiet left by Julian's departure. Adni looked over her shoulder at the double doors marking the exit of her rooms.

"It's Nina," the soft voice of the blonde woman drifted through the door.

"Come in." Adni smoothed her shirt and went to greet Nina in the sitting room.

One of the large doors parted, and Nina stepped inside, shutting the door gently behind her. Dark bags hung under her eyes, and her skin was far paler than Adni had ever seen it. Adni hadn't seen Nina much on the return trip to Palmyra, but she got the impression Nina hadn't slept well in a long time.

"Good morning," Nina said. She nodded politely.

"Good morning." Adni sat on the sofa, inviting Nina to join her. "Are you all right? You look as if you haven't slept in weeks."

Nina sighed. "The minds of the ashen haven't rested much since the battle."

Adni's chest tightened. She didn't know what she could do about that. "I'm sorry."

Nina shook her head. "Don't worry about me, I'll be fine."

"Do you know how Astrid is fairing?" Adni asked.

"Better, I think." Nina shrugged. "Her mind is so jumbled, her thoughts flying in every direction. She's been difficult to interpret since her return."

"Ah. That's how she fooled you in the first place, isn't it?"

Nina smiled ruefully. "I'm afraid so."

Adni sighed. So much had been taken from Haven and Astrid's family because of the dragons. She hoped they could one day find peace.

"You're leaving today?" Nina asked.

Adni smiled. It was polite of her to ask, even if Adni was sure she already knew. "Yes."

"I know you plan on returning, but I'm not sure what might happen in your absence." Nina shifted as if uncomfortable. "Haven's mind is shifting in too many directions, and the thoughts of the other royals are no different. Please promise me you'll return as soon as you can."

Adni nodded. "Of course." After speaking with Haven, she'd already planned to, but with Nina insisting as well, she'd have to make this a quick journey, no matter what she found at home.

"Good." Nina smiled half-heartedly. "King Emeril and his procession are leaving today. You can journey with them if you'd like."

That wasn't a terrible idea. Having some company on the road might be nice, especially if it lent them the fastest possible route.

"We'll travel with them, then," Adni said.

Nina stood. Though her small half-grin remained, her gaze was distant. She had to have a number of things on her mind, and yet the minds of ashen seemed the most present.

"Does distance from them help at all?" Adni asked.

"A little."

"Then why don't you come with us for a time?"

Nina shook her head. "I've had enough of travel, and someone needs to watch over them."

Adni agreed.

"Good luck on your journey." Nina hugged her gently, careful not to touch her skin. "We'll see you when you return."

"Thank you." Adni squeezed her back.

Nina took her leave, taking a dark shadow with her: the weight of the minds of a dozen ashen.

NOT LONG AFTER Adni spoke with Nina, Julian returned from the bathing room, freshly cleaned and ready to go. They picked up their things, their blades and rucksacks, before venturing to the main castle courtyard where King Emeril and Queen Rona greeted them warmly. They invited them on the journey as Nina already had.

Adni readily accepted, and within the hour they had breakfast, found horses and departed for Salander.

Anticipation clawed at her heart over the several days it took to reach the turn off point. When the time came, they reached a cross-roads, one long dirt road heading south for Ithrendel, and another twisting through the trees towards Elmhurst and the mountains.

Along the journey, Adni recounted what brought her out of the mountains in the first place, telling the King and Queen about her loathsome father and his greed.

"We'll find your father, Adni, and when we do, we'll be sure he's served a proper punishment." King Emeril smiled, a sure, dazzling sort of smile that told Adni they could trust him. "I'll have your things returned to you as well, as much as we can find," Emeril added.

"Thank you, Lord King." Adni smiled. Some weight lifted from her shoulders, even as her heart raced. Though they'd been given plenty of provisions to last until their arrival and beyond, it was nice to know someone was looking out for her family besides her—hopefully she would actually have a family left.

"Best of luck, Adni." Rona nodded politely. Though her mouth was grim, her eyes were bright and hopeful.

Adni wished she could borrow some of the Queen's optimism.

The royal procession rode down the path out of sight. Tall pine trees guarded part of the road, concealing the small army from unwanted eyes.

"Are you ready?" Julian asked.

Adni looked at her. Her stomach soured with uncertainty. "As I'll ever be."

Julian nodded, and led the way home.

* * *

THE COLD OF the mountains wriggled through her jacket to her bones. It sent her shivering the deeper they went. She'd forgotten how cold the mountains could be, especially so close to winter. Though no snow had fallen like she'd suspected it would, clouds were heavy on the horizon.

They left their horses with the bread maker, the same kind man who'd taken them to Salander in the first place. Though he'd been shocked to see them, he readily lent a hand, promising to keep their steeds well fed until they returned, hopefully in a few days' time.

Slick rock slipped beneath her boots, threatening to send her into the underground river. Adni squinted in the dark, a dim torch their only illumination until they reached the village.

"Are we nearly there?" Adni asked. Though she felt as if she should be the one to know, her sense of direction wasn't nearly as fine-tuned as Julian's.

"We'll arrive in minutes." Julian looked over her shoulder. Flames flickered through her gaze.

Adni nodded. Her limbs were heavy with weakness. She was light-headed and knew she needed to eat, but with her stomach constantly turning she hadn't been able to eat since the night before. Dried fish didn't exactly appeal to her anymore anyway.

The drip of water on rock mingled with the quiet shuffle of their clothes and gear. Adni shifted the straps on her shoulders. They dug into her skin even through her jacket.

Her heart raced as the tunnel ended and squat wooden homes rose in the darkness. Torches lit the narrow streets and surrounding lake. At least she could see at last.

Chatter rose from the homes, and smoke wafted from the chimneys of some. It had to be dinnertime. No wonder she was so tired.

Her slow steps became leaden as Julian drifted between homes. Her dark blue eyes flashed in the dim light as she looked over her shoulder again and again, most likely trying to gage how Adni was feeling.

Adni twisted her lip between her teeth. She was scared. Scared of what she was about to find. Her family could be dead, their blood dried on the floor. Or they could be alive, and have been this entire time. She wasn't sure what was worse, a swift end or a lengthened demise.

Even if her brother was good at fishing, it wasn't the season for it. They could be starving, or have starved by now.

Her pulse raced inside her ears. She was so close to finding out. After weeks of not knowing and more than a month gone, she was returning home empty-handed.

Something tingled along her senses. Something faint. Her eyebrows pulled together. Her fingertips burned and goosebumps ran over her arms.

Adni squeezed her eyes shut and took a deep breath.

When she opened them again her small house was standing before her. It looked the exact same: a small fence surrounding a tiny yard, wooden boards woven together to create walls, a plank of wood for a door, and a torch lit on the fence post.

Her heart leapt into her throat. The tingle across her skin increased as she unlocked the gate and stepped into the narrow stone yard.

Her palms burned and her eyes watered. For the first time Adni was sensing someone's magic. Someone she never thought had a magical bone in her body.

Her mother.

Adni leapt forward and flung the front door open.

Galia and her siblings spun with wide eyes. Their mouths dropped open as they took in Adni.

"Adni?" her mother asked.

She lunged across the room and wrapped her mother in her arms. "You're alive!" She kissed her mother's head and squeezed her shoulders as magic burned her hands.

"Adni!" her sister cried. Helen leapt from the dinner table and wrapped her arms around Adni's hips.

"We're alive?" Renley chuckled. "You're alive!" He embraced her from behind, her family's collective warmth pulling the chill from her bones.

"I thought you were dead!" Tears slicked her cheeks. Relief flooded every inch of her being. She'd spent so long uncertain of her family's fate, and there they were, alive and well.

"You're the one who's been gone for months!" Renley released her, and so did her sister. They all stepped apart, Adni wiping away her tears as her mother held her shoulders, looking her right in the eye.

"Where in blue skies have you been, Adni?" Galia's eyebrows furrowed and worry clouded her eyes.

Adni smiled as she looked over her shoulder, exchanging a glance with Julian. Where had she been? It felt as if she'd been all over the world, but in reality she'd only seen part of it as she descended to hell and back. She'd gone on a journey she never expected to Salander, to Rythern, and to a dragon city in the mountains. She'd taken a power she didn't understand and gave it all back. She met a half-brother she didn't know she had, fought a dragon who turned out to be her real father, and she fell in love. How in blue skies was she supposed to explain?

Adni laughed at the absurdity of it all. "It's a long story, mom."

THE END

ABOUT THE AUTHOR

Katherine Bogle's debut young adult novel, Haven, came second in the World's Best Story contest 2015. She currently resides in Saint John, New Brunswick with her partner in crime, and plethora of cats.

Follow Katherine for all the latest updates:
katherinebogle.com
TheHavenSeries@outlook.com

facebook.com/AuthorKatherineBogle

twitter.com/KattyB3

instagram.com/katherinebogle

goodreads.com/katherinebogle

ALSO BY KATHERINE BOGLE

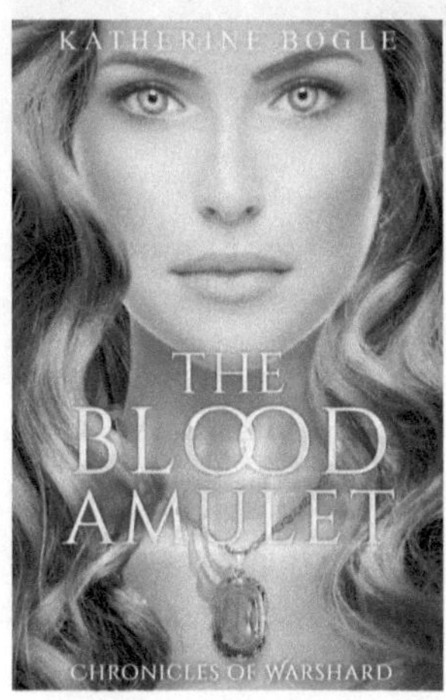

Julian has only ever known darkness.

Having spent most of her life trapped in the mountains alone with her mother, Julian is more than unprepared when her mother drops a bomb on her: there may be a way out.

Entering the six kingdoms, Julian is determined to bring down the dragon overlord's keeping her mother enslaved. But she'll have to face a lot more than crossing a country to find the one magical being with the power to bring down the dragons.

The Blood Amulet is a short story companion to the Chronicles of Warshard series.

Join Haven and her siblings on four unique adventures in a time when war ravaged the six kingdoms...

HAVEN has always hated royal gatherings, and jumps at the chance to sneak away for a race through town on horseback. But when the young princess is injured, her ancestry is brought into question.

Much is expected of the heir to the Rythern throne, but when **LUCIAN** is forced to leave the warfront by his father, his reluctant agreement comes at a price.

The battle for Helms Keep has disastrous consequences for **MARCEL**. Soon he finds himself fighting both enemy forces and his own memories.

ASTRID is sent to the family summer home in the Cinder Mountains for her own safety. Only she doesn't expect the knee-high snow and frigid temperatures. With only her guards to protect her, Astrid must dig deeper than she ever thought herself capable of in order to survive.